# HOOLIGAN ARM

# Brent Purvis

This novel is a complete work of fiction. Although the author grew up in Southeast Alaska and was inspired by its lifestyle and cast of interesting inhabitants, this book is a creation of the author's imagination. All names, characters, businesses, events, and incidents are used fictitiously.

The author acknowledges the trademark status and ownership of various products and companies referenced in this novel. The use of these trademarks is not authorized, associated with, or sponsored by the trademark ownership.

ISBN: 978-1537736716

Editor:                       Tara Neilson
                              www.alaskaforreal.com
Cover Design:                 Joanie Christian Design
                              jchristiandesign@gmail.com
Severed Foot Design:  Ella Purvis

## ALSO BY BRENT PURVIS

Jim and Kram Funny Mystery Series:

*Mink Island*

*Tsunami Warning*

# Dedication

to Ella

my beautiful daughter

what new project are you starting today?

# Prologue

### Monday, November 2nd, 2015

*Muskeg Mama: Memoir of a Klondike Girl* hit the bookshelves and eBooks across the country. Between the intriguing true tale of survival and the mystique surrounding the recent discovery of the lost manuscript, Ellen Cranbrook's detailed personal account, published posthumously, quickly became a best-selling work of nonfiction.

### Saturday, May 7th, 2016 – Prince of Wales Island, AK

At five minutes past midnight in an unpopulated cove several miles southeast of the town of Craig, Alaska, an explosion pounded sound waves across the surface of the water, echoing off the surrounding mountains, and dissipating in the moist air without causing alarm.

### Sunday, May 8th, 2016, Mother's Day – Hooligan Arm, Prince of Wales Island, AK

A tall, skinny redheaded man in his late twenties stood alone on a rain soaked rock next to the entrance of a lagoon. The salt chuck was located at the narrow end of a cone-shaped cove. The outlet was small, not more than twenty feet across. Inside, the body of water opened up to what looked like a small lake. At the far end, a fresh-water river flowed calmly into the saltwater causing white foam to bubble up from the brackish water. At high tide, the lagoon appeared to be stagnant, with water that barely crept through the narrow sleeve, emptying into the saltwater of Hooligan Arm. As the tide changed and the sea level began to rescind, the current of the murky lagoon steadily increased as water rushed out through the restricted opening and into the bay. The lower the tide, the more the current increased, until it almost appeared as rapids in a raging river.

Zeke Melon stood on his wet rock near the entrance of the lagoon at high tide. His brown rubber boots found secure footing on the jagged basalt as the calm, black water seemed to stand still within arm's reach of him. Several yards behind where he stood, two oversized coolers sat empty with their lids open, ready to receive their bounty. About twenty yards down the rocky shoreline, an aluminum skiff had been pulled halfway out of the water onto a gravel bed. Its long bowline had been secured to a tree on the shoreline. Water sloshed against the small boat's transom underneath the outboard engine that had been locked into its elevated position.

The gangly redhead turned a handle and extended a long, fiberglass pole about fifteen feet into the air. At the end of the pole, a sixteen inch round metal hoop supported a twenty-four inch deep, nylon mesh net. Zeke reached into the front pocket of his rain-soaked hoodie and removed a bottle of Nyquil. He briefly fought the child-proof lid before lifting the bottle of cold medicine to his lips. After gulping down a third of the green liquid, Zeke slid the Nyquil back in his sweatshirt's pouch and slowly dropped the dip-net into the water.

Starting with the net close to the lagoon's entrance,

Zeke pushed the net through the friction of the water away from the lagoon toward the expanse of the cove. It took quite a bit of strength as he plunged the net deep, keeping the pace steady and the net positioned accordingly. As he slowly raised the handle toward the surface, Zeke turned the pole so that the net came up even with the sea's plane. Lifting it into the air, Zeke was pleased to see a silvery shimmer appear as droplets of saltwater fell from the net. Several small, skinny fish wiggled as they struggled for life against the bottom of their long-handled trap.

Zeke muttered aloud, "S... s... s... s... sweet!"

Zeke pivoted on the rock until the long handled net hovered above one of the large coolers. With a well-rehearsed flipping motion, eight shimmering hooligan, each only about eight inches in length, were deposited into the cooler. The dip-net fisherman turned back to the water, submerged his net and pushed his arm and back muscles hard as he made another pass.

After close to fifteen minutes, Zeke Melon had only half-filled one of the coolers. The hooligan, which were sometimes called candlefish, were spawning, but it was still a little early in the season. Harvest numbers could be low. He had already noticed the tide change and knew that as the current from the lagoon gained speed, dip-netting would become quite difficult. In addition, the little fish became less apt to make their spawning journey into the lagoon as the water current increased. The hooligan typically pooled up in the cove, waiting for high slack tide to embark into their journey upstream, but quickly became discouraged when the water flow turned to rushing rapids.

Zeke decided on one more pass with the net. The water in front of him swirled as the flow seemed to change by the second. Foam drifted by as it exited the lagoon. The fisherman extended the handle and again plunged the net. Knowing that this was his last round of the day, he pushed the net deep, causing his back and arm muscles to burn. As he turned the handle, directing the mesh toward the surface, it seemed to pull back on him, wanting to stay in the deepest part of the channel. He worked his leverage on the long pole and pushed up hard with his left arm and pulled the handle end down hard with his right. There was one certainty this time. The net was heavy.

Fighting current, friction, weight of the catch and tired muscles, Zeke began to worry about his ability to lift the net from the water. Motivated by the prospect of a net full of fish, he wasn't about to give up. He quickly devised a plan to retrieve the haul. Zeke slid the pole behind him, one arm-length at a time. With the net still submerged, he feared that his catch might escape as he pulled the pole in toward shore, but the heavy weight never seemed to lighten up. Lifting the net from the water was going to be a challenge.

Sensing that the net was nearing the edge, Zeke Melon stepped back off the rock. He pulled hard as he dragged the net out of the water and onto shore. As expected, there were several skinny fish wiggling inside the snare, but there seemed to be something else in there. Zeke walked over and stood above the net. He lifted the hoop off the ground and stared directly down into the pouch. At first glance, there didn't appear to be enough fish to have caused such a heavy retrieval. Among the silver hooligan he discovered the item that had weighed down his catch. Disbelief quickly turned into shock, followed by horror. Zeke Melon stared straight down at a severed human foot.

# Chapter 1

It was Mother's Day. Jim Wekle knew his duty. He picked up the cell phone from the desktop in his office and punched in the contact number. He leaned back in his armchair while it rang.

"It's about time, Jimmy. I thought you forgot about me."

Jim silently rolled his eyes. "Happy Mother's Day, Mom."

Filled with self-importance, the voice on the other end of the line said, "What took you so long to call, dear?"

"It's only noon, Mom."

"Well, it's one o'clock here and that's too late to wish your mother a Happy Mother's Day."

Jim wasn't in the mood, so he quickly changed the subject. "What's the weather like today?"

"What's the weather like every day? It's San Diego, Jimmy. It's perfect."

"And how's Dad?"

"The same. Obsessed with weed killer and television remotes. Won't even take me out to a Mother's Day brunch."

Jim replied in his best Boy Scout voice, "Well, too bad I'm not there. I would love to take you out for brunch."

"You'll have your chance soon enough, Jimmy. I'm

coming up for a surprise inspection." Mrs. Wekle's voice lacked enthusiasm, resembling the curtness of an Army Colonel.

Jim sat up at the unexpected announcement. He feigned excitement, "Wow, Mom. That's great. When would you like to come visit? We usually get some nice weather in August."

"I'll be there on Friday. Make sure you have clean sheets in the guest room."

Jim loved his mother, and would certainly welcome a visit from her, but Friday seemed a little soon. "Friday? Great." Jim's head was spinning. "And Mom, you know I don't have a guest room."

Jim's cell phone beeped, indicating an incoming call. He ignored it.

Vera Wekle ordered, "Well, whatever that tent-thing is you live in… Make sure it's picked up, scrub your toilet, and be prepared to sleep on the couch."

Jim asked, "How are you getting here? You know Alaska Airlines will only get you as far as Ketchikan, right?"

The cell beeped again in his ear.

"I have an internet connection, Jimmy. I'm not an idiot. I'm also not an old, retired fragile soul, like you think I am. Frightening Frankie is flying me out from the Ketchikan seaplane dock Friday evening. He said we should get in around six-thirty."

"You know Frightening Frankie?"

The cell phone beeped three times in a row, signaling

7

the call was going to voicemail.

Vera Wekle's voice changed from Army Colonel to Patronizing Mother. "Of course. We just spoke on the phone last week. That lovely girl of yours gave me his number."

Jim was speechless.

His mother said, "Oh, don't think your mom doesn't know all. One phone call to the station and I could tell that girl, Maggie, is sweet on you, Jimmy."

"Uh… You've been talking to Maggie?"

"And when were you planning on telling me about her? After that train-wreck you called a first marriage, wouldn't you think your mother deserves to know when you're seeing someone new?"

Jim really wanted to change the subject again. He asked, "Is Dad coming with you?"

"Who, Mr. *TSA violates our basic rights as an American and a human*? I think not. Besides, he's spotted a dandelion in the west corner of the yard. All hell is breaking loose."

The office phone on Jim's desk started to ring. Jim spoke into his cell, "Give Dad a hug for me. I've got to go, Mom."

"Sounds fine, dear. Thanks for remembering to call."

"Happy Mother's Day, Mom. Call me before you leave on Friday. Bye."

Jim picked up his office line, "Lieutenant Wekle."

"You need to get down to the marina, boss." The voice was from his youngest charge, Trooper Brett Stilhaven.

Jim asked, "Was that you calling my cell a minute ago?"

"Yeah. It went to voice-mail."

"I was talking to my mother."

Stilly said, "You're a good son."

"Remind me of that on Friday. What's going on at the marina?"

"I've got something pretty ugly for you to see down here, boss. I'm here with some guy in a boat down on the dock."

"Which dock?"

"I'm on the north float. This kid named, uh… Zeke Melon… He scooped something up while dip-netting sardines."

Jim could hear a voice from behind Stilly say, "Hooligan. Not s… s… s… sardines."

Stilly's voice sounded distant as it replied, "Same thing."

Again in the background, "N… n… n… n… no they aren't"

Jim said, "Stilly. I'll be there in a few."

He hung up, grabbed his Stetson, and headed for the door.

A single eye squinted as it moved close to the scope of

a rifle. At first only the magnified image of water glinted back through the scope into the peeping eyeball. As the gun's barrel swung up, the scope's view of the water moved rapidly, flashing round images of the sea with periodic glimpses of clouds and sky. An image of a white mass that clashed against the water and sky backdrop flashed through the eyepiece. The man moving the rifle barrel swung its position backwards a bit in order to focus on the white mass floating atop the water.

"I've got you in my sights, you son of a bitch," growled the man under his breath.

He positioned the crosshairs across the back of the vessel. The name, *Earth's Guardian*, arced like a rainbow across the full width of the trawler's wide stern. The scope moved up to the ship's deck. Several men wearing white pants and blue, white, and red shirts decorated like the French flag were busy moving gear into a white inflatable raft. The scope kept scanning. The man moved the gun's aim up from the stern deck toward the ship's quarters, and finally the wheelhouse. From the apex of the ship, a flag pole extended several feet into the air sporting a white flag with two overlaid black letter P's on it. Outside of the wheelhouse, a small balcony with a white railing surrounded the elevated chamber. A sliding door opened and a short man wearing a white polo shirt, white pants, white belt, white loafers, white socks, and wispy white hair stepped from the wheelhouse onto the balcony. The man stood, looking in toward land, wind causing his hair to dance and his cheeks to chap red.

"Bingo," the man with the rifle said as he positioned the center of the scope's crosshairs on the short, white-haired man.

# Chapter 2

Zeke Melon struggled to get the words out. It didn't help that a small crowd of fishermen, deck-hands, tourists, and Alaska State Troopers had amassed on the slip next to where he had moored his skiff. A cooler had been removed from the boat and sat on the dock next to where Zeke muttered incoherently.

"N... n... n... n... net was h... h... h... h... heavy." The young man's emotions were frazzled, which didn't help his stutter at all.

Trooper Brett Stilhaven was taking notes while he asked questions. "Where, exactly, were you dip-netting in Hooligan Arm?"

Zeke sighed. He knew that L's were difficult. "L... l... l..." He paused and inhaled deeply. "L... l... l..."

"Lagoon?" Lieutenant Jim Wekle asked.

The tall redhead nodded in relief.

"Were you up inside the lagoon?" Jim decided to help the guy out by asking only yes or no questions.

Zeke Melon shook his head.

"You were standing by the mouth, weren't you?"

He nodded in the affirmative.

Jim asked, "Must've been high tide, huh?"

More nodding.

"Had the current just changed?"

More nodding.

Jim thought for a moment, and then asked, "Did you pick up or see anything else out of the ordinary?"

Zeke shook his head.

"Clothing? Life jacket? An empty boat?"

Again, the skinny redhead shook his head.

Stilly asked, "Any bear sign where you were fishing?"

He shook his head, 'no.'

Jim said, "Okay, Zeke. I think we have your contact info, right Stilly?"

Trooper Stilhaven said, tapping on his notebook, "Right here, boss."

Jim continued, "We'll call you if we have any other questions. We'll also need to take your cooler here, okay?"

Jim bent and opened the lid of the large ice chest. Inside were dozens of dead, skinny, oily, six-inch long fish surrounding a gruesome-looking human foot. The foot had been severed savagely just above the ankle, which left flesh and bone exposed in a jagged fashion. The flesh color of the foot was a mix of pale white and beet red.

Zeke Melon said, "But m… m… m… my hooligan." The lanky redhead accidentally farted as he made his plea.

Ignoring the audible flatulence, Stilly replied, "Sorry Zeke, but that's all evidence now. We'll have to take the whole cooler with us."

Jim motioned to his young Trooper for a quick sidebar. Stilly walked up close and Jim spoke softly, "You know how smelly those things get? You don't really want to process all of those stinking fish, do you? "

Stilly curled his lip. "Not really. Those things are already looking pretty ripe."

"Don't you think it wouldn't hurt to give the guy his catch? I mean… What kind of evidence do you expect to get from those little suckers?"

Stilly shrugged. "I don't know. Just following procedure."

Jim said, "Why don't you go up to your rig and get a plastic sack and two pairs of gloves. I'll help you bag the foot."

Zeke Melon overheard the conversation. He smiled widely, exposing a mouth full of perfect teeth. "I g… g… g… get to keep my hooligan?"

"Looks like you get to keep your hooligan, Zeke." Jim grimaced, "You actually eat those things?"

The skinny redhead shook his head.

"Use them for bait?"

Again, a head shake.

Jim asked, "Well, what the heck do you do with them?"

Zeke Melon just grinned, farted, and shrugged, keeping his true intentions a secret.

Phyllis Prescott drove her Ford Taurus up close behind a small, yellow foreign car. While she waited, Phyllis dropped her visor and began to apply lipstick while scanning her image in the driver's side mirror. She put the lipstick away, raised the visor, and looked at the car in front of her. It still sat motionless, exhaust billowing out of the tailpipe. Just to the left of the yellow car, a hut with cedar shingles, barely larger than an outhouse, sat perched in the middle of a gravel lot. A sign hung from the roof that read, *Salmon Lane Coffee Hut.*

The aging lady behind the wheel of the Taurus reached out with a frail hand and turned on the car radio. A transmission from the only radio station on the island filled the car's speakers. A man with a smooth voice was reading a list of items for sale on a segment called *The Island Shopper.*

*"For Sale: A five-thousand gallon plastic water tank, only partially used for five years. Some mildew on the inside. Six hundred dollars or best offer. Call Frank at 826-4479."*

Phyllis craned her neck around the steering wheel, becoming exceedingly impatient as the yellow car still sat next to the window of the Coffee Hut.

*"For Sale: Old suits, fifty dollars apiece. Tool chest, well stocked, a hundred and forty dollars. Four-stroke Honda ten-horse outboard, three hundred dollars. Remington pump-action shotgun, seventy-five dollars. Large black dog, free. Call Wilma soon before husband returns. 826-9087."*

Phyllis gave two quick beeps of the horn. No response.

# HOOLIGAN ARM

*"Wanted: Two six-foot lengths of two-inch PVC pipe. Will pay cash or trade for classic crayon collection. Call Alaska State Troopers office and leave a message for Kram."*

After another couple of blasts from her car horn, Phyllis finally saw an arm emerge from the Coffee Hut. It held a white paper cup, overflowing with brown liquid that dripped down the side of the yellow car. The driver of the yellow car grabbed the coffee, flipped the coffee attendant the bird, and sped away.

Phyllis Prescott turned the radio down, put the Ford Taurus into gear and pulled forward. Swinging her head toward the open window of the Coffee Hut, Phyllis was startled by the sight that stood before her. A smiling man with white hair pulled back into a ponytail was wearing an apron and waving at her with one hand. The apron was completely soaked through with coffee. Whipped cream hung down from the man's chin like a Colonel Sanders goatee. Coffee grounds were stuck to both of the man's cheeks and the elbow of his waving arm. On the counter in front of him, colorful straws were strewn about in a random pattern that resembled a game of pick-up-sticks. Behind him, a tower of paper cups leaned precariously, threatening to collapse at any moment. Steam bubbled ominously from three different machines against the back wall, percolating in a manner reminiscent of a mad scientist's laboratory. Rock music blared from two speakers that hung from the ceiling of the hut.

The ponytailed man, still waving while he bobbed his head to the beat of the music, shouted above the stereo, "Welcome to the Salmon Lane Coffee Hut. What can I get started for you today?"

Scrunching her face, signaling disgust, the older lady shouted, "Could you turn down that rock music, please?"

"One Rock n' Roll special, coming up!" The coffee attendant sprang into action in a cloud of straws, cups, whirling sounds, and steam explosions.

Phyllis shouted, "I just want a vanilla latte."

There was no response from the attendant. Instead, a coffee grinder jammed and grounds flew out the window landing in the elderly lady's hair.

She shouted, "Excuse me!"

The man grabbed a hammer and hit the top of the espresso machine. A steam valve blew hissing scalding, moist air into the hut. It billowed out the open window like fog rolling into the bay. Sludge-like liquid seeped into a shot glass just as the music rose steadily toward an all new decibel level.

"Hot damn," shouted the coffee attendant.

He sang along with the lyrics as he fired up the whipped cream dispenser. Head banging back and forth to the beat, the coffee attendant howled, *"Rock and roll, baaaaaabeeee! Rock and roll, giiiiiirl. Rock and roll, baaaaaabeeee! Give it a whiiiiirl."* He overfilled the whipped cream so much that it oozed down the sides of the white paper cup. He grabbed a handful of chocolate covered espresso beans and pelted the whipped cream tower with them. After slapping a maraschino cherry on top, the coffee attendant winked as he poked the cup out the sliding window, straight through the driver's side of the Taurus, hovering the cup directly over Phyllis' lap.

"That'll be four bucks plus tip, please."

A dollop of whipped cream landed on the woman's tan pants. She shrieked, put the car in gear, and hit the gas pedal. The impact of the moving car caused the coffee attendant to drop the cup into the interior of the Ford Taurus as he yanked back his arm.

As the car sped away, the coffee attendant yelled, "Remember, you owe me four bucks. Plus tip!"

# Chapter 3

The *Earth's Guardian* swung slowly on its anchor line as it sat in a protected body of water wedged between Fish Egg Island and the much larger Prince of Wales Island. Its anchorage was just to the north of the town of Craig, in plain view of all of the local inhabitants. The all-white vessel spanned sixty-five feet in length and had a massive boom arm angled up from its center, capable of lowering inflatable rafts from the ship's deck to the surface below on either side of the boat. The spacious back deck featured flat, dual metal doors that gave way into the belly of the ship. Positioned around the deck were several tall storage lockers, an array of thick dock lines laid out in coils, two gas-powered generators, a large pump, three winches, two scuba stations with large oxygen refilling tanks, and six spaces dedicated to securing large, inflatable rafts near the edge of the deck rail. Only five rafts were in place.

Halfway up from the mid-section of the boat were several doors that gave access to the ship's main cabin. Inside, there were crew quarters, several heads, a galley, lounge area, and a captain's suite. Below deck housed a massive cargo hold, a well-stocked workshop, and a large engine room with two powerful diesel engines, both of which leaked like a sieve.

Perched atop the forward cabin, a wheelhouse shot up high above the deck, ending in a point of antennas that reached to the sky. Just to the aft of the antenna array, the ship's only flag flapped in the wind. A solid white backdrop gave way to two overlapping letter P's.

Pierre Lemieux opened a door and stepped out onto the exposed walkway that encircled the boat's wheelhouse. Decked head to toe in all-white with the exception of the name *Planet Patrol* across his breast, the short man with white hair grasped the railing with both hands, glaring across the water to the town of Craig. Low clouds hid most of the mountain that rose steadily behind the town. Boats of various sizes filled the slips in the north-end marina. A handful of floatplanes sat tethered to wooden docks. Cannery buildings sat perched over the water on wooden stilts that shot up from submerged footings. The color of the day was typical Southeast Alaska grey. The air was moist with the smell of saltwater and seaweed.

"Beanie, get out here," Pierre barked. His cheeks were ruddy and his mood sour.

A dopey kid that barely looked college age stumbled as he exited the wheelhouse. Catching himself on the railing, he reported to his boss by standing tall at attention.

"Yes, sir, Uncle. Captain. Uncle Captain." The kid saluted.

Pierre asked, "Have you set up an audience with the locals, yet? We need Planet Patrol to make a big splash here soon."

The kid wore the ship's standard crewman shirt that resembled the French flag. All of Pierre Lemieux's crewmen wore the same outfit, except that Beanie LeFranc was the only one allowed to accessorize with a red scarf tied around his neck. "Still working on it, Uncle Pierre. There doesn't seem to be a lot of interest in having us offer an informational meeting on eco-friendly commercial fishing." His voice squeaked like he was still going through puberty.

"Then we change the title. We need something to get the attention of these ass-wipes." Pierre Lemieux paced around the circular walkway, with his nephew in tow. "Let's call it something that sizzles. How 'bout, *Commercial Fishing: the Raping of the Sea*? That ought to poke the hornets' nest a bit."

Beanie LeFranc shuffled awkwardly behind his boss and uncle as they circumnavigated the upper portion of the *Earth's Guardian*. Beanie spoke in a tone that lacked both confidence and depth of timbre. "I'm not sure if we can say the word 'raping' in a press release."

"What press release? There is no press around here you dolt. This is an island in the middle of friggin' nowhere. Now, go schedule a meeting room in town, type up a flyer, and print about five hundred copies. I want every idiot on that forsaken rock to read that title. If *Commercial Fishing: the Raping of the Sea* doesn't get their attention, we'll start dowsing their boats in fake fish blood. I want these pricks steaming mad. You hear me, Beanie?"

Fluorescent lights buzzed on the low ceiling of the medical clinic. Jim Wekle stood in the isolated back room next to a tall woman with long, blonde hair. Jim wore his Trooper's uniform, holding his Stetson under an arm, while the blonde woman wore a white lab coat and black-rimmed glasses over her svelte nose. They both stood next to a sterile, metal table that was positioned in the center of the room just beneath a very bright, movable exam light. The table was long enough to support a full human body, but only a single foot was perched on display.

"It's cold in here, Dr. Kim," commented Jim.

"Cold is better than ripe," replied the doctor.

"Good point."

The tall doctor stated, "This might be the only room on the island to have central air."

Kim Dooley had just recently expanded her medical clinic to include a coroner's lab. The facility was as new as was her recent certification in forensic pathology. Once her facility and training had been completed, she easily earned the newly created appointment of Prince of Wales Borough Coroner. Not only did she deserve the appointment, she was the only person on the island that qualified.

"What've we got, Doc?" asked Jim.

"It's a foot."

"Wow, eight years of medical school really paid off."

"Don't get sassy with me, Wekle. I'm married and my husband's huge."

"I carry a gun."

"Touché."

The doctor motioned for Jim to lean in close above the metal table. She moved the light so that it was positioned directly above the foot. The doctor pointed with long, steel tweezers at the base of the heel.

Dr. Dooley said, "Obviously, Caucasian, and I believe, male."

"How can you tell?"

"On average, men have longer feet, while women have narrower and higher foot arch characteristics." Scanning the length of the foot's sole with the tweezers, she added, "Based on heel to toe length, this is a men's shoe size ten. That would be very rare among females."

Jim followed the doctor around the table ninety degrees.

She pointed to the toes, and said, "Also, most women take better care of their feet. Look at those toenails. They probably haven't ever been manicured. They're in desperate need of a good clipping, and there is no sign of nail polish."

"How long do you think it was in the water?"

"Not long. There has been very little decomposition of the flesh. Also, I see hardly any sign of little sea critters eating on it. I would guess…less than a day?"

"Can you tell me about how it got removed from the rest of his body?"

Dr. Dooley's blue eyes peered over the top of the black-rimmed glasses. "I thought you'd never ask." She winked at him.

Jim blushed slightly as he asked, "Any sign of animal attack?"

"There are no teeth marks or claw marks of any kind. Nothing on the foot that would indicate any sort of significant animal activity."

"Was the foot cut off, like with a saw or an axe?"

She pointed at the flesh and bone sticking up from the

top of the injury, just above the ankle. "Look at how jagged and random the skin is here. And now look at the fibula, and here, at the tibia. These fracture marks are completely inconsistent with any sort of saw blade or tool."

The coroner moved around the table again and leaned in close to the severed area, focusing on the skin that surrounded the exposed shinbone. "And look closely at this part here. There appears to be some charring."

"What are you saying, Doc?"

The tall blonde stood up straight and removed her glasses. "The evidence suggests that this foot was blown off by some sort of explosion. Would have had to be a powerful explosive, too, to do this kind of damage."

Jim turned away from the table and rubbed his temples with the thumb and middle finger of his right hand while pacing around the room. He stopped, and asked, "What do you think, Doc? What are the odds that this guy's still alive?"

"Somewhere close to zero. Anything with enough force to blow off some guy's foot? Well, you can guess as to the shape the rest of the body might be in. Factor in the remote locale, water temps, blood loss... Not looking good for our footless friend, here."

"Thanks, Doc. I need to get going." Jim got all the way to the door of the forensics lab when he stopped and asked, "Is there any way to tell if this foot had washed down the fresh water river into the lagoon, or if it's been swirling around the saltwater currents most of the time?"

"I can't really tell for sure, Jim. There's not enough

evidence on the appendage for me to give you a guess."

"But you're certain that the injury happened less than twenty-four hours before the foot was found?"

She nodded with her reply. "More like twelve to fourteen hours, I would say. Water temps are cool, which does slow down decomp, but this foot is in too good a condition to be in that environment very long."

"You rock, Doc."

"Come and visit anytime, Jim."

Lieutenant Wekle gave the doctor a handsome smile as he exited through the door of the lab.

# Chapter 4

Officially titled the eulachon, a six to eight-inch long, oily smelt, it is commonly referred to by two names throughout Southeast Alaska. Many call the little fish that travel in vast schools to their springtime spawning beds, hooligan, which is believed to have been derived from its native designation. They are often called candlefish, which many mistakenly believe comes from the bright, reflective quality of its slender body when swimming in schools just below the surface. In actuality, the candlefish moniker came about in response to the fish being so loaded with natural oils, especially when harvested during their spawn. Once it is dried and run through with a wick, its flesh will support a slow burn, just like a candle.

Dip-net fishing for hooligan is hard work. Finding the proper location is an absolute key to a successful expedition. The fish will school up in deeper pockets, awaiting the tide before making their run into fresh-water for the spawn. A dip-net fisherman must find the perfect vantage point from shore that will allow access to this hole with nothing more than a fifteen foot long-handled net and proper footing to allow leverage for working the device. Zeke Melon had found just such a spot.

Selecting the general area for his dip-net expeditions was first solely based upon the locale's name. He soon found that there was good reason that the cove supporting the lagoon was called Hooligan Arm. It sported one of the best hooligan spawns in the region, and Zeke typically had the entire cove to himself. The little fish were not often sought after by fisherman. If one harvested hooligan for food, they would be subjected to a strong, fishy flavor, similar to a sardine, but with larger bones and more guts to contend with. Some tried catching hooligan to use as a bait fish for salmon or halibut, but once frozen and re-thawed, the bait became mushy and wouldn't stay on a hook for very long. The demand for hooligan was so low, and the supply so plentiful, a dip-net fisherman did not even need a license or heed a bag limit when angling for the little suckers.

Zeke had a plan. He had only lived on Prince of Wales Island for just over a year, but in his time of barely holding down multiple temp jobs working for fish canneries, stevedoring outfits, school custodians, and septic pumpers, he had heard dozens of stories of Alaska's fish and wildlife. One of those stories that kept his attention and stuck in his mind was told to him by a Native Alaskan coworker while pumping outhouses in a remote campground. During a rather testing battle concerning a clogged pump hose and a porcupine carcass, Zeke was told the tale while working the bottom of a holding tank with suction set on high. The older Native Alaskan coworker told the younger Zeke about eulachon candles. The man detailed all techniques involved in the process; including when to harvest, proper drying methods, what type of wick to use, how to thread the wick through the fish, and even how his family used to prop up the candles by using aluminum foil and a screw. Zeke became equally enthralled with the concept of making hooligan candles as he was with the prospect of never pumping out another outhouse. In the spirit of entrepreneurship, the young redhead, cursed by an intense stutter and terminal gas, embarked on his new, upstart career.

Forced to play the tide, Zeke had a very limited window of opportunity to get his fishing done each day. Currently, high tides were coming in around nine o'clock in the morning and nine forty-five at night. Since he was still gainfully employed as a septic pumper and needed that job to pay his rent, the 9am tide was not an option. During the weekdays, he was destined to fish the evening high tide, and each day the tides shifted later by about forty-five minutes. Zeke knew that it was inevitable that, even during the late spring in Southeast Alaska, his evening fishery tasks would soon occur too late at night to operate with the aid of daylight.

At mid-May in Southeast Alaska, the sun was setting around nine-thirty at night. This would be his first return trip in the dark. Zeke geared up with a lantern, headlamp, raingear, dip-net, cooler, rubber boots, three jelly-filled donuts, and a bottle of Nyquil, and he left the docks in Craig at several minutes past 8pm. His fourteen foot Smokercraft aluminum skiff buzzed along the shoreline, powered by an extremely loud, and quite smoky, 2-stroke outboard engine. Zeke sat in the stern of the boat and guided the tiller and throttle with his left hand. The boat traveled at a decent tack, close to twenty miles-per-hour. He skippered his skiff south, passing by the open Port St. Nicholas, weaving between rock outcroppings and tree covered islets, rounding several points, and entering the cove of his destination.

He made the trip out to the mouth of the lagoon at the head of Hooligan Arm in just under an hour. Zeke beached his skiff and secured it to the same tree that he had used several times before and then unloaded his lantern, net, cooler, and the bag of jelly donuts onto the rocks just below the tree-line. The tide wasn't quite high yet. He had just enough daylight left to get everything in place before it was time to fish. Killing the last few minutes before slack tide, Zeke sat down on a large piece of driftwood and pulled the Nyquil bottle from inside his rain jacket. While watching the current literally slow to a snail's pace right in front of the rock where he sat, Zeke downed a third of the bottle, contemplating the rugged beauty of the thick forest of evergreens that coddled the cove.

After a deep breath, Zeke muttered to himself, "Beautiful." He was impressed that his stutter didn't impair the word and assumed that the cough medicine must be kicking in. The air was thick with moisture, but rain wasn't falling yet. The wind was still, and the low clouds immovable, seemingly propped up by the tops of the trees surrounding him. The water inside the cove was calm, even though there was still a hint of a current running from the lagoon. The birds had been hushed by the late hour. As light closed on the day, he was completely alone in a silent Alaskan paradise. Zeke fired up the lantern and placed it close to the cooler. He clicked on his headlamp, devoured a jelly donut, and decided it was time to start fishing.

It was slow at first. He only netted five or six hooligan per pass. Zeke decided to try a slightly different position. He backed off his rock a bit and made a pass with the net a few feet closer to shore. He only picked up two on that pass. Zeke repositioned again and decided to go deeper. He had been reluctant to go deep, as it was much harder work, but the hooligan fisherman wanted more than half a dozen fish per sweep of the net. He plunged the dip-net hard into the water, pulling down with his left hand and pushing up with his right. After reaching maximum depth, he pushed the net downstream. It took almost his entire upper body strength and lower back muscles to make the pass, but once the net made it to the surface, he could hear the hooligan bubbling like popcorn.

A brief moment of anxiety attacked his nervous system as he recalled the fresh memory of pulling in some guy's foot. He shook the thought from his mind and continued to retrieve the heavy load. After pulling the net in close, his headlamp illuminated a full pouch, jammed with fish. Zeke estimated that close to forty of the skinny little suckers had to be squirming around in the mesh pouch.

With his muscles aching and a cooler full of candlefish, Zeke Melon untied the skiff and pushed off into the dark cove. He didn't have running lights on his Smokercraft, but he figured that he would just have to risk running at night. His eyes had already adjusted to the darkness, and there was just enough of a dim glow that he could see faint outlines of the various shorelines around him. Zeke was floating along with the outgoing current, just preparing to fire up his outboard, when he heard the other engine. It sounded like it had just turned into Hooligan Arm, coming from the same direction that he was about to head.

Zeke couldn't see any running lights on the other boat, either. From the sound of it, he guessed the other craft was powered by an outboard engine similar to his own. It wasn't as noisy as Zeke's, but it was definitely a small boat motor. He couldn't see it, but he guessed that it was probably similar in size to his skiff.

Before starting his own engine, Zeke waited until he had a good line on where the other traveler was. He didn't want to risk running headlong into another craft that was running just as blind as he was. From the sound of the outboard, the other boat seemed to be heading into the middle of the cove. Zeke decided it was safe to move as his plan was to stay close to shore. He fired up his engine after the third yank of the pull-cord and made a beeline out of the cove.

On the trip back to town, Zeke Melon's first thought was of his cooler full of hooligan. It was a productive night, and he was proud of a job well done. If he was able to catch this many fish each trip, it wouldn't be long before he reached his goal. After his boat exited the cove, he made a right hand turn and headed north up the island. His mind drifted to the set of circumstances that led to him being all alone on a remote island in Alaska. It was about as far away from where his family thought he should be as he could get. If they could see him now…running a boat alone in the dark of night, just off the shoreline of the second largest island in Alaska, with a full load of fish. Zeke smiled.

He thought of the boat he had just heard back in Hooligan Arm. It wasn't that strange to hear and see boats on the waters of Southeast Alaska day and night. After all, he was out there in a small boat in the middle of the night. But then Zeke's thoughts turned to the severed foot. What a horrific experience that had been. Could the boat that he'd just left behind in the cove have something to do with the foot? What the heck were they doing out there, anyway? It was the middle of the night and they were heading for the middle of the cove. What could they possibly be doing that would cause someone to lose a foot? Were they murderers? Were they insane marine stalkers with implements of torture? Had they seen or heard him? Were they following him? Were they coming to cut off his foot?

His anxiety almost got the best of him. Zeke shook his head to snap out of his paranoia. He focused his thoughts on the task of running his skiff in the impaired vision of the night. It was dark and his body ached from dip-netting. His mind raced in a fog of cold medicine, angst, and exhaustion. He reminded himself of the success of the night, that his cooler was full, and the fact that he was already halfway home. Calming himself, Zeke forced his mind to concentrate on a safe return to town, the impending processing of his night's catch, and the smell of the damp, salty air.

# Chapter 5

Jim was the first to arrive at the station in the morning. He was forced to start the coffee pot. He wasn't sure how, but Maggie always seemed to make a better pot of coffee. Jim would have to settle for his own method. It was only 6am, but it was already light outside. Clouds covered the sky again, but seemed to sit a little higher than the previous day. The rain still held off, but was just one heavenly sneeze away from falling. Other than the coffee situation, Jim liked to be at the station early. It was quiet, he was alone, and he usually used this time get caught up on his paperwork.

This morning, Jim had other things on his mind than getting caught up on his files. He laid across his desk a nautical map of the region. He followed with his fingertip the shoreline of Prince of Wales Island, heading south from the City of Craig. The shore snaked west in towards the center of the island and then back out again, creating the inlet of Port St. Nicholas. Jim spotted his small, self-named, Mink Island perched next to the southern shoreline of Port St. Nicholas. The big island continued south around a couple of small coves protected by smaller islands. His finger went past Culebrina Island, Unlucky Island, Cana Island, and eventually the Prince of Wales shoreline started to turn in again. Hooligan Arm shot in straight west toward the center of the big island. The nautical map didn't have a lot of land detail, but it did show a narrow opening followed by an oval-shaped lagoon at the head of Hooligan Arm.

After refilling his coffee cup, Jim located a

topographical map of the area. The nautical map gave details of the sea, whereas the topo map gave such land details as elevation contours, terrain type, man-made structures, trails, roads, boat docks, and mines. He checked to see if there was a road system or even a trail system that passed close to the lagoon. Jim located the lagoon at Hooligan Arm on the topo map, but it didn't have any indication of land access. The closest road appeared to pass a little less than a half-mile from the lagoon. There was a cabin titled Beaker Homestead accessible by a Forest Service road that ran close to part of the cove's northern shoreline, but the terrain between that area and where the foot was discovered looked to be dense Alaskan wilderness. It would certainly be nearly impossible to traverse on foot. The river that emptied into the lagoon was unnamed and very short, fed by the mountains that surrounded the coastal region.

He was just about to arrange marine transportation to make a trip out to where the foot was recovered, when he heard a knock on the outside window of his office. Lifting the Levolor blinds to see who was standing in the forested area behind the station, Jim had a hunch who he might find. He sighed after discovering a ponytailed man pressing a nose against the window, smiling and waving.

Opening the side door of the station, Jim said, "It's early, Kram."

"Don't you just love springtime, Jimbo?" Kram bolted into the station like he owned the place, skipping like a schoolgirl, making circles around the other Trooper's empty desks.

"I'm still on my first cup of coffee," Jim hinted

gruffly.

Kram bounded into Jim's office, grabbed the stapler from his desk, and sat cross-legged on the floor. "The birds are chirping, grass is growing… Life, it's a miracle, my blue-clad friend."

"We can't grow grass here, and the only birds that chirp are the ravens and the eagles."

"With the rite of spring upon us, it has reconfirmed my mission to enter the American workforce. Laboring with the common man, eking out a living, making ends meet, working nine to five…everybody's working for the weekend." Kram opened up the stapler and began ejecting staples across the room while humming *I've Been Working on the Railroad*.

Jim sat down in his desk chair and rubbed his temples. "How's the job at the Coffee Hut going?"

"Got fired. Guess they received some complaints… Can't imagine why…" Kram raised and tilted the stapler so that the projectiles arced into a potted ficus tree in the corner of the Lieutenant's office.

"Well, at least you gave it a shot."

"One small setback gives motivation to persevere. I shall once again enter the workforce, with a hardhat on my head, gloves on my hands, and boots on my feet."

"You get a job working construction?"

"No. Grocery bagger."

"Ah."

They heard the sound of keys unlocking the side door to the station. Maggie walked in and gave both men a pretty smile. Her black hair looked freshly brushed and she wore a red sweater above brown pants. Kram hopped to his feet, jogged over, and gave the girl a peck on her dark cheek.

Maggie's smile deepened. "And good morning to you, too, Kram."

Jim waved, and said, "Morning."

"That's all I get? At least Kram knows how to make a girl feel special."

Kram chimed in, "Yeah, Jimbo. Least you can do is give her a hug."

Jim shot his friend the look of death. Kram went back to his stapler game. Jim knew there would be issues when he hired his girlfriend to be dispatcher and station manager. He didn't need Kram adding fuel to the fire. "Kram, don't you think it's time for you to get going? Those groceries aren't going to bag themselves, you know."

Kram saluted. "Aye, aye, skipper. Off to work I go." He started whistling the work song from *Snow White*.

Kram stopped halfway to the door, turned and tossed Jim the stapler, saying, "You might want to refill this. Seems to be empty. Can't imagine why."

Maggie hollered over from her dispatcher's desk, "Hey Kram, have you been giving out our number again? There's a message here for you...something about PVC pipe?"

The rifle scope scanned the back deck of the *Earth's*

*Guardian*. There wasn't much activity. Only one deckhand was working, shuffling about filling scuba tanks and tending to some dive masks. The rest of the boat sat still in the morning calm. The man holding the rifle moved the scope up towards the wheelhouse. The windows reflected the light such that he couldn't see inside. The magnified image of the scope scanned up. Only the single flag flew, advertising the double-P pattern, but not affirming any other allegiances.

Suddenly, activity appeared in the lower portion of the scope and the man moved the rifle down so it was again focused on the wheelhouse. The same short, white-haired man that he had seen time and again appeared at the railing next to the wheelhouse door. The man leaned against the railing and lit a cigarette. The center of the crosshairs focused perfectly on the short man's head, just above his reddened cheeks.

"I could take you out right now," muttered the man behind the gun.

Another person appeared on the walkway next to the short man. It was a younger man wearing an outrageous blue, white, and red shirt and had a red scarf tied around his scrawny neck. The younger man was talking fast. The older, shorter man simply stood still, sucking in on the butt of his cigarette, and blowing smoke out his nostrils. The rifle scope moved its focus between the two men, swinging back and forth from head to head.

"Bastards," said the gunman.

The older, shorter man made a quick statement then waved his non-cigarette arm in a dismissive gesture. The younger nodded and disappeared back inside the wheelhouse. After another long drag on the smoke, the short man flicked it away and then disappeared back through the side door.

"Until next time, gentlemen," said the man looking through the scope. "Until next time."

# Chapter 6

Three women wearing replica hats apropos of what a lady might wear in the late eighteen-hundreds, braved the mild drizzle as they met in town near the floatplane dock. Phyllis Prescott, divorced grandmother who lived alone in a one bedroom shack, carried a magnum of champagne and a portable boom box capable of amplifying compact discs. Angel Yu, Chinese widower who inherited over fifty grand in credit card debt from her late husband, carried three champagne flutes and a handful of red, white, and blue bunting, common to what one might expect to see on a campaign trail. Shasta Wilford, famed for her elaborate stories of being married to the late and exceedingly wealthy Lexington Wilford III, carried a folding card table and several hand-drawn posters. The three women walked together toward the edge of the wooden pier that was elevated fourteen feet up from sea level, and set up their makeshift booth next to the top of the foot-ramp that led down to where floatplanes moored.

Shasta pulled out the legs of her card table and set it close to the top of the ramp. Angel secured the bunting to the small table with a roll of duct tape. Phyllis popped the cork on the bottle of champagne and poured three glasses full. They taped up posters that advertised an event titled *Traverse the Tail*, and all three ladies removed their jackets to expose that they each wore a period dress common to a late-nineteenth century bath-house.

When she first heard the low rumble of the turbine engine, Shasta Wilford raised her champagne flute and giggled,

"Here they come, ladies." Three glasses clinked together, and then three glasses tilted back, pouring yellow, bubbling liquid into three mouths. After each glass was drained, Phyllis Prescott grabbed the bottle from the table and topped them off. The Cranbrook Culture Club was fully primed and ready for their first customers.

Frightening Frankie's single engine de Havilland Beaver appeared through a depression in the mountains from behind the town. After flying over the ladies' heads, the floatplane banked to the left, heading south down the shoreline of the island and away from the dock. After close to a minute of flying away from town, the blue and white de Havilland Beaver made a sharp, right-hand turn, positioning its bearing north up the island and directly into the sputtering wind. With the expertise of an experienced pilot, Frankie eased the seaplane down and dipped the floats onto the water's surface like a duck landing on a pond. Several minutes later, the floatplane taxied over close enough for a dockhand to grab the wing line. The pilot cut the engine, jumped out of the side door, and secured the plane to the wooden dock.

The dockhand quickly began unloading several pieces of luggage from the plane's cargo hold onto a wide cart made from plywood and oversized wheels. Six passengers individually stepped from the plane's float and onto the dock by lifting their feet over a short rail made from four-by-four treated lumber. Standing awkwardly on the floating pier, it was obvious that the recent arrivals weren't locals. The passengers all wore raincoats and hats, and each held various items common to tourists; including cameras, binoculars, rainproof fanny-packs, first aid kits, and thick, expensive Alaskan guidebooks that had no more than half a page dedicated to

Prince of Wales Island. Several of the tourists also clutched a copy of the book, *Muskeg Mama: Memoir of a Klondike Girl.*

As the tourists walked up the ramp with the dockhand pushing the luggage cart close behind, the Cranbrook Culture Club went into full swing. Angel Yu pushed her thumb into a button on the CD player and ragtime music that had been recorded on an out of tune piano filtered through the speakers on the boom box. Shasta Wilford opened up a parasol and began to twirl it above her head while awkwardly fluttering a gloved hand below her wrinkled chin. Phyllis Prescott lifted the hem of her dress and began to kick spastically, poorly mimicking old dancehall moves and threatening the future mobility of her lower extremities.

In a loud, nasally voice, Shasta Wilford yelled, "Welcome to Craig, Alaska, on beautiful Prince of Wales Island. Site of where Ellen Cranbrook used to reside after being stranded here during her exodus from the Klondike Gold Rush of 1896. You've just stepped onto hallowed grounds among adventure seekers. We, the ladies of the Cranbrook Culture Club, would like to be the first to greet all women as they step foot onto this historic rock."

The ragtime music moved from a flitting melody to the more syncopated rhythms of the bridge. Phyllis adjusted her dancing appropriately, almost kicking one of the tourists in the crotch. Shasta moved her gloved hand back under her chin and resumed twinkling her fingers with the grace of a truck driver.

Angel Yu yelled, disproportionally loud and with a thick Chinese-American accent, "You ah now standing on the same island where Ellen Cwanbwoooooooook made the famous joooney through the fowest, suviving the hawsh weathew, bittew cold, and waaaaain."

Being out of shape, and not used to exercise in excess of thirty seconds, Phyllis began to wheeze while her dance moves faltered. Her attempts at leg kicks became quite challenging as the wheezing escalated to pulmonary convulsions.

One of the tourists pointed at Phyllis and asked, "Is she all right?"

Shasta Wilford announced, "Sign up now to guarantee your spot in our legendary reenactment called, *Traverse the Trail*. For only three hundred and forty-five dollars, you can secure your place in an all-inclusive historical trek, including an overnight stay in the legendary rainforest while we read stories of survival from Ellen's own pen. This is a once-in-a-lifetime, authentically Alaskan adventure that pays homage to one of the greatest women in our history. Men need not apply."

Phyllis went for her grand-finale move, sliding down to one knee, arms in the air, hacking uncontrollably while announcing, "Just sign this…" Panting. "…form and be sure…" Hacking. "…to give us your…" Uncontrollable wheezing. "…your contact info…" Coughing fits. "…cash only…"

Angel Yu shouted, causing an obese man from Iowa to plug his ears, "Cash only, exact change, and no weefunds." Continuing in a voice that could shatter a plate glass window, Angel Yu achieved an unprecedented decibel level, pitch and timbre rising shrill with each word. "Space is limited. Women sign up now to make sure you claim a place in histoweeeeeeeee."

Wallets were retrieved, purses opened, and hundred dollar bills produced. The female tourists nodded and eagerly smiled as they signed up for any occurrence that mildly suggested an authentic Alaskan experience, especially an experience relating to Ellen Cranbrook and *Muskeg Mama*. Shasta Wilford passed around clipboards and pens, taking names and addresses, and excitedly registered three fresh new recruits. Angel Yu held each hundred dollar bill up to the sky, vigilantly inspecting for counterfeit bills. Phyllis Prescott lowered her arms, but stayed on her knees, wondering whether or not she might need medical attention.

*The chill of that summer's eve might very well have been the bitter bite of winter's own venomous teeth. It was the first of many times that I genuinely believed my earthly life was meeting its final curtain call. But for this encore, there would be no applause, no rabid, bearded man whose clothes smelled as vile as his dark soul, whistling in my ear, tongue lapping at the watered down whiskey that swirled in his glass, while commanding me forward to one final exposé. My last hurrah, so to speak, would not be on the beer-raddled pine boards of the dancehall stage, but rather, it seemed to be one of pure exhaust, and upon a moss covered stump of a former glorious hemlock, no less. I pulled my damp and quivering body upon the arborous relic, preparing to succumb to the imminent darkness that crept over my being, giving one last gaze out to the aquatic burial ground of the lost ship and all its mates. There was only wind, rain, and the silence of death that stared back, leaving only to my resolve, what I thought would most certainly be, my last breath.*

The call came in while Jim was on patrol. Maggie's voice came through the radio and announced that there were reports of multiple four-wheelers causing a disturbance on Williwaw Drive. Jim answered the call and informed his dispatcher that he was already fairly close to the location. Maggie gave him the full address and name of the person that made the complaint. Jim made a quick U-turn and guided his Ford Crown Victoria toward the direction of the call.

While en route, he questioned, as he often did, the wisdom of hiring his girlfriend to be the station dispatcher. He wondered how many successful relationships there were between people that worked together during the day. Maggie was great, both as a girlfriend and as a dispatcher, but shouldn't there be a little separation between professional and personal lives? Plus, he was Maggie's boss. So far, Jim didn't feel as though it was too much of an issue, but he could only imagine what might happen the first time he had to discipline the employee. That certainly might result in the cold shoulder after hours.

Concerned at how his other subordinates might interpret the situation, Jim had already gone over it multiple times with the other Troopers in his charge. Stilly and Brandi both assured their boss that it was a good hire. First, there were no other viable candidates for the job, and second, Maggie was awesome at running the station. They both advised their boss to lighten up on the situation, but Jim sensed that something was there beneath the surface of their words.

It legitimately concerned Jim. He really enjoyed his relationship with Maggie, even, dare he say, *loved* being with her. He also agreed with the other Troopers that Maggie performed her duties as dispatcher and station manager well. Being fairly new to the job, Maggie still had a lot to learn, but in many ways, she had already surpassed the person that she had replaced. Maggie was smart, quick, dealt with emergency situations with a calm head, great with technology, completely trustworthy, had firsthand knowledge of the area and residents, and she even knew how to make coffee just the way he liked it. So why did it still bother Jim that he had hired his girlfriend?

The white and blue Alaska State Trooper vehicle turned onto Williwaw Drive. After only a quarter mile down the gravel road, Jim saw a man standing alone in the road at the base of a short driveway that led to a wood-shingled duplex. He parked on the side of the road, donning his Stetson as he stepped out of the car. The Trooper walked over to the man, projecting the standard stoic assuredness that came natural to wearing the uniform.

"Perfect timing. You just missed them." The man spoke in a nerdy voice that dripped with sarcasm. He was a man of less than average height with thick, fuzzy eyebrows named Cliff Barr.

"Hi there, Cliff. You the one that called it in?" Jim knew the man, as it wasn't the first time he had registered complaints.

"Of course I called it in. Look what they did." Cliff pointed to his mailbox that sat crumpled on the gravel next to the road.

A lady wrapped in a baby blue bathrobe, clutching a small, hairy animal, came waddling down a different driveway. She stopped at her mailbox that still stood erect, light glinting off of its perfectly polished metal top, and removed a handful of envelopes from inside.

Cliff Barr pleaded, "Ask her. She had to have seen

44

them, too. I'm not the only person on Williwaw Drive with eyes and ears."

The woman in the bathrobe turned and shuffled back up her dirt driveway toward her home. The small dog that she held yipped angrily at Cliff as the woman disappeared.

Jim asked, "I'm going to need a few details. How many are we dealing with here?"

"There were three of them. All on four-wheelers and all wearing coats, gloves and helmets. I shouted at them that I was making a citizen's arrest and that they should stop immediately, turn off their engines, and wait for the authorities. They blatantly ignored my commands. Can you believe that?"

"Shocking." Jim jotted a few words in his notebook. "It's not illegal to run four-wheelers on this road. What caused you to call in a disturbance?"

"Are you blind? Look at my mailbox." Cliff Barr spoke in a tone reminiscent of a rebellious teenager. "Also, look at the track marks in the gravel. They ran up and down my driveway several times at extremely high speeds. They spun donuts next to my house and, I'll say it again, they knocked down my mailbox. There's got to be a law against this kind of harassment."

"There is. Okay, I get it. That is definitely called a disturbance."

"*Disturbance?*" Cliff Barr exploded. His furry eyebrows seemed to poke straight out from his face as his temper flared. "This is a Federal case. Isn't the mail controlled by the United States Postmaster General? Call the FBI. I want satellite imagery, phone taps, automatic weapons. These are terrorists.

Call Homeland Security."

"Calm down there, Cliff. We're probably talking about a couple of teenagers out for a little mailbox baseball. I'll try to find them and ask them to stop."

Cliff threatened to come unglued. "*Ask* them to stop?"

"Any idea where they came from?"

Cliff shrugged, scowling.

"Do you know what type of ATVs they were riding?"

Nothing.

"Two-stroke, four-stroke? Arctic Cat? Polaris? Yamaha?"

Silence.

"Red? Green? Blue? Yellow?"

Lip curl.

Jim sighed. "Did you recognize any of the riders?"

Cliff shook his head.

"Do you think these were young kids or adults?"

Another shrug.

"Which way did they go when they left?"

Cliff pointed one way, shook his head, then pointed the other way.

"Okay," Jim said. "Well, I'll look into it."

"You haven't a clue where to find these guys, do you?" Cliff Barr asked.

"Well, I have to admit, there's not a lot of info for me to go off of, Cliff. But this is a small island and word travels fast. Like I said before, my guess is these are teenagers out for a joy-ride. They just need to learn a little respect for personal property is all, and I'll do my best to help them learn." Jim pocketed his notebook and headed for his car.

The short man with furry eyebrows asked, "That's it? What if they come back and terrorize my poor mailbox again?"

Pointing to the crumpled piece of metal lying on the ground, Jim said, "I'm not sure what else they could do to that mailbox. Looks like it's already taken as much terrorizing as it can take."

"Aren't you planning on regular neighborhood patrols? How about a sting operation?"

Stepping into his car, Jim said, "Look, Cliff. If this becomes an issue again, you can give us another call. My advice is, lighten up. The more fired up you get, the more these kids will work you. Try offering them some cookies next time, and they'll leave you alone."

"*Cookies*?"

"Yes, cookies."

Just after Jim closed his car door and started the engine, Cliff yelled, "My tax dollars pay your salary. Why don't *you* bake them some cookies?" The man's overactive brow seemed to dance above his eye sockets when he yelled.

Lieutenant Wekle drove away leaving the distraught and unsatisfied man standing in the middle of the gravel road.

# Chapter 7

Growing up with high levels of anxiety, an intense bout of irritable bowel syndrome, and a paralyzing stutter, it didn't help matters that Zeke Melon came from near-regal stock. Born Ezekiel Daniel Mellon into one of the most influential families in the State of Pennsylvania, the kid seemed doomed from birth. The pressure that was inherited with being a relative of the founder of the Mellon Institute of Industrial Research, and former United States Secretary of the Treasury, was more than Zeke could endure. After barely graduating from high school in Pittsburgh, Pennsylvania, he was granted forced admittance to his ancestor's namesake across town in what was now known as Carnegie Mellon University.

After trying his darnedest to flunk out, Zeke was shocked when he made the dean's list his freshman year. Only attending his classes less than half the time and making sure that he failed most every exam, the young Mellon was convinced that he was being heralded as the college's poster boy for academics solely based on his last name. Baffled by cronyism, Zeke decided to legally change the spelling of his last name by dropping one of the "L's." During his second year of complete ineptitude, half of his college professors didn't put two-and-two together and actually graded him appropriately. By mid-terms of his junior year, Zeke was dismissed from Carnegie Mellon University as a complete failure and family disgrace.

With a desire to move himself as far away from his

family legacy as possible, Zeke began to hitchhike west. This proved to be more difficult than he had figured as hitchhiking had gone out of style years ago. No one seemed eager to jump at the chance to pick up a lanky redhead wearing a backpack and Carnegie Mellon sweatshirt. It didn't help matters that Dateline had recently aired, and re-aired, their special report titled, *Hitchhiking America: A Killer at Every Turnstile*. It took Zeke three weeks of sleeping in bus stations and bumming rides from truck drivers before he finally reached Seattle, Washington. Convinced that Seattle was about as far away from home as he could get, Zeke set out to find work and attempted to make a go of it.

He got a job working at Ivan's Fish Bar on the Seattle waterfront, cooking fried cod that was served to tourists through a sidewalk window. With minimum wage earnings and perpetually reeking of fry oil, Zeke still hadn't found the Zen happiness he so longed to achieve. He was sneaking down on the waterfront marinas at night and sleeping undetected on the back decks of various fishing boats. Zeke showered at work once or twice a week, and used a laundromat sparingly, ate mostly French fries and deep fried clam strips, and spent his off time roaming the streets. His only saving grace was that the deep fryer's sound and odor masked his constant farting and his current job and lifestyle required him to speak very little; a fact that he relished given his propensity towards stuttering.

His life seemed to have stability, at least for a very short time; however, two things happened that had dramatic results. First, Zeke got promoted. He always showed up early and stayed late. He tended to his duties as fry cook with purpose and pride. His manager saw a work ethic in Zeke that wasn't often displayed in your average Ivan's Fish Bar employee. The other workers collectively looked about as enthused as a sloth convention. It showed that Zeke actually appreciated attending to his duties, having a roof over his head, and eating the free meal that came with every shift.

When Zeke's manager informed him that he was being moved to the cashier's window and being given a fifty-cent-per-hour raise, Zeke's response was, "Sh… Sh… Sh… Sh…" The manager interpreted this as, "Sure," but in actuality, Zeke was trying to express a much different four-letter word. His boss never quite got the message that he was horrified at the notion that he would now be forced to interact with humans. The thought of running a cash register and fighting through his stutter for eight hours a day, scared him deeply. The day before his promotion was to kick-in, Zeke Melon decided that drastic measures were in order.

With mostly unpleasant memories of a sickly youth and overbearing parental units, Zeke focused on one of the few bright spots in his memory. When he displayed symptoms of fighting a cold, his mother would often give him Nyquil to help him sleep. Zeke displayed cold symptoms often, sometimes even surprising himself with how a bout of clammy hands and post-nasal-drip became so easy to produce. Most mothers would temper this medicinal treatment by offering their child a watered-down children's version of the cold syrup, but Zeke's mother believed in fighting ailments head-on. After gulping down several ounces of the dark green, licorice flavored ooze, Zeke noticed that in addition to his oft-faux sniffles subsiding, his stutter seemed to all but disappear. Temporary relief from intense stutter should have been listed on the bottle. As far as he was concerned, downing a few gulps of the magical green sludge was one of the best parts of his day. Zeke Melon was a Nyquil junkie.

Although the prohibitive cost and lack of human interaction put his cough medicine addiction into temporary remission, the new promotion to the cashier's window brought back Zeke's craving with a charging vengeance. Literally seconds after his boss informed him of his new duties, Zeke made a beeline up the street for a twenty-four-hour mini-mart that mainly paid its bills with cigarette sales and back door meth transactions. The mini-mart manager was happy to sell Zeke a bottle of Nyquil that had sat on his shelf collecting dust for over three years.

The second dramatic event to hit Zeke right around the time of his Ivan's Fish Bar promotion was simply due to the passing of days on the calendar. As the late winter months moved into solid springtime, Zeke found fewer places to squat in the marina. He had become an expert at secretly locating small covered areas on the back decks of various vessels to sleep in. Most of the boats that he snuck onto happened to be commercial fishing rigs. Most of these boats were now being readied for the impending season, which often required the captain and crew to sleep aboard. As nets were tended, engines tuned-up, galleys stocked, decks painted, and septic holding tanks pumped, Zeke found that more and more of these boats were actually leaving their port along the Seattle waterfront. Whether moving to dry-dock for hull maintenance, or heading north for the season, Zeke's floating armada of nighttime havens was quickly shrinking.

Timing was a crucial factor in the events that led to Zeke Melon's Seattle departure. After getting the dosage wrong before one of his shifts at the Ivan's Fish Bar cash register, Zeke appeared to be quite intoxicated while attempting to count back change to an elderly couple from Butte, Montana. Although his stutter had completely subsided, Zeke's manager spotted him handing over bills one at a time, giggling at the Presidents' faces.

"Abraham Lincoln...Hee hee. George Washington.... He's silly."

Not only was he completely stoned to the gills, but also so totally pleased at the ease with which he spoke, he didn't realize that the manager was standing over his shoulder watching the whole exchange. After enduring a seemingly endless lecture from his boss, Zeke was fired on the spot, given his last pay in cash, and kicked out the back door of the restaurant.

Without purpose and still fuzzy from the narcotic effect of the cough syrup, Zeke walked the docks of the marina. He staggered by a rather large purse seiner named *Ella Maye* just as the captain was cussing out his first mate. The crew was down two members and the boat was scheduled to leave in the morning. The captain, being a boisterous, unforgiving man, took this fact out on a rather innocent first mate by shouting loud enough to be heard three slips over. Just as the captain screamed in his mate's ear about being dangerously shorthanded and desperately in need of a deckhand, Zeke appeared at the deck and said, "I'll do it."

After being hired on the spot, Zeke was told to gather his things and be aboard in time to clean up the dinner dishes in the galley. He would be given a bunk in which to bed down and the vessel would lift dock lines at first light in the morning, heading north. Zeke grabbed his backpack and made a hasty trek for the nearest drug store.

With a diet that had for weeks solely consisted of deep fried foods and cough syrup, mixed with bowels that had a natural propensity toward instability, Zeke's bunkmates were treated to a chorus of flatulence unlike anything they had ever experienced. His gas proved so extraordinary in both timbre and aroma, the other crewmates took to sleeping up in the ship's dining area. Between the gas issues and the fact that the kid downed cold medicine like it was Gatorade, the crew was ready to lynch the guy before the boat had even made it out of Canadian waters and into Southeast Alaska.

When the other shipmates complained, the captain originally told the crew to, "Suck it up," but eventually decided that the Nyquil addiction was actually quite a liability. Fearing that Zeke would fall off the boat in a stupor, the captain gave the go-ahead to the first mate's request to replace Zeke at their first port. Finding a brief moment of cell reception while passing a small town on the British Columbia coastline, the first mate called his cousin on Prince of Wales Island and arranged for an exchange. The captain guided the *Ella Maye* up the western coast of the island and pulled into harbor at Craig, Alaska for one quick overnight stay. Once the first mate's cousin was on board, Zeke was kicked off amid a rainstorm and left standing on the pier with his backpack, Nyquil bottles, and intense gas.

For better or for worse, Zeke Melon had made his way from Pennsylvania to Prince of Wales Island in Southeast Alaska. It was about as far removed from his home and family as he could possibly imagine without leaving the country for a Siberian labor camp. Zeke decided that the community of Craig would be his new home. He immediately sought employment and cheap housing, and over time, the young redhead had saved up enough money to buy a small, used, aluminum skiff.

# Chapter 8

With nothing more to go on other than a disembodied foot, Lieutenant Jim Wekle knew that he had to conduct a search of the area where it was found. He had contracted an official run out to Hooligan Arm with his usual contact for such outings. Sitting behind the wheel of his brand new boat, the silver-haired Hugh Eckley pushed his Boston Whaler 285 Conquest hard against the chop.

"This thing is sure beautiful, Hugh," Jim said while sitting in an elevated seat just inside a small, partially enclosed cabin.

Hugh smiled, expressing self-admiration concerning his recent purchase. "This isn't even half throttle. This baby can fly."

The pristine twenty-eight foot, white fiberglass craft was perfectly suited for the waters surrounding Prince of Wales as it sprayed foam to either side, easily cutting a swath through the sea's surface. The boat had a v-berth up under the bow, full state-of-the-art electronics in the cabin, a back deck perfect for fishing, and twin Mercury 225 engines hanging off the transom.

Jim sat comfortably without the need to hold himself steady. "I am really impressed. This is a fantastic boat." The boat was so clean and new, the Trooper had almost felt guilty wearing shoes when he'd stepped aboard.

"It better be fantastic. It cost almost as much as my house." Hugh Eckley had a passion for the sea. He was as naturally comfortable behind the wheel of his craft as the eagles were in the air, soaring overhead. Hugh adjusted the scale of his electronic chart that sat perched above an array of gauges. "This chart's tied into the radar. We could run blinded by fog or night and I'd know right where we were."

The boat weaved its way around small islands as it sped south down the shoreline of Prince of Wales. It was a fairly mild spring day with high, overcast clouds, no rain and a paltry fifty-two degree temperature. Jim had traveled around the island by boat many times, but he always marveled at the stunning scenery. Land was always green, with cedar, spruce, and hemlocks filling nearly every inch of land. The island shorelines were mostly dark rock, with a white line marking the high tide. The water was, more often than not, a dark, deep blue-grey, with white, foamy caps caused by wind and turbulent current. The sky was usually grey and cloudy, frequently dripping with the very moisture that kept the land intensely green. It was a mostly uninhabited land surrounded by a vast sea, and ensconced in a rugged beauty that many sought to experience, but only a hearty few were brave enough to call home.

"Here it is," Hugh said, indicating that they were entering Hooligan Arm. The skipper guided the boat past a point of land that disguised the cove's opening, and then veered sharply to the left, showing off his new craft's mobility a little. After straightening out, the older man grinned as he glanced over to the State Trooper.

"Handles like a dream," Hugh shouted.

Jim nodded. "Smooth ride, Skipper."

The boat's captain powered back and the Boston

Whaler settled down into the water, easing into a slow chug. Jim grabbed a pair of binoculars and scanned the shoreline on both sides of the cove as they putted their way towards the head of the arm. Nothing but water, rocks, driftwood, seaweed, birds, and trees could be seen.

Hugh dialed in a close-up view of the cove on the digital chart. He had to adjust the scale several times. What at first appeared as a mere asterisk, grew into a jagged oval shape in the middle of the cove as the skipper modified the zoom.

"That little rock is right over there." Hugh moved his finger from the digital chart monitor and pointed through the forward window, straight off the bow. Waves lapped against a round, dark protrusion, no more than fifteen feet in diameter. "That thing is a boat killer. There's good depth on either side, but with the outgoing tide and strong current exiting from the lagoon, I'm not getting anywhere close to that sucker."

Still holding the binoculars, Jim stepped out onto the stern deck and scanned the rocks just below the tree line on both sides of the cove. He used a finger to adjust the focus as he slowly turned his upper body, examining every rock in Hooligan Arm. Over his shoulder, Jim hollered through the opening of the cabin, "Can you get in closer to the mouth of the lagoon?"

"I'll get you as close as I can." Hugh inched up the throttle and the engines churned the boat forward into the inlet.

As the boat idled closer and closer to the head of the cove, Jim was able to get a close-up scan of where Zeke Melon had described standing while dip-netting hooligan. Water frothed as it seemed to get sucked out of the lagoon. The closer the boat got to the lagoon, the more the current seemed to impede its progress.

Hugh shouted, "Current's strong here. Not sure how much closer I feel comfortable getting. Still getting used to this boat, and I don't like strong currents."

Jim nodded in agreement. "You think you can find a place to drop me off on shore?"

"Not with a brand new fiberglass hull," Hugh answered. "I haven't even named her yet. No chance I'm gonna put a rock next to her bow. You can swim."

"Not likely," Jim chuckled in response.

While Hugh performed a tight turn, Jim shifted his position on the back deck so that he could inspect the shoreline on the opposite side of the cove. There was no sign of humanity anywhere. Everywhere he looked, Jim saw lush forest growing straight up from jagged chunks of black basalt rock. Just below the high tide line, brown seaweed and white barnacles littered the surface of the black rocks. Waves splashed at the base of the rocks and chunks of smoothed driftwood bounced against the shore.

Jim was hoping to see some object or some color stand out as he scanned. He wanted to see just one sight that didn't belong in hopes that it was a clue to what happened to the man that formerly owned the foot that had been found. There was nothing other than the rugged nature that stared back at the Trooper.

As the skipper slowly ran the boat up the opposite shoreline that they had entered, Hugh asked, "No cigar this time, Jim? Don't you usually puff away on the back deck on these kinds of boat trips?"

Still scanning with the binoculars, Jim answered, "My girlfriend wants me to quit."

Hugh snorted a little laugh. "Aren't you her boss?"

"It's complicated."

"They're all complicated, Jim, my friend."

The boat had just passed the halfway point of the cove's southern shoreline. They were again even with the small rock that crowned just above the water's surface in the center of Hooligan Arm. Jim dropped the binoculars from his eyes and looked all around, hoping the boat's new position would provide a fresh perspective. As his view passed over the center of the cove, something caught his attention. Just above the water line on the south side of the small rock that lifted up in the middle of the cove, something strikingly white appeared to be stuck in place.

"There," Jim hollered as he pointed toward the rock. Both Jim and Hugh took turns with the binoculars analyzing the white object. Neither man could make out what it was, but they both thought that it was not from the natural environment that surrounded them. They agreed that a closer look was in order.

As the boat slowly moved in towards the rock, Hugh's expression became more stoic and more focused. Jim knew well enough that the skipper didn't like moving his new craft in towards something so ominous. Hugh glanced at his depth reading continuously as he inched closer.

"How's the depth, Hugh?" asked Jim.

"Plenty of depth," was the reply, but Jim could hear concern in Hugh's voice.

Jim found a long-handled boat hook that was propped up next to the outside opening of the cabin. "Do you think you can get close enough for me to reach it with this?"

The boat skipper gave a half-nod. "That all depends on depth and current. I'll give it a try."

The slower that the boat crept, the more the waves bounced them around. It seemed to Jim that maritime maneuvering at low speeds was a very inaccurate art form. The slower a boat motored, the less control the operator seemed to have. He trusted that his skipper's decades of experience on the water would keep them safe, but Jim couldn't help but fear the rock that bounced closer by the second.

The boat turned sideways to the rock. Jim reached out with the boat hook toward what looked like a white piece of fabric of some sort. He made a pass at hooking the fabric, but they still weren't close enough by two or three yards.

"I'll make another pass. Now that I know the depth readings here, I can get you closer." Hugh powered up slightly as he made a quick three-sixty, turning away from the rock and circling back in for a closer run.

Jim stretched out with the hook as the boat nervously passed within several feet of the rock. "A little closer, Hugh. Almost there."

Hugh turned the wheel toward the rock and the boat bounced a few feet closer in. Jim leaned out from the rail of the back deck, risking a fall overboard. A wave pushed the boat in several inches more and Jim was able to slip the edge of the boat hook under the white piece of fabric. With barely a grip on the long handle, Jim didn't have the leverage that he had hoped for. Lifting the object from the rock took all of his finger and hand strength. After elevating the fabric from the rock, Jim feared for a moment that it might drop into the water. He pulled hard and shot the boat hook quickly onto the back deck, successfully securing the object of his pursuit safely on board.

"Got it," Jim yelled.

Hugh Eckley gunned the engines and the boat veered sharply away from the rock, unscathed and without incident. "Next time you have a search and recovery mission, you might think about calling the Ross brothers."

"Hey, we didn't damage anything. Besides, a little scratch in the new fiberglass would give this thing a little Alaskan character. It's way too clean."

Hopping into the elevated chair next to the skipper, Jim brought with him the white fabric that they had just recovered. The piece under inspection was about a two foot long and one foot wide segment that was smooth and purely white on one side, and a rough, off-white underneath. It was made out of strong material, but certainly pliable. The smooth, white side had been laminated and was obviously waterproof and marine-grade. The underside appeared dull and rough. The edges were jagged and appeared to have been torn away rather than cut.

"What do you think, Hugh?" Jim held the specimen out for inspection.

Without taking it from the Trooper, Hugh answered

confidently, "I know exactly what that's from."

After a silent pause, Jim prodded, "I'm all ears, Hugh."

The boat captain exhaled and shook his head slowly. "That material's from an inflatable raft."

"Aren't those rafts pretty tough? Have you ever seen a segment torn apart from the rest of the raft like this?"

"No. If they had hit that rock and punctured the raft, it would still be primarily intact. Just not suitable for flotation. This material is strong, Jim. To be ripped apart like this... There had to be quite a bit of force."

Jim paused a moment before asking, "About as much force as it would take to blow a foot off of someone's body?"

"That sounds about right." Hugh had driven the boat far from the rock, and took the engines out of gear. The wind turned the boat slightly as it safely bobbed in the middle of the bay. Hugh Eckley had a somber look on his face as he turned to his passenger and said, "Something bad happened out here, Jim."

The Alaska State Trooper studied the fragment that he held in his hand as the two sat quietly for a moment, allowing the boat to drift in the wind and current. Jim broke the silence. "We may not know what exactly happened out here, yet, but at least I know what to look for. We're still missing a lot of body parts and quite a bit more of this raft."

"We can look all you want, but with currents like these, I think we are lucky to have found anything. It could all be sitting down at the bottom or washed half way to Russia by now."

"I think we're done searching out here for today. I need to go back into town and look around a bit."

Putting the boat back into gear, Hugh asked, "Oh Yeah? What're you looking for there?"

Jim turned his head. "I'm looking for someone that's missing a white inflatable raft."

# Chapter 9

"Is the sky ever blue in this friggin' place?" barked Pierre Lemieux while standing on the lower rear section of the *Earth's Guardian*, again decked out head to toe in all white clothes. His voice bellowed with more of a Midwestern American accent than that of his French namesake. His white shoes had received a recent fresh polish and gleamed despite the lack of sunshine.

Beanie LeFranc busily tussled with a stack of papers that threatened to blow away from his hands in the ever present wind. "This is Alaska, Uncle Pierre. What did you expect? Sun, sand, babes in bikinis?" The awkward kid laughed, snorting nasally at his own questions. He again wore the same ship's outfit of white pants, French flag shirt, and his own added charm: a bright red scarf tied around the neck. Regardless of how he accessorized, the kid couldn't help but look like a dork.

"Shut up, shit-brick, and climb down the ladder." The two men opened a gate at the edge of the ship and descended the side of the vessel, stepping into a white inflatable raft. A crewman sat at the back of the raft ready to provide the two with transportation. Once everyone settled on board, the crewman fired up a small, but noisy, outboard engine. Plumes of blue hovered around their three heads as the engine sputtered through the choking process. The small raft shoved away from the larger ship and began buzzing across the bay toward town just as rain started to fall from the low, grey clouds.

While being pelted in the face with tiny raindrop pellets, Pierre Lemieux growled, "Where did you schedule our town meeting? City hall?"

Beanie shook his scrawny face and shouted above the engine noise, voice squeaking at high decibel, "No. It wasn't a big enough meeting space. Ever since you had me hang up posters that called commercial fisherman the *rapists of the sea*, we seem to have drawn a pretty big crowd for tonight."

"Good. That's what we want. So where are we holding the meeting?"

"In the warehouse portion of the cannery over there." Beanie pointed toward one of the larger buildings on the Craig waterfront. The drab building stuck out over deep water, suspended on large pilings that plunged down, supporting ocean-side moorage for a long fish-buying vessel.

Pierre Lemieux hollered back, "So let me get this straight. We are about to unleash a shit-storm of environmentalist eco-babble rant concerning the ills of commercial fishing while standing in the middle of a fish cannery, centered in a town that mainly subsists on the very industry that we are attacking?"

"That's sounds about right, Uncle."

"We'll be lucky to make it out alive."

"You told me to poke the hornets' nest, if I remember correctly."

"You contact local law enforcement?"

"No. Was that a mistake? They usually attend when we cause this sort of ruckus."

"One can only hope." Pierre Lemieux attempted to light a cigarette, but failed due to the constant onslaught of wind and rain.

As the small raft pulled up close to the city dock, four strong looking bearded men wearing jeans, flannel shirts, and brown Xtratuf boots stepped out from a couple of the fishing boats moored at the dock. The fishermen walked slowly toward the edge of the city float. One of them held an ominous looking gaff hook. Another held a wooden club commonly used as a fish-bonker. The four figures stood tall at an open section of the pier, gritting their teeth and puffing out their chests in a symbolic display of manhood.

As the inflatable raft approached the pier, the fisherman holding the gaff hook yelled, "Dock's closed. You'll have to turn back."

The man piloting Pierre Lemieux's small craft cut the throttle down to an idle and looked at his boss, waiting for instructions. Pierre Lemieux gave a sinister grin while giving the signal to turn back. "Well, Beanie, my boy. It looks as though the hornets' nest has truly been kicked. Let's head back to the ship. I have a phone call to make."

As the raft made a quick circle away from the city dock, Beanie asked excitedly, voice warbling as always, "Does that mean I should cancel the public meeting?"

"Not at all. We'll be showing up tonight. But instead, we'll be walking in with full armed escort." Pierre Lemieux smiled widely as the white inflatable raft skated over the water's surface away from the city. "Looks like we will be contacting that local law enforcement after all."

It had been a rough morning for Cliff Barr. He had several hours and close to fifty bucks invested in replacing the mailbox that the thug four-wheeler gang had crushed and knocked over. Chores like this didn't come easy for the man, either. He had worn out his small stock of profanity and invented several new words in the process. The man was a writer by trade, and any amount of physical labor stressed him to the core of his being. Frazzled, exhausted, and emotionally drained, Cliff Barr didn't have the gumption to work toward his various writing deadlines that faced him. Instead, he decided to go grocery shopping.

Binging on ice cream, soda, and Pringles seemed prudent to the writer. He filed through the aisles of Ocean Market in Craig, filling his metal shopping cart with nothing but junk food and the occasional staple. His cart brimming with chemical-laced snacks, Cliff pushed into an empty checkout stand and began unloading his sweet and savory treats onto the black conveyor belt. A young girl wearing a name tag on her apron that read, "Savannah," assessed the load of groceries to be just large enough that she radioed in for backup.

"Customer assistance on check-stand three," echoed through the store's sound system.

Within seconds, a pony-tailed man that appeared much too old to be a bag-boy came sprinting up to the end of the checkout stand, grinning excitedly. A name tag that hung upside down on his stained apron indicated that he was "In Training."

"Hello, sir," exclaimed the aging bag-boy wearing jean cutoff shorts. "I am here to make your grocery shopping experience as smooth and enjoyable as humanly possible. Would you like paper bags, plastic bags, cardboard boxes, or should I just carry your wares to your vehicle, one armload at a time?"

Savannah rolled her eyes as she scanned across a box of Ding Dongs.

Cliff gruffly replied, "Plastic will be fine."

The ponytailed bagger shouted, "Hot damn! Plastic it is." He started peeling off plastic bags from the checkstand in a flurry. "I'll triple-bag 'em for extra support." Several bags had gotten away from him and sailed like parachutes away from the counter. "The real trick here is to line up the handles like so." Kram held up an empty trio of plastic bags for customer inspection. Cliff ignored him and dug out a credit card from his wallet.

Kram leaned over the checkstand, and fixated on Cliff Barr's face. Exuding fascination, he said, "You have the most fantastically furry eyebrows that I've ever seen."

Savannah interrupted the fixation by passing him a tube of cookie dough. "Hurry up. You're falling behind."

The bagger stuffed groceries into the triple-bagged pouch with the speed of a maniac on caffeine pills. "The way I see it, the more we fit into these things, the fewer trips it will take you from your car. It's raining out there, and you'll thank me for sure if I can reduce this down to one trip." A crunching sound was heard as the bagger crammed a half-gallon of ice cream on top of a Doritos bag.

Cliff Barr cringed. "Hey, uh, take it easy on the chips there. I was planning on eating those."

While juggling a can of chili, a Hershey bar, and a box of Triscuits, Kram exclaimed, "I bet you've never seen this move before." He tossed the three items high in the air, and caught each in an open grocery bag one at a time. The can of chili pulverized the chocolate bar.

Savannah said in a bored monotone, "That'll be sixty-three, forty-two, please."

Mesmerized by the scene of his bag-boy balancing a summer sausage on his nose, Cliff automatically swiped a credit card through the digit scanning machine. Savannah tore the receipt from the cash register and handed it to the customer without saying a word. The receipt dropped during the exchange and fluttered to the floor.

"I've got it, don't worry." Kram shoved the summer sausage into Cliff's chest and dove to the floor like a lineman going after a fumble. He reappeared within seconds, clenching the receipt close to his eyes. "Ah, there you go, uh, Mr. Cliff Barr..." Upon reading the name, Kram froze with the receipt half extended toward the customer. "Wait a minute. You're seriously named, Cliff Barr? I love those things. I pack Cliff Bars when I go hiking. The Macadamia Nut/White Chocolate are my favorites; nourishing yet enormously delicious. Cliff Barr. I would kill to have that name."

Kram dropped the receipt to flutter back to the floor and grabbed the intercom mic. Pressing a button, the entire store filled with Kram attempting a faux deep voice: "Cliff...Barr... Paging a Mister Cliff...Barr... There's a coconut almond butter here with your name on it." Changing voices, Kram mimicked a southern drawl, "Cliff Barr...Ya'll come back to the deli department where we'll be sampling blueberry crisp all afternoon. It's reeealll goooood." Switching to a thick German accent, "We've got da carrot cake, und da oatmeal raisin for da Cliff Barr. They be vundabar!" Kram burst into uproarious laughter, still depressing the button on the intercom microphone. His cackle echoed off the freezer coolers.

Cliff stormed out of the store carrying sixty-three dollars worth of groceries stuffed into two bags ready to burst at the seams. He loaded them into a blue Toyota Rav4 and pulled out of the store lot fuming over being ridiculed by a grocery bagger. His mood didn't improve when he returned home. He turned the Toyota onto Williwaw Drive only to find that his newly installed mailbox had been once again pummeled into the ground.

# Chapter 10

Zeke Melon's rental reeked. He lived in a one-bedroom duplex off of Williwaw Drive about a half-mile outside of the Craig city limits. The neighbor that lived in the other side of the duplex had already threatened to call the cops if he didn't get rid of the smell. Zeke sensed that his neighbor enjoyed calling the cops and had done so frequently in the past.

After pumping septic tanks and outhouses for weeks on end, Zeke considered the scent of eighteen-hundred dead fish lying around his apartment to be quite innocuous. Zeke was, however, worried that if the neighbor did turn him in for drying fish inside his rental, the word would spread to his landlord, resulting in a possible eviction. There was no way he was going back to being homeless. The last thing he wanted to risk was losing all the time and product he had invested into his hooligan candle operation. At this point, it seemed he had no other options for a drying location.

He thought about moving the dead fish to an outdoor location, but he was confident they would get eaten by insects, birds, or could even attract bears. He considered renting a storage unit, but between rent for the duplex and all that he had invested in his boat and dip-net supplies, Zeke was tapped financially. He even went as far as to ask his boss at the septic pump shop if there was room in the back for him to lay out a couple thousand hooligan to dry. His boss quoted several potential health code violations. For some reason it was considered unsanitary to store a household product next to a ripe shit-pumper. Zeke Melon was stuck with drying fish in his apartment.

There were fish lying atop wax paper in almost every inch of his rental. The kitchen and bathroom counters were completely covered. With the exception of narrow pathways leading around the apartment, most of the floor space was taken up as well. To force a quicker drying process, Zeke turned the heater up and left it on high day and night. The reaction of constant heat mixed with dead, oily fish created one of the ripest stenches one could possibly imagine. The odor infiltrated every piece of clothing, every inch of furniture fabric, every crevice of every orifice attached in any way to Zeke and his apartment. Zeke Melon went about his business, happily coexisting with hundreds of dead fish, blissfully oblivious to the stink.

The plan was to amass at least two thousand of the little suckers, sufficiently dry them, and run each through the anus and out the mouth with an eight-inch length of wick. Once impaled, each hooligan would be mounted on a small stand crafted out of a recycled aluminum beer can and a three-inch nail. Over several days while the hooligan dried, Zeke decided to be industrious and do some prep-work. Cutting the bottom portion of a beer can was both tedious and hazardous to Zeke's health. After using a hack saw on close to a hundred cans per day, his hands had been cut so many times that Zeke's Band-Aid budget was becoming a concern. It wasn't until his left hand was almost completely covered with fresh cuts and bandages that he started wearing gloves.

Being a college dropout didn't prohibit Zeke from performing simple multiplication. If he could sell two thousand hooligan candles for fifteen bucks apiece, he could rake in thirty grand. The process of production wouldn't be his only overhead, though. Zeke knew that his venture required a larger pool of tourists to market his product to than what Prince of Wales Island had to offer. He needed to be on the docks in Ketchikan when thousands of cruise ship patrons stepped off their ships every day during the summer months. Zeke was hopeful that he could sell his entire stock within a couple of weekend trips, if things played out just right.

He would need some demo product, for sure. Not only would he need to show the tourists how these fish would burn like a candle when he peddled them on the Ketchikan waterfront, but Zeke knew that he needed to trial run a few of these candles at home, just to make sure the little suckers would actually burn. He shuffled along his fish-laden apartment, carefully stepping over layers of hooligan, until he located a batch from one of his first dip-net outings. He selected one of the dead fish that looked especially old and wrinkled, assuming that it had been drying the longest and possibly ready for a test fire.

Running the wick through proved challenging. The young entrepreneur had selected a thin wick and routed it through the back end of a long, thick needle. He ran the needle up through the butthole of the smelt-like creature and angled the needle so it would hopefully come out between the fish's teeth. During the skewering of the hooligan, the fish buckled and the needle shot straight out through the small scales of its fleshy side. Not submitting to frustration, Zeke calmly rerouted the needle back into the middle of the fish and eventually it found its way to the head portion. Missing the mouth by a fraction of an inch, the tip of the needle protruded straight out one of the hooligan's eye sockets, taking the dried eyeball with it.

It looked gruesome, but it would work. With a wick streaming up from an eye and a nail sticking in through its underbelly, a skinny, shriveled hooligan sat perched atop the bottom of a sliced open Schmidt beer can, ready to be lit.

"H... h... h... here goes n... n... n... nothing," Zeke said to himself as he flicked a lighter. His hand trembled in anxious anticipation as the flame moved close to the beak of the fish. He touched the wick with the lighter and instantly the flame transferred. The wick quickly burned down, but slowed when it reached the face of the fish. This was the moment of truth for Zeke's blossoming enterprise. For a brief moment the flame looked as though it would extinguish, but then, to the amazement of his own widened eyes, the nose of the fish sizzled and began giving off a thin whisper of black smoke as the hooligan began to burn slowly, just like a candle.

"Woooohoooo!" After yelling loud enough to wake his neighbor, Zeke turned off all the lights switches and cranked Pink Floyd's *Money* on his boom box. With the pulsing sounds of bass and electric guitar playing riffs in seven-four time around the cha-ching of a cash register, Zeke Melon danced alone around his hooligan candle, all the while being careful not to step on any of the drying fish.

"I was thinking, halibut burgers down at *Porty's* then a quick evening harbor cruise on my boat. I think your mom would love that, don't you, Jim?" Maggie was sitting at her dispatcher's desk looking over her shoulder as she spoke.

Jim stood in the middle of the station, giving his full attention to the piece of inflatable raft that he had salvaged from Hooligan Arm. "Yeah, that sounds good, I guess."

"I can't wait to meet her in person. We've had a few great chats on the phone. She really seems sweet." Maggie paused, hoping for a reaction from her boyfriend. Finally she said, "Am I boring you? Or are you just not that excited to see your mother? What's going on, Jim?"

"Everything's fine." Jim walked away, entered his office, and shut the door.

Maggie looked over at Trooper Brandi Sitzel and asked, "What's with him?"

Brandi replied without looking up from her computer, "I'm not involved in this conversation."

The switchboard lit up as two lines rang simultaneously. Maggie punched the first button and spoke into her headset. "Dispatch, is this an emergency? Okay, please hold." She switched over to the other line and said, "Dispatch." After several seconds of listening and making notes, Maggie replied, "Give me your full name, address, and phone number, please… Okay, I will send a Trooper right over to investigate." She punched a couple of buttons and then said, "Dispatch, thanks for holding." After a few seconds of listening, Maggie said, "Hold on one moment. I will patch you through to our Station Commander, Lieutenant Wekle."

After pushing a few buttons, Maggie held out a piece of paper and said to Trooper Sitzel, "This one's yours. Stilly's on the other side of the island."

Brandi stood up, grabbed her jacket from the back of her chair and asked, "What is it?"

"Disturbance. Loud music and something about a

horrible smell coming from the apartment next door."

"Location?"

"Williwaw Drive."

"Wasn't Jim just out there recently?"

Maggie replied, "Yep. Same address. Probably the same guy. He likes to complain a lot. Have fun."

"Don't I always." Trooper Sitzel grabbed the piece of paper and made for the side door of the station.

Just as the side door closed, Jim emerged from his office and ordered, "Maggie, get Stilly back over to this side. I'm going to need his help tonight. It turns out that we will be needing to play bodyguard for the island's least popular person."

Maggie replied, "I didn't think we were in the bodyguard business, boss."

"Well, we are if it keeps people from getting killed. I'm heading down to the docks. Have Stilly meet me at the cannery warehouse as soon as he can." Jim donned his Stetson as he made his way for the side door of the station.

Maggie said, "Be careful, Jim."

Jim stopped and turned. "Remember what we talked about, Maggie. If this thing is going to work... me being your boss... us working together at the station... Well, you can't treat it like you're worried I'm going to get shot every time I leave on a call."

"I know. It's just that..."

"And all this talk about my mom coming to visit?

Let's save that for after hours, okay? We shouldn't be talking about our personal life while at work. Especially in front of the other Troopers."

"Ten-four, *boss*." She immediately swung around and began typing loudly on her computer.

Jim wasn't the best at picking up on the subtleties of women, but this signal was loud and clear. His girlfriend, who also happened to be his employee, was pissed. He said, "I've got to run, but we can talk about this later, okay?"

Jim waited for a response. When none came, he left the station through the side door, closing it behind him. "What did I do now?" he asked himself as he started his car.

# Chapter 11

The view through the rifle scope displayed a familiar sight. For the second time that day, the man holding the rifle watched the short, white haired leader of Planet Patrol descend a ladder on the side of his ship and step down into the bow of an inflatable raft. And for the second time that day, the leader's scrawny sidekick followed, taking a position in the middle of the buoyant craft. A third man sat in the stern with his hand on the tiller of the outboard engine. As soon as the raft pushed away from the side of the larger vessel, the man looking through the rifle scope picked up his cell phone and dialed a number.

"Looks like we didn't get the message across. They're heading your way again."

The voice on the other end said, "Got it, Gretch. We'll give them the same welcoming party as before."

Gretch Skully replied in a low, harsh tone, "I've got you covered."

After ending the phone call, he continued to follow the inflatable raft with the crosshairs of the rifle scope. The raft was making its short trip across the harbor between where its mother-ship was anchored near Fish Egg Island and the much larger Prince of Wales Island. There were a few other boats maneuvering in the same waterway, but for the most part, the raft was able to buzz in a fairly straight line from the *Earth's Guardian* over to the docks at the City of Craig's northern marina.

Keeping the raft centered in the crosshairs of the scope was fairly easy for the man. Not only did Gretch Skully have plenty of experience with a gun, but he had his rifle on a pivoting tripod making it fairly easy to manipulate while scoping a moving target. He centered the scope on the wispy, white hair of Planet Patrol's leader. Gretch's loathing almost foamed as the leader named Pierre Lemieux crossed over towards his home island with an expression of indignation on his petty, reddish face. This was war, and Gretch Skully wasn't about to go down without a fight.

"You son of a bitch," rumbled Gretch, pure hatred percolating in the depths of his soul.

When the inflatable raft neared within a hundred yards of the dock, Gretch punched a button on his cell phone. The single word, "Now," was sent to four separate phones. Gretch moved the scope's view over to the City Float and within seconds he saw four strong looking men step off of four different fishing boats that were all moored closed in. The four men walked quickly to the outer dock where the inflatable raft was fast approaching. One of the men carried a gaff hook, while another held a wooden club. The four fishermen spaced themselves evenly on the outer portion of the dock and stood strong with their legs apart and broad chests bulging. They were putting on the same show that had scared away the Planet Patrol representatives earlier that day.

Moving his view back to the inflatable raft, Gretch Skully was astonished when he saw the environmentalist leader give a smug smile and a cute little wave towards his greeting party.

"We'll never let you set foot on our island, you piece

of garbage," Gretch said aloud but only for himself to hear.

As the small boat bounced against the side of the dock, the four fishermen converged on the spot, standing shoulder to shoulder, blocking any attempt for the Planet Patrol men to disembark from their craft. Gretch smiled to himself as he watched the scene unfold. There was no chance those guys were getting out of that boat. They wouldn't even be allowed to tether a dock line.

A new figure suddenly appeared at the edge of the dock. A tall man wearing a Stetson and a blue uniform stepped behind the four fishermen. Gretch immediately recognized this man as a lieutenant with the local State Troopers station.

He grumbled, "What the hell are you doing here, Wekle?"

The Alaska State Trooper stood back from the fisherman, but had apparently ordered them to step away. The Trooper had his right hand resting on his holstered weapon, but had not drawn in yet. The fisherman stepped away from the edge of the dock and two Planet Patrol representatives were allowed to climb out of their raft. The raft's pilot pushed away and began its return trip to the *Earth's Guardian*.

The two men from Planet Patrol were allowed to walk along the dock and up a ramp that ascended to street level. The State Trooper followed a few feet behind, leaving the fishermen on the dock. It was obvious that Planet Patrol had arranged for an escort.

Gretch Skully punched a button on his ringing cell phone. "Not to worry. They managed to get on the island, but this thing is just getting started. We'll converge at the meeting. Get the word out. I want everyone there in half an hour."

After ending the call, Gretch lifted his rifle from its perch atop the swiveling tripod stand and walked to his pickup truck. He started his truck and made his way down the hill, heading toward the cannery warehouse in town, the rifle lying on the seat next to him.

Trooper Brandi Sitzel was frustrated. She had welcomed the transfer to the Prince of Wales Island station with the prospect of working more independently and being on the fast track for a promotion. Over the past year, Lieutenant Wekle proved to be a good boss and a respectable man, but the promotion to corporal had never arrived. In addition, she often found herself saddled with the younger and less experienced Trooper Stilhaven. She typically wouldn't mind the assignment of mentoring a younger officer, if it weren't for two exceptions. The first reason was that Brandi Sitzel couldn't technically pull rank on the younger officer. They were both listed as Trooper in status, and Stilly was starting to use that as an excuse to boss her around in return. This bothered Brandi as she pretty much outsmarted and outperformed the young officer in every aspect of the job. She even could best him in acts of physical strength. None of these facts seemed to register with the younger, male Trooper, who continued to act as an equal, if not superior to the more experienced female.

The second reason that Trooper Brandi Sitzel was starting to resent often being assigned to share duty with

Trooper Brett Stilhaven, was that the kid was completely infatuated with her. She was a knockout, and everyone knew it. Brandi was tall, perfectly proportioned and had long, blonde hair. Her face was as stunningly pretty as they come. She even made the uniform look hot, which was certainly a challenge.

Brandi often used her appearance as an advantage in her job. It was easy for the Trooper to instantly have the upper hand when entering an adverse encounter with an unruly man. One look at the stunning officer with the long, blonde hair pulled back into a ponytail, and most men were putty in her hands. Even if a suspect didn't melt by her appearance, they often assumed that she was a creampuff; a serious error on the part of anyone hoping to escape unscathed. It didn't help matters that, when approaching these tense situations, she had a similar effect on the Trooper that she was partnered with.

Trooper Brandi Sitzel considered it a nice change of pace to be sent out on a call individually. She exhaled calmly as she guided her vehicle, alone and free to deal with situations as she saw fit. She understood why her boss preferred her to partner up on most calls, as it was always best to have someone backing you up, but Brandi felt just fine heading out solo. She turned her Alaska State Trooper Jeep Cherokee off from the main highway and onto a gravel road marked as Williwaw Drive. About fifty yards down the road, she noticed a man standing by a crumpled mailbox, waving her in.

"Did you call in something about loud music and a strange odor coming from your neighbors?" Brandi asked through the window of her Jeep.

The man was sinking a steel pole into a vat of concrete in the ground. "I most certainly did. Where's the other guy?"

"He's busy. You're stuck with me." Brandi reminded herself to have patience.

"I prefer to deal with the Lieutenant. We have a history."

Patience. "Well, you've got me. Why don't you tell me why I'm here."

The man smoothed out his feral eyebrows with a swipe of his hand, then said, "Look. I am a writer. I write from home. I am dependent on my being able to write as a source of income." The man's voice was rising in intensity as well as timbre with each word. "Instead, I am battling a rogue gang of four-wheelers that seem to have some vendetta against my mailbox, and my neighbor seems to be rotting away in a pungent cesspool of heavy metal and rancid fish. I have a deadline at the end of the month. Ten thousand words on the mating ritual of bald eagles, and I haven't made it past the first paragraph." The man was nearing hysterics. "You need to do something right now. I demand immediate action on this."

Trooper Sitzel opened the door of her Jeep and stepped out. "Sir, you can just calm down, now. I am here to see if there is anything I can do. Tell me your name, please."

"Cliff Barr. And you should already know that. When your boss was out here a few days ago ineffectually investigating my mailbox that got run over, he took down all my information. By the way, they did it again." He pointed to the gnarled remnants of a mailbox that sat next to his feet.

"Okay, Mr. Barr. Why don't we discuss the mailbox

situation first?"

He straightened the pipe in the concrete with a post leveler. "No way. I'm taking matters into my own hands. Let's see those little shit-eating punks bust this thing down. I'm using quick-drying cement and a steel pole this time."

Trooper Sitzel said, "Okay, tell me about why I am here, then. What's going on with your neighbor?"

"Just head up the driveway and you'll see. Or should I say…*you'll smell*." Cliff Barr pointed a thumb over his shoulder. "It's a duplex. His unit is the one on the right."

After stepping back inside the Jeep Cherokee, Trooper Sitzel drove up the driveway. The narrow road had a line of young alder trees and short salmonberry bushes tight on either side as it curved slightly to the right. The road opened up to a small parking lot that sat in front of a single-level, brown-sided duplex. Parked in front of the left unit, was a newer model, dark blue Toyota Rav4. In front of the right side of the duplex was a dented 1982 Datsun pickup. The miniature truck had originally been painted white, but now was mostly orange as it had more rust on it than white paint.

Trooper Sitzel parked the Jeep next to the Datsun, turned off the engine and opened her door. As soon as the door of the Cherokee opened just a crack, pungent air came rushing into the cab of the vehicle.

"Oh, man." She put her left hand up to her nose. "This guy wasn't lying about the stink." Brandi considered herself to be a fairly strong individual, and she had come across some gruesome odors in her career, but the air was so ripe with the odor of dead fish that it caused her to squint as she approached the right door of the duplex. There was some music playing inside the home, but nothing that would be considered excessively loud. The smell, on the other hand, could definitely be considered excessive and worthy of further investigation.

Brandi knocked on the front door. Within seconds it opened and a young, skinny redheaded man appeared. He was wearing shorts, a t-shirt, flip-flops, and large, protective goggles over his eyes. His right hand held a hacksaw and his left was protected by a work glove. The young man's red hair hadn't been combed in a while and it stood frazzled above the eye goggle strap. The guy's jaw hung agape. The last thing he expected to see was an Alaska State Trooper standing on his doorstep.

The Trooper spoke first, "Hello sir, we've had a complaint regarding the smell coming from your home." She almost choked as waves of rotten fish scent wafted from inside the house.

The red-haired man stood frozen and speechless. He looked as though he was slipping into a panic. His flesh tone went from pale to completely white, and his right hand that still clutched the hacksaw began to tremble.

"Do you mind if I have a look around?" Brandi asked as she pushed her way past the speechless duplex tenant.

All that emanated from the man was a guttural, throaty, "G... g... g..."

Stepping past the redhead and into the small living space of the rental, Trooper Sitzel gazed at a scene unlike anything she had ever laid eyes on. There were hundreds upon hundreds of small, dead, skinny, shriveled fish everywhere. They had been placed strategically in straight rows, spaced about an inch apart from each other, covering most every floor and counter space within the walls of the home. Their number was so immense and they were lined up in such an organized fashion, that Brandi was amazed by how much effort had gone in to creating the scene. It reminded her of the patience and care that went into arranging an elaborate array of dominos.

There was a small work station at a round table close to the kitchen that was left clear of little fish. Under the table was a pile of empty beer cans, some of which had been cut off close to the bottom. Littered on the table was a mess of tiny aluminum shavings. A sack of long construction nails sat open close to the table and a box of short strings sat open next to the nails. In the center of the kitchen stove, surrounded by dead fish, a single candle sat burning away, casting glowing images on the walls behind it. It appeared to the Trooper that the candle flame was burning right through half a fish.

The Trooper found words hard to come by. "I… uh… I'm not exactly sure what's going on in here…" Her words tapered at the end when she saw several empty bottles of cough syrup propped up in one corner of the room like a small pyramid.

The red haired man again uttered, "G… g… g…"

The Trooper cupped her left hand over her nose in an attempt to make the smell bearable, and said, "I think you're going to need to explain this."

# Chapter 12

The cannery warehouse was cold and devoid of inventory. In preparation for the impending season, the cannery workers had cleared as much floor space as possible. The walls were painted a sterile light-blue color that rose all the way to the tall, trussed ceiling. Empty fish boxes lined an entire wall. A half-dozen yellow handtrucks stood parked in a straight line at the ready next to the rows of empty boxes. Freshly cleaned, nylon covered cutting benches stood between stainless, shimmering metal troughs. Gut buckets and rolling plastic tubs were neatly packed into a corner opposite the wall of fish boxes. The cannery warehouse was clean and sterile, and soon it would endure several months of processing thousands of salmon that would slide down the metal troughs and work their way through the "slime line."

By the time Jim and Stilly arrived with the men that they escorted, the warehouse was already packed with people. As soon as the two representatives of Planet Patrol walked in from the sidewalk, ducking underneath the open loading bay door, a chorus of "boos" erupted throughout the crowd standing in the expansive warehouse. Several individuals hurled insults, barking quips such as: "Go home, jackasses!" "Environmentalists suck," and "Bite me, Planet Pussies!"

Jim and Stilly helped block through the center of the crowd as Pierre Lemieux and Beanie LeFranc made their way to the head of the warehouse where a makeshift podium had been constructed out of a stack of fish-boxes and a clipboard propped up on a large sponge. Pierre was shorter than his nephew, white hair shooting out above a red-cheeked face, wearing a white shirt, white belt, white pants, white socks and white shoes. Beanie wore his trademark red scarf around his neck and held an expression on his face that made him appear to be straight out of high school. Neither of them appeared remotely up to the task of debunking the angry mob. The two men approached a plastic Walmart microphone plugged into an equally pathetic sound system that sat perched at the edge of the podium.

An angry voice from the crowd shouted, "Hey, Wekle, how could you protect this slime?"

Jim knew that any response would be the wrong response, so he kept his mouth shut. He was a peace officer, and that's exactly what he intended to keep in mind. These two men were guests to the island, no matter what their politics or agenda, and they had as much right to be there as anyone else. He would do his best to protect everyone's rights, whether local or antagonistic, no matter how heated the subject matter.

Stepping up to the microphone, Pierre Lemieux spoke the first few words of his prepared speech, "Residents of Prince of Wales Island." He voice came out excruciatingly loud and distorted. High frequency feedback reverberated off the walls of the warehouse, causing Beanie LeFranc to cover his ears to shield them from the painful squelch.

The crowd roared in laughter. Many pointed in ridicule. Multiple middle fingers shot up at random, similar to concert goers holding up lighters during a Nineteen-Eighties power-ballad. An older lady in the back hurled a live mussel shell toward their hated guest speaker. It missed its target by inches and shattered on the back wall.

Upon seeing the shellfish flying through the air, Jim nodded at the younger Trooper, signaling for Stilly to move close to the person who threw it. The technique was reminiscent of an elementary teacher moving close to an off-task student, using body position in order to discourage misbehavior. Jim kept careful watch over the crowd, scanning from the front of the audience to the back doors where people still kept entering. The locals were fired up, and they had a right to be. This outside entity had just marched in uninvited and with the full intention of pissing everyone off. These "off-islanders" were about to tell this community that had subsisted primarily on the fishing industry for over a century, that everything they stood for was wrong. Jim well understood the volatile circumstances that appeared ready to erupt at any moment. He started to question his own logic in only bringing one other Trooper with him.

Pierre Lemieux stepped back from the sabotaged sound system and pulled a bullhorn out of a backpack that his nephew carried. Hitting the trigger on the bullhorn, Pierre announced loudly, "Residents of Craig, Alaska. It's time that you all faced the shocking impact that the commercial fishing industry is having on the environment."

One of the locals in the front row yanked a small rope and the makeshift podium tumbled. As multiple fish boxes, a clipboard, and a sponge crashed raucously at the feet of the hated guest speaker, the crowd burst into uproarious applause.

"Mock me all you want," started Pierre, but the applause continued. "I said, mock me all you want." It was beginning to seem as though the crowd's clapping and carrying on was not going to end.

Pierre hit a siren button on his bullhorn, shocking the audience into somewhat of a calm. Switching back to loudspeaker mode, he announced, "Mock me all you want, but you can't ignore the data that my team of Planet Patrol environmental experts has assembled. I have their report right here in my hand." Pierre Lemieux held up a stack of papers in his left hand. A teenager walked up, removed a wad of bubble gum from his lower lip and stuck it to the middle of one of the data reports. The crowd stared to clap again.

A man carrying a long, straight object entered through the back of the crowd and made his way over to a staircase that led to an elevated cannery office. He climbed half the steps, turned and sat perched, a few feet above the rest of the crowd. Jim saw the man and immediately made his way toward him by skirting along the edge of the assembled mass. The Lieutenant climbed the stairs and stood directly in front of the man.

"You didn't need to bring that here, Gretch. This is a peaceful protest," Jim said, pointing to the rifle with the scope that sat at the man's side. Jim kept one hand close to his holstered sidearm.

Gretch Skully seemed to stare right through Jim. He was stone faced, his steely eyes displaying the look of a man possessed. Gretch's low, gravelly voice replied, "I can quote you the second amendment, if you like."

"Don't give me that line, Gretch. This isn't about your rights. It's about keeping everyone in here safe. At best, you came here with your weapon as a means of intimidation. Don't give me any reason to draw my weapon and arrest you right here. You know I am serious." Jim paused a moment, then said, "Let me hold that rifle. I'll give it back, unloaded, when you leave."

Standing before the angry mob, Pierre Lemieux shouted statistics related to the world-wide decline of salmon populations, as well as data concerning the pollutants left in both the air and water from the fleet of commercial fishing vessels that swarmed the Alaskan waters every summer season. His nephew, Beanie LeFranc, cowered, pinned between the dismantled stack of fish boxes and the back wall.

After letting a few tense moments pass, Gretch Skully released his grip on the long-barreled weapon. Jim reached down slowly and retrieved the rifle. The Trooper calmly emptied five rounds from the Remington Gamemaster 760 and deposited the bullets in his front shirt pocket. He held the rifle in his left hand while descending the stairs, and rejoined the back of the crowd.

The activist continued his speech, spewing forth rehearsed rhetoric that provoked the frothing audience to hurl every obscenity in the English language in return. One Norwegian fisherman even fired off some Nordic profanities. As the short man with wavy white hair grew in intensity toward the climax of his diatribe, his cheeks turned ruddier and his arms flailed about frantically. Pierre Lemieux launched into a personal testimony as to the merits of his organization, Planet Patrol, and he shouted quick examples of locations from all corners of the globe where they had invoked positive change for Mother Earth "on which we all live and breathe!" A beer-bellied fisherman belched loudly.

Sensing that the speech was nearing its end, Jim worried about how he might safely extricate the environmentalists from the incensed mob. Just as he was coming up with the exit strategy, he recognized a woman entering the warehouse, making her way through the crowd. The woman was middle-aged with dark black hair and wore a blue windbreaker above Levi jeans. She carried a piece of paper in one hand, and politely excused herself to each member of the crowd that she pushed past. She moved with a refined elegance - for a woman in rubber boots - and the locals gave way, showing her proper respect.

Jim found Trooper Stilhaven on the edge of the crowd, pointed toward the woman and asked, "What do you think the Harbormaster's got to say about all this?"

With stoic grace and panache, Cheryl Lawson stood in front of Pierre Lemieux, interrupting the closing remarks of his speech. She turned to face the crowd, her back to the guest speaker, and held high the piece of paper in her hand, displaying it for the whole audience to see.

The Harbormaster spoke loudly and with clarity, "I am officially serving this document, signed by the judge only moments ago, to Pierre Lemieux of Planet Patrol. This is an official injunction which bars his ship, the *Earth's Guardian*, and all its subsequent marine vessels, from moorage and passage within one mile of the city limits of our town, Craig, Alaska. By law, Mr. Lemieux and his counterpart must immediately exit these premises and travel back to their boat. They have exactly one hour to leave the one-mile radius of our city, or the Coast Guard and State Troopers have full authority to take action."

The crowd erupted in a chaotic chorus of cheers, applause, high-fives, belching, and obscenities. Jim and Stilly quickly made their way to the front of the room. Jim accepted the document from the Harbormaster, Cheryl Lawson, and scanned it for authenticity. After verifying that it was legitimate, he handed it over to Pierre Lemieux and motioned toward the door. The crowd eagerly parted down the middle, making an aisle to allow for a quick exit.

Lieutenant Wekle said to the short, white-haired man, "I think you had better leave now." Jim and Stilly followed the representatives of Planet Patrol as they exited amid a massive salute of middle-fingers.

Once they hit the sidewalk outside the cannery, Jim said, "Trooper Stilhaven, see to it that these men go straight to their boat and leave our docks immediately." The crowd again cheered, then broke out into a loud song. As the men wandered up the street, a soulful rendition of "*Nah-nah-nah-nah, hey-hey-hey, good-bye*," bounced off the buildings that lined the city street.

Meeting Jim at the sidewalk outside the cannery, Cheryl Lawson asked coyly, "How do you like them apples?" The Harbormaster possessed that rare quality of grace combined with down-to-earth reasonability. Jim liked her style.

The Trooper responded, "Nothing like coming through at the perfect moment, Cheryl. A couple minutes later, and we would have had a situation on our hands. How did you get the judge to go for it?"

The Harbormaster grinned. "Piece of cake. His family tree is filled with fishermen. Also, I served with his son back in my Coast Guard days. I took advantage of an inside deal." She patted the Trooper on the shoulder. "Sometimes it pays to be me, Lieutenant." She flashed him an infectious smile as she sauntered down the sidewalk.

It didn't take long for the bulk of the crowd to disassemble. Hardworking locals, many of which wore flannel and Xtratufs, dispersed in various directions from the cannery warehouse. Gretch Skully walked up to Jim and asked, "Can I get my rifle back?"

Jim held it out with the barrel pointing toward the sidewalk. "Here you go, Gretch. You can pick up the live rounds at the station later, provided you show up without your gun in hand."

Accepting the rifle from the Trooper, Gretch replied, "Keep 'em. I've got plenty more where they came from."

# Chapter 13

In the three days that I convalesced under cover of cedar boughs and a hand woven blanket, my trepidation underwent a keen metamorphosis, with a resulting feeling somewhere between gratitude and relief. The people that I first feared to be my captors, I soon beheld as my rescuers. With dark hair, brown skin, and the ability to do more with the natural wilds than I ever imagined possible, the clan that was native to the island of my recent besiege proved caring and hospitable to my every basic need.

What I now believe to have been hypothermia, my mental state at the time deemed severe illness. I was in no immediate condition for transport by foot over miles of forest and mountain. With sheltered rest and the nourishment of dried fish and a leafy vegetation whose name and origin is still a mystery to me, strength seeped slowly into every crevasse of my being. On dawn of the third day, it was obvious that the clan would be making a journey of some sort, and that I would be traveling with them.

With silent efficiency, camp was broken and duties divided among man, woman, and child evenly. It seemed that not a word was spoken, but each individual knew well their role in the venture. Hardly a human sign remained when we first stepped onto the damp soil of a hidden trail. The respect for which these people held for each other and the land they walked upon was unequalled by any past experience that I had held. Automatically, I joined in the silent reverence and took foot to the trail, embarking on the journey of a lifetime through the lushness of the island wilds that I had been shipwrecked unto only a few days into the past.

It had been a long day and Jim was ready for a little decompression time in his private sanctuary on Mink Island. The drive around Port St. Nicholas was a pleasant one. The evening turned out to be beautiful with the temperature close to sixty degrees and the sun threatening to shine through breaks in the clouds. Daylight hours were certainly increasing, as it was almost eight o'clock at night and still appeared plenty bright out. Jim rolled down the window of his Ford Crown Vic and let the salt-filled air blow against the side of his face, through his nostrils, and deep into his lungs.

As the highway meandered along the shoreline, Jim knew exactly where to glance to his right in order to spy views of the water between patches of trees. It was a calm night, with little wind and only a slight ripple on the water's surface. A boat was trolling close to shore. Mid-May was certainly on the early side of the season, but king salmon could still be caught.

For several miles the highway headed east, straight toward the center of the long island. At the head of the bay, it made a sharp right-hand turn and followed the opposite shoreline as it worked its way toward the western edge of Prince of Wales. About halfway up Port St. Nicholas' southern coast, Jim put his turn signal on and guided the State Trooper vehicle onto a very secluded, private driveway. The short, gravel road soon opened up to a small lot, just big enough to park only a handful of vehicles. The only other vehicle in the lot was a red Vespa scooter.

"Looks like my landlord has stopped by for a visit," Jim muttered to himself as he parked his vehicle. After gathering a few things from the Crown Vic, Jim locked his car and made his way down a narrow dirt path with tall vegetation on either side. Within seconds, the path opened up to a stunning view of Port St. Nicholas and the small, tree covered, Mink Island that sat perched in the cove, just offshore. Beyond the tiny island, across the expanse of the cove, the City of Craig sparkled as buildings and windows reflected the late evening sunlight.

As Jim stepped onto the ramp that led down to his floating boat dock, he noticed long, white hair fizzing out from a ponytail across the back of a man bent over inside his skiff. Jim wished the ponytail was a little longer, as Kram was showing off some significant plumber's butt above a beltless line from a pair of hand-cut denim shorts. The sound of a socket wrench clicked away as Jim's landlord knelt with his head just below the starboard gunwale. Two seven-foot-long, white PVC pipes had been attached atop both the starboard and port side rails of the aluminum skiff. The two-inch diameter pipes had been attached to supports that allowed the PVC tube to angle up at the bow. The pipes stepped up in diameter as they approached the stern. The tail end of each pipe sat close to where the boat operator would sit, and it was the thickest portion of the tube, at eight inches across.

"What the hell are you doing to my boat?" Jim asked in an unnaturally high pitched tone.

Startled by the voice, Kram jerked his head up, slamming it into the PVC pipe he had just secured. Tools rattled inside against the metal hull. Jerking around while rubbing the back of his head, Kram smiled sheepishly. "Oh, Jimbo. You're home. I was hoping to have this little project completed before you saw it. I'm almost done, just a couple more nuts and bolts here."

"Kram, why are you bolting down plastic pipes to the side rails of my boat?"

Chuckling a little, Kram said, "Well, technically, these are polyvinyl chloride pipes, not plastic. And technically, this is my boat, not yours."

"Yeah, but…"

Standing up tall, balancing with both feet spread wide, Kram announced, "Jimbo, I hereby give you what every man needs. This is no longer just a simple open bow, three bench seat, stern operated aluminum skiff. This is now just what you've been waiting for your whole life. I hereby dub this vessel *Conan the Bohemian Warship*." He spread apart both arms in a grand gesture as if anticipating a huge round of applause. "My friend, Jim. You are now looking at a watercraft mounted with dual potato cannons. You can take down your foe from a hundred yards away. Each cannon is equipped with a state-of-the-art model JX-14 barbeque igniter switch, easily accessible gas pressurization chamber, my patented potato loading portal, and for those of us that like to play battleship, we have a fully adjustable angle mechanism that will allow for an increase of projectile trajectory by up to thirty degrees."

Stunned, Jim responded simply, "Um… Great." After a confused pause, he asked, "What happens if the boat's engine conks out? The pipes are blocking the oar locks."

"That's all part of the experience. Come on, hop in and let's give it whirl." Kram yelled joyously as he bent back down into position and finished ratcheting the last bolt into place.

Stepping into the bow of the boat, Jim noticed a sack of red potatoes and several bottles of hairspray rolling around the floor. His counterpart hopped up and fired the outboard engine with one pull of the cord. Releasing the lines, the two men were propelled away from the dock. After about half of the short distance between the shore and Mink Island, Kram goosed the throttle and turned toward the middle of the cove while the boat lunged up on step. Stopping several yards past the island, and with the bow angled out toward the center of the bay, Kram killed the engine and retrieve the bag of potatoes and one of the hairspray bottles.

"This... will... be... radical!" Kram said giddily as he opened up a small chamber at the base of one of the tubes. He loaded a medium sized red potato into the chamber and secured the loading door shut, cramming it down, conforming the spud to the shape of the tube.

Picking up the hairspray, Kram exclaimed, "Air tight. That's the key." He attached a small rubber tube to the top of the hairspray bottle and turned a valve at the base of the canon's gas chamber. With gusto, the ponytailed man punched a button on the top of the hairspray bottle. His mad cackle equaled the volume of the hairspray hissing flammable gas into the pipe chamber. Turning the valve shut, Kram lifted a push-button barbeque igniter with black and red colored wires. The wires dangled in his grasp, eventually attaching to bare screws that pierced through the PVC pipe into the gas chamber. The screws angled into the chamber in a V-shape, their tips almost touching inside, but allowing the perfect space for a tiny electric arc.

"*Fire in the hoooooole!!!*" Kram slammed his thumb down on the barbeque igniter. An immediate whooshing sound ensued, followed by a red, circular object firing out of the bow-end of the canon barrel, arcing high in the air.

"Whoa," muttered Jim. The red potato held flight much longer and much farther than Jim thought possible. It launched so far, Jim almost lost sight of the spud before it plopped down in the water well over a hundred yards out from their boat.

At the top his lungs, Kram screamed, "*Hot Damn!*" The man was so excited he was vibrating.

Jim said, "Let's do that again." He had to admit, he, too, was a little giddy.

Kram didn't need to be told twice. He jumped down and scooped up a couple of potatoes. This time he loaded both potato guns and filled two gas chambers. He handed the igniters to Jim, who accepted them and stepped forward to sit in the boat's middle bench seat. Jim turned so that he was facing out the bow. Kram fired up the outboard engine again, and put it into gear. He wrenched the throttle and the small skiff thrust forward, rising up so that it skimmed the water's surface while it playfully bounced across tiny waves. Water frothed from the back of the boat as Kram gunned it to full throttle. They were flying as fast as the little skiff could carry the two men.

Kram screamed, "*Yeeeeeeeeehaaaaaaw. Hot damn and fire in the hooooooooooole…*"

Jim slammed both of his thumbs down hard on the red igniter buttons. Both tubes created a *thunk* that could barely be heard above the hum of the outboard. Potatoes fired fast out the end of both PVC pipes and small red projectiles soared far into the air, turning into small little dots on the horizon. They disappeared into the saltwater far in front of the boat, plopping down with a tiny splash ring, resembling the markings of where a small fish jumped.

Loosening his grip on the throttle, Kram asked, "What do you think of that, Jimbo?"

Grinning widely, Jim had to admit the potato canons were pretty cool. "Not bad. Let's find something to aim at."

The two men took a few more turns test firing the new canons at a green channel buoy before guiding the boat back toward Mink Island. They secured the skiff to the wooden dock that floated on the protected side of the small island, and walked up the ramp to the trail system that led to the yurt.

Jim said, "You head up to Lookout Rock. I'll grab us a snack and be right up."

"Oooh, snacks." Kram scurried up the trail like a squirrel.

Jim entered the yurt and gathered a plate of smoked salmon, crackers, pepper jack cheese, grapes, and a couple bottles of water. He wandered up the boardwalk to where two reclining deck chairs were positioned atop a huge rock that sat under an umbrella of cedar trees. By the time Jim arrived, Kram was already playing with Oscar the mink.

"I taught her to fetch, Jimbo. Watch this." The ponytailed man in denim cut-offs tossed a red bandana that usually stuck up from his back pocket. As soon as the bandana landed in a fern, the little mink scurried over, snatched it in her teeth, and quickly brought in back to Kram, offering it by standing on her back feet. Kram accepted the bandana from the mink and threw it again for her to fetch, giggling.

"And you used to slaughter those little creatures," Jim

said while placing the plate of food on a wooden stump between the two chairs.

"Still might. There's good money in mink pelts, Jim-Kahn. Plus, my freezer's getting low."

In a disgusted tone, Jim snapped, "You eat these things?"

Nodding while munching on a cracker, "Not much meat on them, but very lean, and low in cholesterol."

"That's really quite disturbing."

"I mostly was joking."

"You're odd."

"Thanks."

They snacked on some crackers for a moment, then Jim said, "Kram."

"Yeah?"

"Don't eat Oscar, or I'll shoot you."

"Roger."

Once food became part of the equation, Oscar the female mink quickly lost interest in chasing the red bandana. She found her usual perch next to Jim and waited for a snack. Jim dropped a piece of smoked salmon and the mink gobbled it up immediately.

The two men sat chatting, while staring out through a break in the trees at a stunning view. The water across Port St. Nicholas had grown even calmer, with barely a ripple. As daylight waned, lights from the City of Craig began to twinkle on the shoreline across the sound. The town's glow pulsated as it reflected across the smooth bay. To the right of the city lights, land rose sharply in elevation, every inch seemingly covered by thick evergreens as land sloped higher and higher. A bald eagle playfully soared over the cove. Several gulls stood at attention on a log that jostled in the surf just off shore. It was a gorgeous scene, one that Jim had grown to love.

Jim asked, "How's the new job at the grocery store going?"

"Got fired," Kram answered curtly.

"What happened?"

"Creative differences."

"Ah…"

After they finished off the plate of food, Jim pulled a cigar covered in a cellophane tube from his shirt pocket. He snipped the end and lit it up in a plume of smoke and fire.

Kram asked, "Speaking of creative differences, I thought your girlfriend made you quit those things."

"She did."

"Ah… Wanna talk about it?"

After he ensured that the end of the cigar was evenly lit, Jim pocketed his torch lighter and answered, "Not really very much to talk about. Maggie wants me to quit smoking cigars. I don't want to quit smoking cigars." Jim took a puff on his imported stogie. "Plus there's this issue with Maggie having trouble separating our personal relationship from our work relationship. At work I'm her boss, but I feel like she gets pissed off every time I give her an order. I think she expects me to be all lovey-dovey all the time, but I can't do that at work. I am the commanding officer of that station and have to maintain a dignified image that comes with that responsibility. There's a lot of pressure there." Jim took one puff then jumped right back into it. "Oh, and talk about pressure. My mom arrives tomorrow. I think she and Maggie have been scheming. I didn't even know the two of them had made contact, but apparently, they're good buds. Not to mention that I've got a severed foot from some dude that apparently got blown to bits and a community on the verge of rioting against environmental freaks."

Kram said, "Not very much to talk about. Indeed." He leaned back in his chair and assumed his best Sigmund Freud pose, steepling his fingers below his chin. In a calming tone, he said, "Tell me about your mother."

"Typical mom stuff. Fears that her single, divorced son is going to grow old, unhappy and be alone for the rest of his life. Wants grandkids and will do anything to make it happen, including passive-aggressive pressuring techniques that she's somehow mastered in her menopausal stage. She quite possibly recently learned the skill at an aging evil-mother convention."

Pretending to take notes on an invisible notepad, Kram asked, "And your father?"

"Oh, Dad, he's cool. He's more concerned about the clarity of his flat-screen than he is about becoming a grandfather. Don't get me wrong, Kram. I love both of my parents. They've been good to me. I just don't trust my mother's intentions with regard to this visit. I think she's got an agenda regarding my relationship with Maggie and is coming up here to set that agenda into motion." Jim tapped his ash onto the ground. Oscar scurried over to inspect where it landed.

The faux therapist asked, "And the cigars? What are your intentions there?"

"To smoke them whenever I damn-well feel like it."

"Ah, I see."

"Look. I don't drink. I don't gamble. I don't spend money frivolously. I don't carouse with men who chase other women. I try to eat fairly healthy. If I want to have a cigar every once in awhile, you can damn-well bet that's what I'm going to do."

"Damn-well," Kram agreed. "And this severed foot you mentioned. Sounds both intriguing and perplexing."

Jim paused for a moment while gazing at the view. Sunlight had disappeared and the faint glow of the day lifted gently above the caps of distant islands. After taking a puff on his cigar, Jim said, "It's a strange case. I think a pretty large explosion occurred aboard a very small boat and all that's left is a foot and a small piece of laminated marine fabric. With the currents out there, we probably won't ever find any other evidence, and there is little chance we can I.D. the foot. We sent out for DNA results, but that'll take weeks and in my experience with people up here, finding a match in the system is extremely rare."

Kram sat silent, but slowly nodded in an encouraging way. After another puff of the stogie, Jim continued, "What I find strange, is that this happened days ago and there have been no reports of anyone missing. That's pretty unusual. To tell you the truth, I'm not even sure if a crime has been committed. The explosion could have been a result of a horrible accident. Maybe someone dropped a cigarette inside a full gas tank? I don't know. Our new coroner seems to think that it would take a rather large explosion to result in this type of damage, so if it was an accident, it had to be catastrophic." Jim paused for a moment and examined the butt-end of his imported cigar. "I really don't know much yet, but I do have one lead that I am planning on following up. I've arranged a little helicopter reconnaissance trip in the morning."

Nodding and tapping his fingers on his chin, Kram said, "I see, I see… It sounds as though our little session was productive this evening." He stood and bowed toward Jim, then descended the rocks in front of where he sat. As he approached the edge of the island, Kram said, "We'll continue next week. Shall we say…same time, same place? My secretary will schedule with you and arrange for payment."

Kram waded out into the water, carefully placing his feet atop slippery rocks. "Be well, Jim. Be well." Kram plunged forward, diving into the frigid sea. He angled to the right, swimming away from Mink Island and over towards the wooden dock on Prince of Wales, arms arcing, feet kicking, water sloshing all around.

"Goodnight, Kram," Jim shouted.

A hand rose from the water and waved briefly. Jim turned his head to the right and could see through a small break in the trees. There was just enough light and just enough of a view for Jim to watch his friend reach the wooden dock on the other side. Kram lifted himself out of the cold water, shook his whole body like a wet dog, and trotted up the ramp, disappearing on the trail that led to the parking lot. Moments later, Jim heard the faint sound of a Vespa motor-scooter heading down the highway.

# Chapter 14

Morning brought low clouds and drizzle. It was the type of day that reminded one that Southeast Alaska was one large rainforest. Everything was wet. During the brief skiff ride over to the main island, droplets pelted Lieutenant Wekle in the face. Dirty water sloshed around Jim's feet as the boat bounced along. Jim's car even felt damp inside. Perspiration oozed from the dashboard and seats and the gas gauge of the Crown Vic had fogged up inside the plastic window pane. Misty haze seemed to blanket the trees during his drive up Port St. Nicholas. For a short time, Jim thought that his helicopter charter might have to be postponed due to the low ceiling, but by the time he reached the chopper pad, the clouds had lifted enough to allow for the trip.

Bush pilot, boat skipper, and helicopter extraordinaire, Hugh Eckley, was cleaning the outer windows of the red and white MDH when Jim Wekle drove through a gate in a chainlink fence and up a rocky drive to the paved landing pad. The small chopper sat perfectly centered in a circle that had been painted on the pad. The helicopter's roundish body shape and bubbled windows exposed an interior capable of carrying up to four people. It had two windows on each side, and a wide front window that curved below the pilot's feet, allowing for great visibility when flying. The small craft was perfect for quick trips and getting in and out of tight spaces.

"You able to make the run this morning, Hugh? The cloud cover seemed to have lifted a little bit." Jim grabbed a small backpack out of the trunk of the Crown Vic.

"Piece of cake. I've flown below cover so low you could see ants at a picnic. Hop in and we'll get this thing fired up." Hugh Eckley wore a brown jacket over a flannel shirt. A ball cap hat on his head displayed a logo featuring a helicopter flying above a sketched tree line. The words *Southeast Enterprises* were scrawled in large font below the chopper image. Hugh's company featured an array of helicopters that could be contracted for use in needs that ranged from logging support, remote construction, search and rescue, aerial surveys and photography. Lieutenant Wekle had long ago secured their services for aid with remote investigations, both land and sea, pertinent to the Alaska State Troopers' caseload.

As the blades began to rotate above their heads, the two men strapped in and readied themselves for the quick flight. The helicopter lifted up smoothly, rising well above the tree tops before turning south. Despite the drizzle outside, the windows stayed clear of rain droplets as wind from the powerful blades hurled them away. The *Southeast Enterprises* property was located just north of the Craig city limits. In a matter of seconds, the two men were passing directly over the town. Jim looked down at the waterfront where there was the usual morning activity. Several small boats were passing through, creating white V-shaped wakes in the harbor. A purse seiner was just starting to chug its way out of the marina past the breakwater. Several people were moving down the ramp to the floatplane dock. Jim assumed that Frightening Frankie was getting ready to make his morning flight over to Ketchikan, as soon as the clouds lifted a bit more. A scattering of people scurried between buildings on the connecting sidewalks, reminding Jim of Hugh's ant comment from earlier.

The experienced pilot continued guiding the helicopter

south. Soon, they were over water, as the island's shoreline moved inward, creating the large cove named Port St. Nicholas. Jim could see his home of Mink Island, a small circle of trees just off the southern shore. A glimpse of the yurt flashed through the trees. Jim looked to his right to see a few odd shaped islands close by, all covered in dense, green trees. Beyond the islands, there was nothing but clouds and ocean; both of which shared a very similar grayish hue.

In a matter of seconds, they were again flying over land. Jim was always amazed at how the Prince of Wales Island shoreline snaked in and out of wide coves and narrow inlets. The island was massive: 140 miles long and 45 miles wide, but with all of its curved bays and jagged points, the island's shoreline logged in at close to a thousand miles. Most of the island's 2500 square miles of land was uninhabited rainforest that sprawled from coast to coast over mountains and interspersed with hundreds of fresh water lakes and sparse green muskeg bogs. There was evidence of logging and mining to be seen, but the island was truly a remote and rugged Alaskan paradise, only sparsely touched by human hand.

As the red and white MDH helicopter banked left, turning into Hooligan Arm, Jim could see the rock sticking up in the middle of the bay where he had found the laminated fabric fragment. It looked much smaller and much less ominous from his elevated position. The pilot slowed the aircraft to a hover and turned so that Jim had a perfect view of the lagoon. It was a kidney shaped body of water that appeared to be pitch-black in color. A river ran in at the head of the lagoon, and the narrow opening to the saltwater appeared calm as the tide was fairly high. Just as Jim had suspected, there were no roads that led in close to the lagoon and no sign of any remnants of boats. About a mile up the northern shoreline from the lagoon, Jim could see a rugged forest road entering from the dense trees and snaking briefly along the shore past what appeared to be a dilapidated cabin. There was no sign of people or indication of recent activity anywhere on shore. If there was any further evidence from the explosion that resulted in the severed foot, it was most likely at the bottom of the ocean somewhere and would never be found.

The pilot moved the helicopter back out of the lagoon area and over toward the wider part of the cove, away from the rock in the middle. They flew directly over the main object of their morning mission. Jim took a camera out of his backpack and turned it on. He waited until they had the perfect angle before snapping pictures of the ship that sat anchored below them.

After being banned from the waters surrounding the City of Craig, the *Earth's Guardian* had made its way south and sought refuge in the protected waters of Hooligan arm. In order to give plenty of room for the ship to swing on its anchor chain and stay clear of the cove's rock protrusion, the vessel was anchored fairly close to the mouth of the cove.

They hovered above the water just off the ship's stern. A ring of rainbow colored diesel fuel polluted the saltwater that surrounded the boat. Jim motioned with his finger for them to descend slightly, as he wanted a good look at the back deck. He raised the camera and snapped a few shots. There didn't seem to be any activity on the deck of the ship. It was hard to see from up high, as everything on the vessel was painted the same color of white, but as they dropped in elevation, Jim spotted exactly what he came for. Positioned three on each side of the ship were stations for inflatable rafts, all easily reached by the tall boom arm that jutted away from the back of the cabin area. The little rafts each looked just like the one that Jim had seen previously when Pierre Lemieux and his sidekick had come ashore for their town meeting. He was certain that there hadn't been a white inflatable raft already in the water buzzing around near the cove, as he had kept a careful watch during the short flight over to Hooligan Arm. He was also fairly certain that the piece of white laminated fabric that he had retrieved during his previous boating trip was likely a perfect match to the material that the inflatable rafts were made from. Now, he had enough evidence to verify his suspicions.

It was obvious to Jim that, positioned below him on the back deck of the *Earth's Guardian*, there were six identical stations suitable for holding an inflatable raft. Each station held blocks and straps for securing the little crafts to the deck, and each station had a gas can, oars, and other equipment pertinent to the small boats. Five actual rafts sat secured to deck, each with two straps hugging their sides. Each raft was white and, as far as Jim could tell, appeared to be a match in color to the material evidence that he had covered. There was one anomaly on the ship below, and it was an inconsistency that Jim fully expected to see. A sixth raft station sat empty, its straps lying in a jumble on the decking next to the blocks. There was one inflatable missing, and Jim was certain that a piece of it was sitting in an evidence bag in his office.

The *Cranbrook Culture Club* was a fan club of sorts, and

the club's three members couldn't have been more dissimilar. Shasta Wilford had spent a life of living in luxury and complete boredom. Her late husband, Lexington Wilford III, had been born into the kind of old money wealth that dated back to the seventeen-hundreds. The man served on the various boards of his various family trusts as a profession, which meant that he only actually worked about four weeks out of the year. The man spent the other forty-eight weeks on the calendar doing whatever old rich white dudes tended to do; most of which included heavy consumption of Scotch.

Shasta got married to Lexington in the late Nineteen-Seventies. Being a proud, rich, white southern family, Lexington's father belonged to most of the prominent country clubs in the region. The Wilford's nuptials occurred at the famed Augusta National Golf Club in May of 1979; just a month after Fuzzy Zoeller had won the Masters Tournament. Two years after they married, Shasta gave birth to their only child, and the wealthy couple named him Fuzzy in honor of the event.

For the next decade and a half, Shasta's main responsibility was to oversee the nannies that were raising her son. Young Fuzzy Wilford turned out to be what one might expect from a rich, entitled childhood, and Shasta could barely stand to be around the brat. This circumstance promptly led to the hiring of more nannies, far removing the chance that actual parenting might occur. Finally, when Fuzzy had reached adulthood and left home for a private university, Shasta withdrew several thousand dollars from the 'homemaker's discretionary fund' that her husband allowed her to manage, and she hopped on a plane bound for the Northwest. Upon landing in Seattle, Washington, Shasta boarded a cruise ship where she spent ten days alone touring the Inside Passage of Southeast Alaska. She had told Lexington that she was going shopping for school clothes and dormitory decorations for Fuzzy, and her husband didn't bat an eye about her mysterious two-week absence.

The excursion was short-lived, but never forgotten. Years later, Lexington croaked when his heart burst, leaving him face down in a pile of his morning grits. Shasta rarely ate with the man, but had chosen that morning to discuss an increase in her homemaker's discretionary fund. When the man started emitting an odd gurgling sound from lips that were mushed directly into his breakfast, Shasta rolled her eyes and stormed out of the breakfast nook in a huff. "You'd do anything to get out of allowing me more money," she accused as she stormed off for the wine cellar. Several hours later, when the maid staff determined that Lexington wasn't actually sleeping one off, Shasta did her best to mask her joy as her late husband's body was covered and carted away.

Shasta inherited only a mild chunk of the family fortune, but it was enough to give her independence and freedom from a former life that she had despised. With fond memories of her recent solo experience on board a north-bound cruise ship, Shasta moved to an island in Southeast Alaska in search of solace and a cure for the intense boredom which she had been immersed in most of her adult days. A short time after settling in a home on Prince of Wales Island, Shasta Wilford read the book *Muskeg Mama*, and an idea sprang to life. The *Cranbrook Culture Club*, titled after the author's namesake, came into existence as a way for Shasta to seek out and experience a bit of adventure. She was determined to never be bored again.

Club membership had to be restricted as only a certain type of lady would do. Living most of her life around the 'old-boys-clubs' of the South, Shasta was no stranger to membership restrictions. She came up with several qualifiers in discerning which local island women would be recruited. The first and most important prerequisite was that only unattached women could join the club. No husbands, no boyfriends, and no attachments of any type would be allowed. Living a life filled with watching men sip imported whiskey while telling lies and sexist jokes had left Shasta jaded. Her club membership would need to be filled with ladies who were free of such entanglements.

The other qualities that Shasta looked for during the recruitment phase of her project were mere notions, not deal-breakers. She wanted her membership to be at least above the age of fifty. A fondness for champagne, regardless of the time of day, would certainly help. The ability to look straight into the eyes of a man and lie wholeheartedly to his face was a desirable trait. The women would also be required to read *Muskeg Mama* and be interested in supporting the principles of the book set forth by the author and main character, Ellen Cranbrook. These principles are three-fold. One, women are strong. Two, men suck and cause most of what's bad in the world. Three, it's perfectly acceptable to be uncouth.

Simple, yet profound.

While consuming a bagel and a cup of coffee at a local diner, Shasta crossed paths with her first recruit. Angel Yu served her breakfast. The two women got to chatting while the waitress was refilling Shasta's coffee cup. In between helping café customers, Angel kept returning to Shasta's table in order to tell her story. She and her husband had worked for

115

years as caretakers of a fishing lodge called Cedar Cove Resort that was stuck in a remote peninsula on the northeast corner of Prince of Wales Island. The lodge owners hired the husband and wife team to handle the bulk of the in-house duties. Angel did the cleaning and tended to the guests while her husband ran the kitchen. Her husband was quite a chef and responsible for feeding grand Alaskan meals to the wealthy Cedar Cove Resort patrons. Between the two of them, they had always managed to keep the resort running smoothly and both lived a comfortable life in the wilds that surrounded the Alaskan lodge.

Always trusting her husband to manage their personal finances, Angel Yu had no reason to suspect that there were any concerns. When he passed away from a heart attack at age sixty-two, Angel was forced to pay attention to the bills that kept appearing in the mail. Soon, she learned that her husband had charged up over fifty thousand dollars on various credit cards. With a paltry internet connection at the fishing resort, the man had managed to find the only on-line poker game with such low-quality graphics that he was able to participate. As his addiction grew, he refused to acknowledge that the computer graphics weren't the only sub-par aspect of the game. It was rigged.

The remote life quickly lost its appeal. Soon after her husband's death, Angel Yu moved from the Cedar Cove Resort into the town of Craig in search of a few more housing and employment options. Upon hearing the Chinese widow's story, Shasta scooped her up into the fold of the *Cranbrook Culture Club* as the organization's first recruit, and the two ladies instantly struck a kinship. It quickly became clear that Angel possessed certain qualities that Shasta held dear. She appreciated Angel's quirkiness. She snickered at her new friend's verbal assault on the English language and was totally amused by the lady's insistence on using pure, fresh-squeezed lemon juice to aid in all household chores. Mainly, Shasta liked the fact that Angel felt burned and betrayed by her late husband, and she'd found that sipping champagne at ten o'clock in the morning seemed to light a fire under her.

The third member of the group was a natural fit. Phyllis Prescott loathed men. Every man in her life had been nothing short of horrid. Her father used to beat her as a child. Her ex-husband was a verbally abusive drunk, and her son, a convicted felon. Phyllis' only bright spot on her family tree was a granddaughter that had just turned six-years-old. Phyllis held out hope for the little girl as, first and foremost, she was wholeheartedly not a male. She loved dolls, tea parties, the color pink, and almost every other stereotypically girly trait. This was as much encouraged by the grandmother as it was by the child. For several years, Grammy Phyllis spent most weekdays in charge of the granddaughter while the kid's mom worked. They were like two peas in a pod and spend most of their time fully engaged in non-masculine enterprise.

When Phyllis' son hit the parole board with a song and dance about how he was reformed and wouldn't even think about stealing catalytic converters from underneath parked cars again, the degenerate was released from prison. Being that he had been convicted in the State of Oregon, and crossing state lines would be a strict violation of his parole, the man's estranged wife found it in her heart to forgive him, snatched up Phyllis' granddaughter, and drove on the next ferry off the island. Phyllis was crushed. She considered following the little girl south in order to live close by, but her son pleaded to be allowed a fresh start with his small family. Reluctantly, Phyllis stayed on Prince of Wales, dejected and with a refueled animosity toward all-things-men.

After a chance meeting in the produce section at the local grocery store, Phyllis Prescott was recruited into the fold, and with membership soaring, Shasta Wilford decided that three warm bodies were enough to start making some local waves. Shasta walked into Ross Brothers Land and Sea and paid cash for three identical, fully decked out, Yamaha Grizzly four-by-four ATV's. She purchased three sets of helmets, goggles, gloves, protective body gear, and threw in an extra two-hundred bucks for riding lessons. It took several lessons before the three elderly ladies were confident enough to ride independently, but soon, the Cranbrook Culture Club was hell on four wheels.

Being adamantly anti-men, and recently armed, each with four wheels and a souped-up engine, the club set out to terrorize a local author that lived down the road from Angel Yu on Williwaw Drive. The author was a bit of a ninny, always complaining that the slightest bother would thrust him into the throes of intense writer's block, but there seemed to be some underlying additional hatred for the man that Angel Yu possessed. Coming to the support of one of their three members, the Cranbrook Culture Club sprang into action and embarked on timely missions designed to pulverize Cliff Barr's mailbox.

The first couple of outings were a piece of cake. The mailbox had been posted on a wooden two-by-four that had hardly been secured to a road-side tree. One or two passes with the ATVs and an aluminum baseball bat, and the mailbox was easily obliterated. They could tell that they were getting under the author's skin. After ascending the side of a nearby hillside on an old, defunct logging road, the three ladies had popped the cork on a magnum of champagne. They passed the bottle between them, giggling like little girls while they waited for the cops to show up down below. The ladies smirked and pointed from their secret vantage as they watched the object of their terror mission flail his arms dramatically while describing to the State Troopers how he was a victim of a criminal organization.

Soon, the four-wheeled mailbox assaults became a little more challenging. Cliff Barr had thrown a wrench into the mix by sinking a metal pole into concrete and solid rock, and having a rigid, iron mailbox welded onto the top of the pole. This little setback was easily eradicated with nothing more than a tow-chain. Two of the four-wheelers had run circles around the irate author, keeping him at bay, while the third motorized machine utilized the chain in order to yank the metal pole right out of the ground. They dragged the iron mailbox, bouncing along behind the ATV, all the way up the old logging road and used it as a platform to set their champagne bottle on while they celebrated, watching the scene below.

# Chapter 15

The clouds had lifted above the peaks of the mountains that surrounded Craig, Alaska. Life surrounding the small town seemed to buzz with activity. A tugboat chugged slowly away from the waterfront, pulling a barge full of multi-colored containers. A couple of fishing boats were entering and exiting the protected harbors. A pile driver hammered noisily on a tall metal piling that shot down into the water just offshore. Cannery and dock workers scurried about the waterfront, prepping their businesses in anticipation of the summer season. And a single engine floatplane hummed as it crossed between mountain peaks, readying an approach to the channel that passed in front of the town.

Lieutenant Jim Wekle was wearing his Alaska State Trooper uniform and Stetson as he stood at the top of the ramp that led down to the seaplane dock. He watched Frightening Frankie bank the de Havilland Beaver into the breeze and set down the aquatic aircraft onto the water's surface with ease. Despite what his nickname indicated, Frightening Frankie was one of the best bush pilots in the region. He only received the moniker due to his eagerness to fly early morning trips in variable weather when other local pilots seemed to enjoy an excuse to sip coffee while telling lies in *Porty's*.

Small waves bounced off the seaplane's floats as it taxied over to the dock. A teenaged dock worker wearing shorts, work boots, and a long-sleeved drab shirt grabbed a short rope that hung from the plane's wing and pulled it in close. With the engine cut and the plane secured, the red-headed pilot with reflective aviator shades and a dark blue Seahawks hoodie hopped out a door and stood on one of the floats. He helped several passengers exit from the plane, including Vera Wekle.

Having already descended the ramp to the floating dock below, Jim was there to greet his mother with a large hug and a smile. "Mom, you look fantastic. Welcome to Prince of Wales."

Returning the hug with her eyes clenched shut, Mrs. Wekle was choked up. She looked at him, cleared her throat, and managed to speak. "Jimmy. It's so good to see you." It had been just over three years since they had last met in person, and you could see true longing in her eyes. "How are you, son?"

"I'm fine, mom. It is good to see you, too."

"Are you eating right? You look too skinny."

"I'm trying."

"Are you take D-vitamins?"

"Mom…"

Frankie handed Jim a large suitcase from the plane's cargo hold. The Trooper nodded to the pilot, then escorted his mother toward the ramp that steeply angled up from the water's surface. Jim asked, "How's dad doing?"

"Oh, you know him. Washes and waxes the car once a week, mows the grass at a forty-five degree angle to the sidewalk, and wears white socks that he pulls up to just below his exposed knees."

"So, retirement is treating him well? Is that what you're saying?"

"Oh, of course. He seems to stay busy enough, between his chores around the house, golfing with the men's club, and volunteering with the local Little League." Vera Wekle was happy to be with her son. She walked with an air of elegance. Vera was a tall lady with streaks of silver throughout her curly, black hair. Her facial features displayed an attractive woman with hints of crow's feet at the corners of her eyes. She wore a thick, winter coat. "It's freezing here, Jimmy."

"You're from San Diego, mom. It's actually a pretty nice day here." Jim waved to two figures that stood at the top of the ramp as he pulled his mother's suitcase along behind him amid the other seaplane passengers. Two smiling figures waved enthusiastically in return. Maggie grinned widely as she waved. Kram bounced up and down like a puppy dog in eager anticipation.

Jim guided his mom past three ladies in antique clothes sipping champagne from skinny glasses. One of the ladies with a thick Chinese accent boasted obnoxiously about something called *Traverse the Trail*. Jim and his mother ignored the ladies and approached his friends. Motioning toward his girlfriend, Jim announced, "Mom, I'd like you to meet…"

Interrupting, Vera Wekle said, "Maggie. It's so nice to meet you in person. You are such a pretty girl." She reached out and gave Maggie a polite hug and a peck on the cheek.

Still hopping up and down excitedly, Kram saluted. "Present, accounted for, and ready for inspection, ma'am."

"Mom, this is my friend, Kram."

Vera extended her hand and said, "Pleased to meet you. Kram is an interesting name."

Ignoring the offered handshake, Kram jumped forward and embraced the woman in an intense bear-hug. "This is one of the greatest days of my life," he said, choking back tears.

"You hungry, Mom? *Porty's* serves a mean halibut burger." The four people walked toward the State Trooper's Crown Victoria. Jim put the suitcase in the trunk, as Vera and Maggie loaded up in the back seat. Jim asked Kram, "Are you coming? I'm buying."

With a regretful expression, Kram replied, "Can't. I'm late."

"New job?"

"Yep."

"First day?"

"Yep."

"What'cha doing this time?"

"Gas station attendant."

Concerned, Jim said, "That might be, uh… dangerous."

Kram grinned excitedly. "Exactly!" The pony-tailed man in jean cut-offs bolted, sprinting across the parking lot and up the sidewalk.

Gretch Skully was nearing his breaking point. He had grown up in a family of fishermen. The Skullys had fished the waters surrounding Prince of Wales Island for three generations and the industry had always provided. They were a hard working family filled with a passion for the sea and the salmon that swam in it. Historically, salmon always provided well for his family; however, Gretch found it to be more and more difficult with each year that passed. Commercial licensing fees, insurance premiums, fuel and vessel maintenance costs were through the roof. Although the price of fish was high, scarcity was such an issue that in combination with overhead soaring, it was increasingly difficult to make ends meet for the small, independent fisherman. Gretch feared that he wouldn't be able to afford to fish for too many more seasons.

With his profession in the toilet, Gretch Skully's emotions were already on the verge of a meltdown. When the Planet Patrol vessel floated its way into the region, filled with its anti-fishing propaganda and industry damaging agenda, Gretch was ready to flip out. Fearing for his livelihood, he formed a small coalition of local like-minded fishermen that were prepared to do whatever it took to severely deter Planet Patrol's efforts. Three men sat in a garage on folding chairs while Gretch Skully paced behind them.

"We could sink it. One well-placed hit from a kamikaze mission at full ramming speed should punch a hole big enough to send them swimming," said a man wearing yellow rain pants held up by suspenders.

Another fisherman with a massive beer-belly spoke up. "Who would be crazy enough to ram that ship with their own boat? I couldn't do that to my boat."

A tall man holding a gaff hook said, "Besides, ramming a boat like that would probably kill you."

Yellow rain pants retorted, "Thus the word, *kamikaze*, dumb-ass."

Gaff hook snapped, "That plan sucks."

"Up yours."

Beer belly asked, "Does anyone have any type of grenade launcher or mortar firing device?"

Rain pants replied, "I have a few bottle rockets left over from last fourth-of-July."

Gaff hook said, "You guys are the biggest collection of dipshits…"

"Gentlemen!" The voice was sharp and quickly stopped the banter. Gretch Skully had finally decided to speak up. He had an idea. "I know how we can get rid these scumbags for good." He lit a cigarette, inhaled deeply, and then blew dual smoke streams out his nose. He had the full attention of the other fishermen in the room. He continued to pace, letting the silence sink in.

After another deep drag on his cigarette, Gretch stopped pacing and made eye contact with all three of his henchmen. He tapped the ash of his cigarette and it fell to the floor of the garage. An evil smirk appeared on his face, curling the right side of his upper lip. Fixing his gaze on the man holding the gaff hook, Gretch asked, "Vinny, you still have that tranquilizer gun, right?"

# Chapter 16

Lunch at *Porty's* was awkward. They were positioned in a curved, corner booth, with Jim in between his mother and his girlfriend. The two women jawed back and forth to each other about such subjects as the weather, recent movies, pie recipes, politics, religion, menstruation, menopause, Jim's childhood, Jim's unfortunate habits, Jim's teeth, Jim's hair, Jim's butt, and stupid things that Jim likes to do. Jim wanted to leave…bad.

"One time, when he was just a toddler, he took off his pants and diaper while I was standing in line at the post office, and he dropped a little poopy, right there on the floor. As you could imagine, I was completely mortified. The postmaster had to call in the night janitor just to get it properly sterilized." Vera Wekle's voice reverberated off the walls of the bar and had started to draw the attention of several of the locals. Jim noticed some old-timers sipping from beer cans chuckling.

The standard lunch crowd of locals filled *Porty's*. Some sat at tables and booths, while many sat at the bar. Most patrons drank beer, but some chose hard alcohol, or coffee, or just plain water. Some had ordered food. Some chatted with acquaintances, while others sat alone and quiet, listening intently over their shoulders, fully entertained by the banter from around the bar. The room was dimly lit and smelled of stale beer and fry oil. Pictures of shipwrecked boats and local aircraft crashes lined the walls of the joint, as a tribute to the men and women involved with disasters that occurred all too often in the region. Most of the locals that frequented *Porty's* were connected in some way to at least a handful of the pictures that covered the walls. The photos were monuments to friends and family that had passed, to the lucky ones that survived, and to the brave teams of search and rescue personnel that engaged at a moment's notice.

After chewing a French fry, Maggie asked, "What was he like as a teenager? Was he a lady killer, or a total nerd?"

"A little bit of both. I remember this one time…"

"Mom!" Jim interrupted his mother's story. He reached across the table and grabbed the ketchup bottle.

Vera retorted, "Oh Jimmy, you know that I have to tell her this story." She picked up a glass filled with red wine and took a sip.

"Why don't you talk a little louder? I'm sure the whole town would like to hear. Maybe they could get you a microphone, or publish a column in the local gazette titled, *Stories from Little Jimmy's Childhood.* Subtitled, *The Death of a Lieutenant.*" Jim's sarcasm was ignored by his mother. Maggie punched his leg under the table. He exhaled and then lifted his coffee cup while rolling his eyes.

Mrs. Wekle continued, saying, "Jimmy and his best friend had dates to the homecoming dance. They were just sophomores, so young, you know. I think it had to be his first actual date. He was so nervous. I remember him specifically freaking out over a pimple on his nose. The boys were planning on taking their dates out to dinner at a restaurant and then over to the school for the dance. Our house was walking distance to both the restaurant and the school, so their dates were going to be dropped off at our home. Well, poor Jimmy had managed to wake up with a cold the day of the dance. A pretty bad one, too, but he refused to cancel the date. His pimpled little nose was so stuffed up, he could barely talk. Shortly after his date arrived Jimmy decided to try and pin on the corsage that he had bought this cute little girl. While attempting to work the pins, he sneezed hard into the palm of his hand. When he removed his hand, a string of snot stayed attached between his nose and his hand. The poor girl was repulsed. Jimmy was mortified. His father taped the whole thing on the camcorder."

Maggie, along with several of the locals that sat up at the bar, howled. Jim frowned and stared straight forward. His mother took a bite of her halibut burger. "Hey, you're right. This fish is pretty tasty."

"I am so glad you told that story, Mom. Thank you. Thank you very much."

They continued to eat their lunch, Maggie encouraging more Jimmy-stories to be told. Just as they were finishing their meals, a woman wearing a blue windbreaker, Levi jeans, and rubber boots approached the table. She said, "Good to see you, Lieutenant Wekle.

"Hello," Jim acknowledged. "This is my mother, Vera Wekle. Mom, I'd like you to meet our Harbormaster, Cheryl Lawson."

Vera said, "Pleased to meet you."

"Nice to meet you, too. You know, I have your son to thank for my job here on this island."

"Oh?" Vera turned toward Jim.

"I served on the hiring committee for the Harbormaster's job," Jim said. "It was a slam dunk. Between her experience as a Coast Guard salvage specialist and her quick wit during the interview, she had the other candidates beat by a mile."

Cheryl and Jim exchanged a pleasant glance. Maggie wrinkled her nose.

Cheryl said, "Welcome to Craig, Mrs. Wekle. I'm sure your son will show you around the island. It's quite a beautiful place."

"Harbormaster? That seems like an important job in this town," said Vera.

"I love it. I feel that I get to be a strong woman living in a man's world." Turning her attention to Jim, she said, "I heard you did a fly-by of our recently departed not-so-welcome guests."

"Yeah, did a quick chopper trip. They're swinging on the anchor chain just inside Hooligan Arm."

"Fools. Hope they hit the rock and sink. You find anything interesting out there?"

"Well, they seem to be missing a boat. But that's about it."

"Hopefully, they'll take the hint that we don't want them here." She gave Jim a pretty smile as if to say goodbye. Before walking away, Cheryl turned to Jim's mother and said, "Again, nice to meet you, Vera. You guys enjoy those halibut burgers." Cheryl Lawson waved to a few other people around the room before opening the door and exiting the bar.

"She seems nice," said Vera Wekle.

Maggie spoke up, "I don't like her."

Jim shook his head, "Just because she's nice to me?"

"She always makes a point of talking to you. And did you notice, she didn't even acknowledge that I exist." Maggie was obviously jealous.

In a reassuring tone, Jim said, "Maggie, you're being crazy. Besides, she's much older than me. Why would I even be interested?"

"So? I'm younger than you."

"Exactly. And you're beautiful. And you're sweet. And you're really good to me."

Chewing on another French fry, Maggie said, "And don't you forget it."

The rest of the meal was fairly uneventful, but still mildly painful. When Jim got up to pay the bill, three men at the bar all began to repeatedly fake sneezing into the palm of their hands, pulling away their hand with a look of disgust as they pretended to examine fake snot.

A man sitting close to the cash register asked, "Can I borrow a handkerchief, *Jimmy*?"

"Duke," Jim said pleasantly, but meaningfully, "I think your truck's parked illegally. Good thing I brought my ticket book."

After paying the tab, Jim escorted the two ladies out the door and into the gravel parking lot next to the bar. Moist, sea air greeted them. The smell of tidal activity was ripe. Ravens squawked, an eagle chortled, and a hummingbird buzzed by impatiently. The hum of a floatplane taking off could be heard in the distance, and the dull rumble of a diesel boat engine rose from the dock below. Jim asked, "How do you like Southeast Alaska, Mom?"

"It certainly has a rugged beauty. I can understand the allure, but I don't think I could live here."

Maggie nodded. "Most people can't live here. Especially on Prince of Wales. It's pretty remote. That floatplane that you flew in on today, it was also carrying our mail. That barge over there." She pointed toward the water. "It's carrying our groceries for the week. Sometimes it takes patience just to get supplies and basic services here."

"No Amazon orders with free shipping and second day delivery?"

"No, not exactly."

Vera Wekle asked, "Does some of that get old and bothersome?"

"Not in the slightest. I grew up here. My family has been here for a long time. It's home and I wouldn't trade it for anything."

Jim added, "That's why our population stays pretty small. It's not a way of life that everyone can take."

Maggie continued, "I love it. Besides, there are some pretty great people that live here." She turned to give Jim a sly, cute smile. Her black hair framed the dark, smooth complexion of her face. She was a very pretty girl.

Nudging him with her elbow, Jim's mother said, "She's a keeper, Jimmy. Now, where am I staying? I've been traveling all day and I think I need a little rest and to freshen up a bit."

"We'll head home, Mom. You'll enjoy the drive. There's some beautiful scenery along the way." Turning to Maggie, he gave her a kiss on the cheek and said, "See you in the morning."

"Thanks for the meal, *Jimmy*."

"Don't call me that, please."

Mrs. Wekle butted in. "Jimmy, she can come, too. It's the twenty-first century, and I'm a progressive mother. If you're girl usually sleeps over, who am I to bat an eye?"

Mortified, Jim said, "Mom…"

Maggie smiled. "Thank you, Vera, but I'll leave you two alone this evening. I actually live right over there." She pointed toward the marina.

"Where? On a different island, like Jim?"

Jim said, "No, Mom. She lives on her boat. It's moored in the marina over there."

"How peculiar. You live on a boat. I bet that is such an interesting experience at times. Can you get cable television shows?"

Maggie gave Mrs. Wekle a hug. "I'll give you the grand tour sometime. We'll have to go for an evening harbor cruise before you leave."

While walking away toward Jim's car, Vera Wekle announced in a voice loud enough for Maggie to hear, "She's the one, Jimmy. Beautiful, smart, young, and she owns her own boat. You need to marry that girl."

"Mom!"

The phone rang shortly after four o'clock in the morning. It was just as well. Sleeping on the couch wasn't providing Jim with the best night's rest anyway. The call was from the Emergency Call Center, a sort of professional off-hours answering service for remote law enforcement. Jim was showered and dressed in his uniform within fifteen minutes of the call.

In a quiet voice, Jim informed his half asleep mother, "Mom. I've got a call and I've got to go. I'll come back and check in on you soon." She turned in his bed and gave a muffled reply of acknowledgement.

Jim craved coffee during the quick skiff ride from Mink Island, but he knew that it would be a while before he was able to have a cup. The call was a reported explosion. That couldn't be good. He had phoned in for back-up by calling Trooper Brandi Sitzel soon after the initial ECC contact. She was already on the scene when Jim turned his State Trooper car onto Williwaw Drive. A man with oversized eyebrows, wearing a bathrobe and slippers was frantically waving his arms.

Stepping out of his Crown Vic, Jim heard his female officer saying, "Sir, you need to settle down first if you'd like us to help you."

Cliff Barr was irate and hysterical. Punctuating every third word by throwing both hands into the air, he squawked, "I have called you jokers four times in the past two weeks.

You know what kind of help you've given me? Nothing. Precisely and exactly nothing!"

Walking up, flanking his officer, Jim said, "Good morning, Mr. Barr. I was told something about an explosion. Why don't you explain?"

"Explain? Explain? You want me to explain? They blew it up." The words reached a high-pitched squeal. Cliff Barr's flailing arms finally settled long enough for him to point in the direction of where his mailbox used to sit. With the morning light still dim as the sun was rising, Jim illuminated the spot with his flashlight. There was no sign of the mailbox or its brand new support pole. All that was left in the vicinity was a charred crater the size of a beach ball.

Trooper Sitzel asked, "What did they blow up, sir?"

About ready to freak out, the man struggled in his reply. "My... my... my mailbox, you twits."

"Who blew it up, Mr. Barr?"

"Who? Who?" His voice trailed up in pitch with each word. "Did you actually just ask that? Who? I'll spell it out for you. The bastard, shit-eating, piece of scum, dirt-bag, fart licking, four-wheeled gang of degenerates that I've been calling you idiots about for weeks now. That's who. Do your job. Find these jack-offs and shoot them. Shoot them in the eyeball. Each of them, one at a time, right in the eye socket. Bam." He fired a fake gun with his finger and thumb.

Jim calmly said, "We will not be shooting anybody, Mr. Barr."

Examining the crater with her flashlight, Trooper Sitzel said, "Jim, come here and take a look." After Jim approached, Brandi continued, "This crater in the ground, it dug down pretty deep into concrete and solid rock. That would take an explosion with considerable force."

"Yeah." Jim nodded thoughtfully. "I bet enough force to sever some guy's foot. Is that what you're thinking?"

"I'm just thinking there seems to be more than one big explosion going on around here. Could be a coincidence. Could be a connection." Turning to the man in the bathrobe, Brandi asked, "Do you have any idea who's riding these four-wheelers and where they're from?"

"If I had an idea, don't you think I would have told you by now?" Cliff Barr frowned at them. "They appear out of nowhere and disappear just as fast. Their faces and bodies are completely covered with riding gear. There are three of them, and all three are riding identical looking machines. That is all the information I have. I don't know who they are, but I can only guess that they are probably young men that belong to some sort of terrorist organization. I think it's time to call in the friggin' National Guard."

"Settle down, now." Jim gave him a searching look. "Do you have any idea why they are targeting you, Mr. Barr? Have you had any recent disputes or arguments with anyone lately? Have you angered anyone recently?"

Cliff's raised voice approached the nasal hum of an armature oboist. "I have disputes or arguments daily. You, of all people, should know this. Your lady cop, here, just dealt with my neighbor and his stink-fest up there the other day. And once again, your outfit's incompetence resulted in no change whatsoever. What is wrong with you people?"

Jim turned to Brandi Sitzel and asked, "The

neighbor?"

"You know him. Zeke Melon. The guy that found the foot. He's got some sort of fish drying operation up there. Mr. Barr is correct in that it stinks to high heaven, but seems innocent enough, and until the landlord gets involved, there's not much we can do."

"Innocent?" Cliff Barr was shouting now. "Innocent? You are the biggest bunch of dinks…"

Jim said to the other Trooper, "I'm sure you're right, but I think we should have another conversation with Mr. Melon. Let's go wake him up."

"He's not home." Cliff seemed oblivious that his bathrobe had fallen open in front, exposing tight, black bikini briefs.

"Close your hole, Cliff." Trooper Sitzel, pointed to the lapse in garment coverage.

Jim asked, "When did Zeke leave?"

Tying a knot in his bathrobe, Cliff said, "He left last night, fairly late, too. Never came home. Still reeks up there. The stench has literally crept through the walls and permeated my clothes. Here, smell this." The man held out the lapel of his bathrobe, offering it up for a sniff. He didn't get any takers. "Did I tell you that I am a writer? I make my living working from home. And writing takes full concentration and full brain power. How am I expected to meet my deadlines with distractions like this? How am I supposed to write eloquently and creatively when my home smells like a rancid sardine can and I'm being tormented by a rogue gang of motorized terrorists?"

Concerned about Zeke's disappearance, Jim turned to the side and told the other Trooper, "I'm going to check the dock for Zeke's boat. He's been dip-netting during the high tides, which was fairly late last night. You check his home, and look into this so called gang of four-wheelers. I don't want any more explosions in the middle of the night."

"Roger, boss." Turning back to Cliff, Trooper Sitzel asked, "Have you got a key to your neighbor's door?"

"No, but he's got all the windows open because of the stink. Come on, I'll show you."

Jim hopped into his Crown Vic and sped away for the city docks with his red and blue lights flashing.

# Chapter 17

The morning was full of damp chill. As daylight rose over the mountain on the eastern side of Hooligan Arm, Beanie LeFranc battled with scuba gear alone on the back deck of the *Earth's Guardian*. He was topping off an oxygen tank with deep diving gas as a shiver ran up his extremities. Between the slight breeze and the damp, cool morning air, Beanie was chilled to the bone. As soon as Beanie unhooked one of the cylindrical tanks, he left the back deck area to retrieve a coat, hat, and gloves from inside the cabin. When he returned to the outside area of the boat, he failed to notice, for the second time that morning, the white tarp covering a large lump atop the stern-most inflatable raft. The white lump rested on the port side of the ship and inconspicuously rose and fell steadily as if the tarp itself was taking lumbered breaths.

Bitter after being assigned early morning duties while the rest of the crew slept one off inside their bunks, Beanie cursed under his breath while he sorted out masks and hoses. "Damn grunt duty. This sucks. I thought I was supposed to be the number two man around here." He often spoke to himself when in self-pity mode. "Beanie, fill the hypoxic tanks. Beanie, scrape barnacles off the rudder. Beanie, someone barfed in the head. Sucks."

Needing to fill another dive tank, Beanie walked toward the back of the ship where several tanks sat empty next to the aft deck rail. He lifted a tank with his right arm and had just spun around when something caught his attention out of the corner of his eye. A lump under a mysterious white tarp seemed to have wiggled.

"What the hell *is* that, anyway," the skinny kid asked aloud in a cracked voice. Beanie strolled over close to the covered inflatable and examined the odd circumstances. The small craft was hooked up to the winch that was attached to the ship's large boom arm. He knew that it was not proper protocol to leave something attached to the boom. "That's not right," Beanie said to himself, tilting his head in confusion as he examined the raft station. "Some drunk fool must have gone for a joyride last night. Damn idiots onboard this ship."

The straps that secured the raft to the ship had been removed and sat in a jumble to either side of the small boat. Beanie knew that this was completely out of place. His uncle would never allow a boat to remain hooked up to the boom arm overnight, and especially, he would never allow the inflatable to sit on the deck without being secured. Someone was going to be in huge trouble if Beanie ever found out who was responsible.

Beanie looked puzzled at the mass that covered the inflatable raft. *What in the hell was with this white tarp?* The large bulge under the tarp, inside the raft, appeared to be moving. He stepped closer and poked it with the butt end of an oxygen tank.

A snorting sound, followed by a low rumble emitted from the lump. Beanie dropped the oxygen tank. The tarp moved again. There was something alive under it. Baffled and now more curious than concerned, Beanie LeFranc grabbed a corner. He thought for a moment that maybe one of the crewmen had gotten drunk and passed out in the inflatable under the tarp.  The guy must be snoring while he slept it off.  The bulge looked much too large to be one of the crewmen, but what else could it be?

Convinced that he was about to bust one of his passed-out shipmates for snoozing on the back deck, Beanie prepared himself at the edge of the raft.  He clenched the tarp with a gloved hand, securing a firm hold on a grommet at the corner.  In one quick motion, Beanie LeFranc jerked away the white tarp, yelling, "Aha!"

The bear was groggy and just coming to.  With the tarp removed, the shock and terror was equally shared between Beanie LeFranc and the black bear.  For a brief second, the two creatures made eye contact.  Pure fear filled Beanie's entire being.  He turned pale white and mildly soiled himself.

The bear stumbled as it tried to rise to its feet.  It teetered to its left and caught itself from toppling over by pressing a paw firmly into the side of the inflatable.  Air hissed loudly as sharp claws pierced the side of the inflatable raft.

"Holy shit," Beanie screamed as he made a run for the cabin.

The bear groaned as it slowly leaned to its right.  It was confused, disoriented, and coming out of a drug induced slumber.  The confusion turned to anger when orange fireballs began whizzing by its head.

In a complete panic, Beanie LeFranc had grabbed several loaded flare guns from a supply cabinet and had started firing toward the large omnivore.  In his current state of shock, terror, and urine-soaked pants, the kid's aim was horrendous.  He missed the bear by several feet with each firing.  The flare shots hissed past the back rail and were extinguished by the saltwater of Hooligan Arm.

Spooked by the whole situation, the bear decided to take it out on the row of inflatable rafts that sat on the left side of the boat. By the time Beanie's screaming and whimpering had woken up Pierre Lemieux and the rest of the crew, the bear had lit into the white laminated fabric of several of the life-boats. The groggy-eyed men appeared at the railing of the elevated deck next to the wheelhouse, and watched a pissed-off black bear rip half the remaining fleet of inflatables to paltry shreds.

Shouting down at his young nephew, Pierre Lemieux asked in an accusatory tone, "What the hell is going on down there?"

"Bear! Bear! Bear!" Beanie LeFranc was petrified. Only single, one-syllable words were possible.

"It's destroying our boats. Do something, you dolt."

Beanie grabbed the one remaining loaded flare gun from the storage cabinet and took a trembling step toward the enraged animal. He took aim. His arm shook.

The shot missed the bear, whizzing a fireball well above its head. The black bear groaned, showing its teeth.

Pierre shouted down, "That bear looks pissed. See if you can get it to mellow out some."

"How?" Beanie screamed.

"I don't know... Sing to it."

Beanie LeFranc was frozen, mouth agape, and jaw rigid while cocked to the side.

Pierre hollered, "Don't just stand there like a statue.

You look like an idiot."

The bear groaned and lumbered out from one of the pulverized rafts. It took a step toward Beanie and growled again, this time a bit more menacingly. Shaking its head back and forth several times, the bear suddenly launched into a full gallop, heading directly for the ship's First Mate.

"Stop, Drop, and Roll," yelled Pierre Lemieux from up above.

The bear loped diagonally across the back of the boat in a matter of seconds. Beanie was still in shock. He didn't move. He just stood there, immobile from internal panic. The only bodily function that Beanie could muster was closing and squinting his eyes. Just inches before completely destroying Beanie LeFranc in a fury of claws, teeth, fur, and a red scarf, the bear made a sudden and quick turn. It whizzed by the side of the kid so close Beanie felt wind on his arm. The bear bounded over the railing on the edge of the deck, falling more than fifteen feet to the water's surface. The animal landed with a massive splash, submerging for a short time before floating its head above water and swimming for shore.

"You okay, kid?" yelled Pierre.

Beanie LeFranc collapsed in a puddle of his own bodily discharge.

The bear proved to be an adept swimmer. It quickly crossed the bay and made it to shore. It sauntered up the rocks to the tree line and turned toward the boat. After shaking off water like a wet dog, it opened its mouth and bugled a long groan before slipping into the trees, disappearing into the wilderness surrounding the cove.

Daylight was in full swing by the time Jim reached the dock in town. Walking down the ramp to sea level, he wondered if he would ever get tired of the smell. When he had first moved to the island, Jim thought that he would never get used to it, but now the mixed scents of seawater, tidal activity, and fresh Alaskan air were such a part of his daily life that Jim took pleasure in breathing deep through his nose anytime he was on the waterfront. It was a moist, eclectic scent that some would classify as stink. Jim thought it smelled better than roses.

"Boy, you sure like to call a lady early in the morning." Cheryl Lawson was standing in front of an empty slip, holding an iPad in one hand. She again wore the blue windbreaker. It was embossed with the City of Craig Harbormaster logo on its front left side. She must have just gotten out of the shower as her flowing, black hair was still damp. She wore blue jeans that fit tightly over her slender legs.

"Thanks for meeting me here, Cheryl." Jim walked up to the edge of the empty boat slip and shook hands with the Harbormaster.

She said, "Obviously the boat's gone. I pulled up the recorded feed on the webcam while I was waiting for you." The Harbomaster lifted the iPad and punched in a few finger initiated digital commands. "Here. Look at the time code. Nine-forty-seven PM."

Jim leaned in close to the woman and shielded the iPad screen from the daylight with his palm. The grainy view showed the opening at the breakwater where every boat entering and exiting the marina had to pass. After a few seconds of inactivity, a small skiff with only one person sitting close to the stern entered the screen.

"There he is," said Cheryl, pointing at the image of the boat. She pressed the glass screen of the iPad and froze the image in place.

"What the hell's he got loaded into the bow of that thing?" Jim pointed at the front of the boat. The pixilated view from the webcam made detail difficult to discern, but it appeared that several large tubs had been packed into the skiff.

"Look at that." Cheryl Lawson zoomed into the middle of the boat by spreading apart her thumb and middle finger on the glass.

Jim said, "Gas cans. Also looks like some large plastic tubs. He was loaded up pretty good. Where the hell was that kid heading that late at night?"

Cheryl took the iPad back and looked Jim in the eye. "We don't really make it a habit of going after every boat that doesn't return here, Jim. We'd be chasing our tails if we did. What's your concern here? The weather wasn't too bad last night. It's a weekend. Maybe the kid's staying out there on shore somewhere and those tubs are filled with camping gear. It's Saturday morning right now, so he probably isn't due at his day job."

"Maybe." Jim had his cell phone out and searched his contact list for a number. "What concerns me, Cheryl, is where he's been doing his fishing."

"Ah. Hooligan Arm."

"Right. Something's been going on out there, and I'm hoping this kid isn't smack dab in the middle of it."

"You think he's somehow related to that severed foot? Wasn't he the one that recovered it?"

"Yeah, he was. I don't know, Cheryl. I'm struggling to make sense out of all of this."

The Harbormaster rested a foot on the boat rail. "It would take a fairly large blast to separate a foot from a leg, Jim. You might look into whether or not Zeke has any experience with explosives. We're talking C-4, dynamite, or something equivalent."

"I appreciate the insights." Jim put his cell phone to his ear, waited for a couple of seconds, and said, "Morning, Hugh. You up for an early boat ride? Looks like I might go over budget with you this month, but the pencil pushers over in Ketchikan will have to deal with it."

After arranging a time for meeting Hugh Eckley at his boat, Jim pocketed the phone and turned his attention back to the Harbormaster. "Cheryl, I'm heading out to Hooligan Arm with Hugh. I'll scan the cove to see if that's where this Zeke Melon kid ended up, but I've got another task in mind while I'm out there."

"You dropping in for a little chat with our friends from the Planet Patrol?"

"Exactly. They may not let me come aboard, but at least I'll let them know that I've got my eye on them."

The Harbormaster smirked. "Good. Stick it to 'em, Jim."

After taking in a large breath of salt air through his nose, Jim said, "I might need a favor from you, Cheryl. I think I need to get below deck on board the *Earth's Guardian*. I know that you've got connections with a judge that isn't too fond of those guys. I was hoping you could call in another favor. I'm going to need a search warrant."

"That might take a while, Jim. The kings are firing up around here. I think the judge will be fishing all weekend." She looked at Jim, who flashed back a cute smile. She asked, "On what grounds will the warrant be based?"

"The grounds are thin, but I think doable with a sympathetic judge." Jim informed her of the laminated fabric that he had found on the rock in Hooligan Arm, and the missing inflatable raft that he saw on the back deck of the Planet Patrol vessel during his helicopter flyby. It seemed to indicate that the severed foot had a connection to their ship.

"You're right. Pretty thin." Cheryl Lawson paused for a moment in thought, then asked, "What are your suspicions here, Jim? Somehow, a guy in one of the Planet Patrol boats gets himself blown up out in Hooligan Arm. And this is before their boat was anchored out there?"

"Yep."

"Any motive?"

"Nope." There was a lull in the conversation. Jim broke the silence by saying, "Think about it Cheryl. Someone recently lost their foot and most likely their life out there. Don't you find it odd that there has been no report of an incident? No missing persons report? Nothing. I think that Planet Patrol is involved, and I need to check them out."

"Agreed. I'll work the judge on the warrant, but don't hold your breath for the weekend. It'll most likely be Monday. Or later. In the meantime, I'll keep an eye out for your dip-net fisherman. If he shows up, I'll give you a call." Cheryl started to walk away toward the ramp. She stopped and turned back toward Jim, flashing a pretty smile. "Don't you usually light up one of those sweet smelling stogies when you're down here waiting for a boat ride?"

"You like the smell of those things? I thought most women hated them."

"I'm not most women." She gave him a flirtatious look.

Jim watched the woman walk up the ramp. He wished that she hadn't been wearing the blue jacket as he admired her figure. He also wished that he had brought a cigar with him.

# Chapter 18

Locating and tranquilizing the bear was the easy part. All Gretch Skully and his crew had to do was head out to the local landfill. They didn't even have to wait long before an adult sow came ambling in looking to root through the day's trash. Gretch was elected to be the shooter, and he expertly stuck two darts squarely into the bear's hind quarters. Once the animal had collapsed, the men nominated Vinny to poke the creature with his gaff hook in order to ensure that it truly was asleep.

The next step required a feat of strength. Dragging a three hundred and fifty pound animal up and onto a rolling cart took about all the force the four men could muster. Dead weight was one thing, but the bear's fur created an unexpected amount of friction. They decided that the best technique was to have each man grab a paw and lift heartily. Once on the cart, the men fairly easily pushed it up a ramp and secured the bear to the back of a flatbed truck. After transportation to a seaside industrial complex, the cart was then rolled down a ramp and loaded into the front of a landing craft that one of the men owned.

The midnight run out to Hooligan Arm was nerve racking. All four men silently imagined the bear waking up and wreaking havoc while they sat trapped inside the landing craft. For good measure, Gretch fired another tranquilizer dart into the large beast's butt. Still, three of the fishermen stood careful watch over the bear, weapons in hand, while the other man ran the boat.

They chose the landing craft for the water portion of the transportation process for two reasons. First, it was certainly the easiest marine vehicle for loading up a tranquilized bear. Second, the fisherman with the large beer belly promised the other men that it had the quietest engine out of any boat he had ever heard. Beer Belly proved to be right as they were able to successfully slip up next to the *Earth's Guardian* in the dead of night, without ever being detected.

Yellow Rain Pants had worked cranes and pulleys before, so he was the natural choice to secretly shimmy up the ship's side ladder and operate the boom arm. When the electric motorized pulley fired up, the men feared that the noise would wake the entire crew. Luckily, the captain and crew of the *Earth's Guardian* had partied pretty hard that night, and all laid in their bunks passed out and oblivious.

Once the white inflatable raft had been lowered to the water's surface next to the landing craft, the last challenge was figuring out how to get the drugged bear from the rolling cart onto the white inflatable. The men finally put dock lines around each of the massive animal's paws, and heaved with all their might. Once off the rolling cart, the bear rolled down the landing craft's ramp like a very large sack of spuds and, luckily, plopped perfectly in the middle of the white inflatable raft.

The boom arm creaked and groaned a little more than usual while lifting the raft back up the side of the ship. Yellow Rain Pants repositioned the small boat where it had previously sat, but instead of taking the time to strap it down, he simply threw a tarp over the bear and quickly exited the vessel. The landing craft quietly chugged away from the larger ship and slipped undetected into the night. Three of the men giggled as they considered the success and possible outcome of their little escapade.

"I bet it eats one of them," Beer Belly said, snorting a juicy laugh at the thought.

Gaff Hook Vinny said, "That bear will be so pissed when it wakes up, it very well might eat them all."

"I almost wish I could be there to witness the havoc. I bet they *bearly* get out alive. Get it? *Bearly…*" Yellow Rain Pants laughed alone at his lame pun.

On the three men went, pleased with how their mission had gone and in near hysterics about how it might play in the morning. Gretch Skully guided the landing craft slowly back towards its dock, silent and solemn.

Several hours later, Beanie LeFranc was the first to emerge on the back deck of the *Earth's Guardian*, bitter from his morning duty assignments, and cold from the damp chill. Several moments after that, the bear woke up.

The busy cruise ship season in several ports throughout Southeast Alaska starts ramping up in late April every year. By mid-May, waterfront towns like Ketchikan will see up to as many as six massive ships pull into port each day. Each ship is filled with a few thousand tourists, all armed with matching rain parkas and wallets full of credit cards, eager to disembark from their flotillas for a real Alaskan experienced crammed into about four city blocks. In order to offer this real Alaskan experience, shops stuff their shelves with trinkets made in China to be sold by store clerks that are often implants from the Lower Forty-Eight. Most of the store employees wouldn't know a humpback whale from a tuna fish, but they do a half-hearted job of faking it during tourist season. And the tourists don't seem to know the difference.

Ketchikan, Alaska is located on Revillagigedo Island and sits about sixty miles directly east of the city of Craig, as the raven flies. It is a much more populated town than Craig and better connected to the rest of the world. Residents of Ketchikan have access, just across the Tongass Narrows, to an airport with a runway just barely large enough to land commercial airline jets. Ketchikan has also created large docks and space for anchorages in the protected Narrows for hordes of ships to moor. It has a shipyard and a major port for the Alaska State Ferry system. Ketchikan is called Alaska's First City, as it is the southernmost city in the state. It is often both the first and final stop on an Alaska cruise, and people are eager to spend their money when they come ashore. The town's shift from a logging and fishing community to a tourism mecca has allowed its local economy to boom, at least during the summer months.

A Craig to Ketchikan flight on a floatplane is really a pretty quick trip at just over sixty miles. In a boat, however, getting from downtown Craig to the Ketchikan waterfront is not an easy task. First, the mariner would need to navigate south for close to ninety miles, following the snaking coastline of Prince of Wales Island and staying inside of Suemez Island, Dall Island, and Long Island, which would offer some protection from the open sea. Eventually, one would need to travel around potentially hazardous Cape Chacon, the exposed southernmost point of land on Prince of Wales. After rounding the cape, a boat would need to cross a wide expanse of water where Dixon Entrance meets Clarence Strait. This is a major body of saltwater wedged between several massive islands, Canada, and the seemingly endless Pacific Ocean. After making the open sea crossing, a little more protected passage between Annette and Gravina Islands would soon lead to the Ketchikan waterfront. The route certainly had its navigation challenges, even on large boats with a full array of electronic aids. The 140 mile journey was especially difficult in a small, open skiff in the middle of the night. One might even say stupid.

Zeke Melon had reached his goal of two thousand hooligan candles and was chomping at the bit to get them on the market. Knowing that he only had the two day window of the weekend before he had to go back to pumping raw sewage, the young man loaded up several dozen items of his finished product into sealed tubs and made his way for the marina in town. He packed his open bow with the tubs of hooligan candles, a couple of full gas jugs, a bag packed with fresh clothes, a small cooler stocked with food and water, a sleeping bag, a hand held spotlight, a headlamp, a couple of nautical charts, a compass, and four bottles of Nyquil. Zeke Melon left port just before ten o'clock on a Friday night and gunned the engine, making his heading south down the island. With the added weight in the bow, the boat rose quickly onto step and sliced through the water at a fairly quick clip.

The trip down the west coast of the big island was pleasingly uneventful. Zeke snaked his way around some of the smaller islands and successfully maneuvered through the maze-like conditions with one hand on the outboard tiller and one on a nautical map. He had just made it past the inlet that led to the village of Hydaburg when daylight completely ran out on him. With the cloud cover obscuring the moon, Zeke had to greatly depend on his headlamp for scanning the maritime chart. He also relied on the handheld spotlight while scanning upcoming islands and other landmarks, and for looking out in front of the boat for any floating logs that presented a hazardous obstacle.

It was almost three in the morning when the skiff rounded Cape Chacon. He killed the engine and topped off the gas tank before leaving the safety of the island for the open waters. Luckily for Zeke, there was very little wind during his midnight run, but swells from the open sea presented some challenges. He guided his boat directly to the northeast using nothing more than a cheap compass that tossed and turned as much as his small boat did in the swells. He was only a third of the way across the large expanse of open water when his nerves started to fray. He was running completely blind in hazardous waters with no landmarks in range of his spotlight. The swells seemed endless and with the lack of vision, they came at unexpected intervals. He thought about taking a swig of Nyquil to help control his anxiety, but the kid was too scared to take his hand off the tiller in order to crack open the bottle. Trembling from the knowledge that he had made a very poor choice with regard to his midnight skiff ride across big water, the young man from Pennsylvania forced himself to muscle-up and persevere. The open-sea crossing was the longest ninety minutes of his young life, and almost brought him to a whimpering breakdown.

He hit the southern tip of Annette Island just after four o'clock in the morning. Glow from the rising sun had illuminated just enough of the shoreline for Zeke to get his bearings. He guessed correctly at which landmass he was approaching and guided his boat to the left of the large island.

His assumption was confirmed when he saw lights from the village of Metlakatla passing off the starboard side of his skiff. He was especially confident in his course when he buzzed past one of the enormous cruise ships that was heading towards the same port as he. As his skiff bucked over the ship's impressive wake, Zeke wondered if any of the ship's sleeping passengers would soon be purchasing his candles.

Zeke's skiff passed several other charter boats heading out for their morning fishing trip. As he neared Revillagigedo Island, there seemed to be a buzz of activity even at that early morning hour. He could see cars passing on the highway south of town, boat activity increasing for the day, and even a couple of floatplanes hummed overhead as dawn broke on the Southeast Alaskan community.

After tying up safely to an open spot on the City Float just after 6am, Zeke Melon dosed himself with cough medicine and started carrying tubs up the ramp to the wooden dock in front of the heart of the tourist district. Zeke positioned himself where it appeared to be a central location. It was hard to tell as, without all the ships at dock, the heart of the tourist area was devoid of activity. He set up his small presentation booth using the tub lids as table tops for displaying his product. After setting out his hand-drawn sign, confident that he was ready to peddle his product, Zeke threw out his sleeping bag behind the tubs and attempted to catch a few winks before the boats came into port.

Cliff Barr needed to escape. His nerves were a wreck, he wasn't sleeping well, and he often found himself getting startled at the slightest and faint engine noise. With an imminent deadline, the writer loaded up his laptop and his notes, and decided to find some solitude away from the smell of fish death and away from threat of being run down by ATV's. He piled into his Toyota RAV4 and set out for a campground on the far end of Klawock Lake. There was a covered picnic area overlooking breathtaking views of the lake and the mountains beyond that would be the perfect locale for typing up three thousand words on kayaking the Misty Fjords.

Turning from Williwaw Drive onto the main highway, he heard a ping from the dashboard of the RAV4. The gas light was illuminated and Cliff made a detour to a gas station in town. Parking next to a pump, he opened the car door and started to swing his legs out of the Toyota.

"Stay in the car, please, sir." A voice boomed throughout the station and startled Cliff. "Company policy." A ponytailed man wearing jean cut-offs bounded from a small glass cage in the center of the station and flew over to where Cliff had parked, sliding across the hood of the Toyota and landing between the driver's side door and the pump.

"You are in for a good old fashioned pump station experience, sir. Where the term *full service* takes on new meaning in this modern world of impersonal push-button chaos. Love those eyebrows, sir. Like two woolly caterpillars home to roost. Sit back, and relax, and I'll make your short stay with us as comfortable as possible." Kram shoved the man's feet back into the car and slammed the door shut. He motioned for the man to roll down his window by turning his arm in circles.

Cliff rolled down the automated window and asked,

"Didn't you used to bag groceries?"

Shoving a clear plastic cup filled with red liquid through the driver's window, Kram announced, "Enjoy. It's my special concoction of Kool-Aid and grapefruit juice. It's tart, it's packed with vitamin C, and it's delicious." He plopped a paper umbrella in the cup and feverishly went to work on the front window. He sprayed Lysol across the outer windshield and retrieved an electric buffer from beside the gas pump. A loud whirring sound wafted off the roof of the station as Kram moved the buffer in circles, streaking the sterilizing spray across the width of the car's window.

Tossing the buffer to the side, Kram rapped on the front of the car with his fist and hollered, "Pop the hood, please." On cue, the hood jumped up an inch. Kram lifted the hood and quickly located the car's engine oil dipstick. Speed walking back to the driver's side, Kram ordered, "Stick your hand out, please, sir."

Cliff Barr did as he was commanded and put his left arm directly out the open window. Kram knelt next to the open palm and lifted the oil compartment's dipstick by holding it in the center of its flexible band of metal. With his other hand, Kram bent the oily end of the dipstick back and flicked a considerable amount of dark oil directly into the palm of his customer's hand.

"Gunk. You see it?" Kram grabbed the man's wrist and bent his arm into the cab of the vehicle, suspending the palm within an inch of Cliff's eyeballs. "I recommend our full service lube, oil, filter, and massage. I use nothing but fully recycled motor oils during the massage portion of the service. You'll instantly feel rejuvenated."

Stunned, Cliff Barr replied, "Not today, thanks."

"Suit yourself. Let me check those tires for you. I find that uneven pressure is the best way to keep your car's suspension working like new. You're not rotating them, are you? Biggest scam in the tire industry. That's how they get you. Rotate every three thousand miles, my butt. Hey, did anyone ever tell you that you smell remarkably pungent? Like rotting fish? What type of aftershave are you using, anyway?"

Ten minutes later, Cliff Barr pulled forward and turned back onto the highway with a confounded expression, underinflated tires, and an empty gas tank.

# Chapter 19

Early in the summer of 1896, the steamship *SS Aberdeen* left the Port of Seattle, packed to the gills with hopeful prospectors, and chugged its way up the Inside Passage en route for the boomtown of Skagway. After unloading passengers that were destined for an arduous journey over White Pass on their way to stake a claim in the Klondike, the steamship's captain didn't waste any time on making the return trip to Seattle. Hordes of paying customers awaited him back at the Seattle waterfront, and the quicker he returned, the quicker they would hand him their cash.

Only a handful of return passengers booked passage on the SS Aberdeen's trip south. With the gold rush just firing up, most of the travelers were northbound, but a few were ready to go back. Among the returnees was Wally Weatherford, one of the few early prospectors lucky enough to actually strike it rich in the Klondike. Wally had hired a small posse of tough looking goons to help him transport and protect his heavy load of gold. In addition, the man of recent importance had hooked up with a dancehall girl from one of the Skagway saloons. Wally and the girl had actually fallen for each other, although most in the town thought the young lady to be a gold-digger. Literally.

After loading up the gold, the SS Aberdeen left its Skagway port with only the ship's captain, crew, Wally, three goons, a dancing girl, and two cases of Canadian whiskey. They were all completely smashed by the time the boat exited Lynn Canal, including the captain. Normally, a southbound ship would turn inward past Juneau and head south through the Wrangell Narrows, meandering safely through the protected waters of Southeast Alaska's Inside Passage. With such a small contingent of passengers, the captain of the SS Aberdeen let his guard down and was halfway through his second bottle of whiskey when he let the boat chug right on by his turn.

Several hours had passed before the captain even realized his mistake. The Aberdeen passed between Chichagof and Admiralty Islands, past Baranof Island, and hit the open sea before it dawned on him that he was making the wrong heading. Hoping to escape the huge swells that rolled in from the Pacific Ocean, the captain guided the steamship toward the western coastline of Prince of Wales Island, seeking refuge by snaking inside the series of small islands just offshore. The Aberdeen had actually made it halfway down the west side of Prince of Wales when the storm hit.

Waves crashed against the wooden hull of the ship, tossing the boat around like a cork. With gale force winds whistling in from a southeasterly direction, it made sense to the ship's captain to seek refuge in one of the protected coves that shot inward toward the center of Prince of Wales Island. The SS Aberdeen dodged huge waves and took spray over the bow as it slowly chugged into what the captain hoped would be a safe haven. Unbeknownst to the captain, it was high slack tide and the lagoon waters sat temporarily dormant in what would later be dubbed Hooligan Arm.

The captain had tucked into the entrance of the cove, just passed a protruding rock, and was preparing to drop anchor when the current began to pick up. With the storm pounding the steamship on one side, and the outgoing tidal current beginning its rage on the other, the SS Aberdeen was tossed uncontrollably, twirling as if in a violent whirlpool. The ship struck the rock in the middle of the cove with a ferocious, ripping sound, as the impact crushed a gaping hole into the hull of the vessel. Seconds later, current and winds pushed the steamship from the rock and into the middle of Hooligan Arm. It sank straight down, just over 200 feet to the bottom, with all of Wally Weatherford's gold.

The captain and crew, as well as Wally Weatherford and his goons, were tossed back and forth in the chilling waves. They sobered quickly as they realized the direness of their situation. Some went down rather quickly, while others fought for survival, swimming frantically until their bodies seized from the cold and from panicked exhaustion. Only one person made it to shore that day.

By total chance, a dancehall girl named Ellen Cranbrook washed over the side of the sinking SS Aberdeen just as a wave picked up a flotation ring from the side of the boat. She clung to the life ring and saved her energy, allowing the current to take total control of her. Be it luck, destiny, or by the hand of God, Ellen Cranbrook's hypothermic body washed up onto the rocky shoreline of Hooligan Arm close to where a clan of Tlingits stood, protected inside the tree line, watching the tragedy unfold.

Years later, in her memoir titled, *Muskeg Mama*, Ellen Cranbrook offered the only detailed description of the shipwreck and subsequent events. She wrote about the cove where it occurred, how she gripped the flotation device, closed her eyes, and let the sea toss her at will. She described coming to shore, being tossed into the rocks, finally opening her eyes, barely alive, and seeing solemn, dark faces emerge from the trees. She speculated that, had she not been female, the Native clan would have probably left her for dead. Instead, Ellen gave a detailed account of how the Tlingit group gathered her up and warmed her in a huddled mass of bodies for several hours. They fed her, clothed her, and nursed her back to health around a temporary fishing camp that they had established near where the clan had watched the boat sink.

In her memoir, Ellen described how it took a few days for her to regain strength. The clan watched over her, displaying kindness despite grand language and cultural differences. After several days it appeared that Ellen had made a full recovery and the clan was ready to move. The group of Natives gathered all of their belongings in a quick and efficient method. They set out from their camp and made a rather long trek across the western part of the island to what is now known as the village of Klawock. They used a primitive trail system that, at times, dove deep into the rainforest. At other times, the trail appeared to follow the shoreline, and sometimes the trail rose over mountains, giving grand views of the sea. The group of travelers spent two nights along the trail, but Ellen speculated that she probably slowed them down. She had the feeling that the clan could have made the trek in half the time, but slowed their pace out of respect for their guest.

Ellen Cranbrook lived among the Tlingit clan in the village of Klawock on the west side of Prince of Wales Island for several weeks. She was definitely an outsider and not allowed to participate in many of their ceremonial rituals, but the Native Alaskans treated her with kindness and provided food, shelter, and all the comforts that they could offer. Ellen couldn't speak in their tongue, but quickly got a feeling for how they communicated based on vocal tone and body language. She slowly picked up words and developed a sort of compromised survival speech that seemed to work. After close to two months of living in the Native village, Ellen sensed that some members of the clan were preparing for another journey. She was right, and they wanted her to go with them.

This time, the journey was a bit longer and a bit more arduous. The trail took them inland, up and over a tall mountain, toward the east side of the island. Even though Ellen Cranbrook had returned to full health, she wrote that the cross-island trek left her feeling exhausted and sore each night that they camped. Every morning, it was a struggle for her to restart as muscles ached and feet throbbed inside inadequate footwear. The fourth night that they camped, Ellen got a sense that they were approaching their destination based on how several of the Tlingits addressed her. She had gotten the feeling that the whole trip was dedicated to her well-being, and had begun to wonder what might lie ahead for her. Were they about to leave her in the middle of the rainforest, alone and cold, to fend for herself? Or was there a destination in mind; a camp of some sort that would host her in adequate fashion? She tossed sleeplessly that night as she speculated.

The following day, the group rose, ate dried salmon, and again hit the primitive trail. The hike was shorter this day as they soon saw views of the water and knew they were nearing a destination of some sort. They reached the eastern shores of Prince of Wales Island and arrived at a gold and copper mining community called Hollis. There was a white-skinned population that lived and operated the mines. The Tlingit clan stayed at the tree line, close to the small town, but they made it abundantly clear to Ellen that she had been delivered to her own people. She was incredibly grateful and attempted to offer hugs to her rescuers. The Tlingits reluctantly allowed her to hug each of them before turning and disappearing back into the lush rainforest from which they'd come.

Ellen Cranbrook lived in the mining community of Hollis for two years before returning south to the United States. In that time, she set out to handwrite a personal account of her adventures. Her memoir started from the time she first traveled to the Klondike region, her exploits as a dancing girl, the whirlwind love affair with the suddenly rich and lavish Wally Weatherford, the disastrous journey aboard the SS Aberdeen and the captain's fatal error, and the kind, respectful treatment that she had received from the Tlingit clan of rescuers. Her memoir ended up being a substantial document, spanning page after page of handwritten personal accounts. It was eloquently penned and colorfully described an honest story of perseverance amid hardship.

According to the forward of the recently published *Muskeg Mama: Memoir of a Klondike Girl*, the original document traveled south with Ellen Cranbrook, eventually settling into the bottom of a steamer trunk that survived for more than a century, untouched, in the attic of a country home in Eastern Washington. A distant descendent of Ellen Cranbrook was tasked with clearing the old home for demolition when the ancient chest and subsequent document was discovered. The relative read the extensively written memoir and was immediately enthralled. Understanding the true treasure that they had discovered, the family hired a professional writer/editor named Greta Gleason to prepare the document for publication. Greta Gleason typed up the document, touched it up with professional literary aplomb, and met with multiple publishers. The manuscript was quickly scooped up by a national firm and released within a month. One hundred and eighteen years after it was penned, Ellen Cranbrook's epic personal account hit the shelves and stormed its way to the top of the non-fiction rankings.

# Chapter 20

Hugh Eckley hit the horn with three long blasts. The Boston Whaler's signaling device echoed back from the hull of the *Earth's Guardian*. Jim stood on the back deck of Eckley's boat, smoking a cigar while peering up the side of the Planet Patrol vessel. There was no response from the members of the Planet Patrol.

From the captain's chair, Hugh hollered over his shoulder, "Aren't you glad I brought you that stogie. Gives you something to puff on while we float around out here, honking our horn repeatedly to absolutely no response."

"Hit it one more time," Jim ordered. Finally, this time a head appeared above them at the edge of the larger ship.

"What the hell is going on with all the horn blasts?" Pierre Lemieux demanded. His cheeks flushed red below white hair that hadn't been combed in a while. "What do you want, Lieutenant?" Pierre barked.

"Permission to come aboard? I have a few questions for you, Lemieux."

"Now's not the best time, Lieutenant. We are undergoing some repairs this morning and are quite busy."

"What kind of repairs?"

"Repairs to our lifeboats, not that it's any of your business. Now get the hell out of here." Pierre's head disappeared from the edge of the ship.

Jim puffed on the cigar a couple of times, then yelled,

"I can come back on Monday with a court order, Lemieux. That would give me access to every nook and cranny of that rust bucket. Why don't you just save us both the time and hassle, and let me up to the deck."

Pierre Lemieux's head stayed absent from the rail. Jim thought he could hear voices from on the ship, but he wasn't sure. After several seconds passed, Beanie LeFranc appeared at the railing with a naïve, yet happy smile. Beanie waved Jim up, and yelled, "Permission to come aboard granted, Lieutenant. Climb up the ladder."

Hugh Eckley carefully and expertly slipped the Boston Whaler within inches of the *Earth's Guardian*. Jim stood on the gunwale of Eckley's boat, holding onto the roof of the cabin with one hand and clenching his cigar in his teeth. Once in range, Jim grabbed hold of a ladder attached to the side of the larger ship. Jim hopped over, pushing away from Hugh's boat with his left foot, giving the Boston Whaler a parting shove. After scaling the vessel's starboard side wall, Jim was greeted at the deck above by a scene that appeared close to that of a circus. Crewmen were scrambling across the deck, gathering shards of laminated fabric, repairing dock lines, and removing outboard engines from damaged inflatable rafts.

"What the hell happened up here?" Jim asked.

Beanie LeFranc answered, "We had an issue with some of the local wildlife."

"Wildlife?" Jim asked, with sarcasm in his tone.

The young crewman's voice squeaked as he spoke. "Yeah, wildlife. We're still sorting it out. Actually, you probably wouldn't believe it if I told you."

"Try me." Jim listened as Beanie LeFranc retold the tale that sounded too far fetched to be fiction. The kid's arms flailed as he recounted the havoc wreaked by the bear. He mimicked holding a pistol as he retold the firing of multiple flare guns. Jim wanted to be skeptical of the entire tale; however, there were burn marks that could have come from flares being fired on the starboard side deck rail. In addition, the shreds of inflatable raft very well could have come from a bear's claw. Indeed, it looked as if a pissed off animal made mincemeat of half the inflatable fleet.

"Where's your boss?" Jim eventually asked.

Again, with a nervous squeak, "He, uh, he's indisposed up in the wheelhouse at the moment. He instructed me to answer any of your questions."

Jim picked up a piece of the raft's fabric from the deck of the ship. He also pulled out an evidence bag from his back pocket that held the fabric sample that he had retrieved days earlier. Jim held up both pieces in front of Beanie, and asked, "Do these two samples look identical to you?"

The kid shrugged. "I don't know. I guess."

"Are you missing any of your inflatable rafts?"

Looking around the mêlée that surrounded the two men, Beanie answered, "Uh, you can see the shape that some of our rafts are in here. It's hard to discern one raft piece from another."

"I didn't ask if any have been damaged by a bear. I asked you if you happen to be missing any lifeboats. I count six inflatable stations, three per side. I only count five rafts, and that includes the damaged units by this so-called bear intruder."

"How can you tell?"

Jim replied, "Count the outboards, Einstein."

Beanie's voice became even more disturbed. "I don't know what you're talking about, officer man. We aren't missing anything."

Jim could tell the kid was lying. He was about as easy to see through as a glass of water. "How many crew members do you have aboard?"

"Counting me and my Uncle Pierre?" Beanie paused, obviously deep in thought. "Seven? No six. Yes, I think we have six members of our team aboard. You know, we do the Earth's bidding across the globe. We have but one ocean that connects all the continents that we must care for before the Earth is ruined at the hand of mankind."

Jim blew smoke in the kid's face. "Save the rhetoric, kid. Your boat, here, leaks oil like a sieve. Can I look inside at your crew quarters?"

"No." Beanie was quick to answer.

"Can I question the rest of the crew?"

"No."

"Are any of your crewmen missing a foot?" Jim asked, simply for the shock value.

Appearing to be legitimately stunned, Beanie squeaked, "Not that I know of."

"You guys see any sign of a redheaded male in a small skiff buzzing around here last night? The guy might have been dip-netting at the mouth of the lagoon."

Beanie shook his head. "No. I know who you're talking about. I've seen him before, but he wasn't out here last night. It was pretty quiet around here."

"Except for the bear that somehow climbed aboard your ship," Jim corrected sarcastically.

Squeaking, "Uh, I guess so, yeah."

Before signaling down to Hugh Eckley that he was ready to be picked up, Jim wandered the back deck of the ship. He noticed an extensive amount of scuba gear, underwater lights, waterproof video cameras, baskets, small powered winches, portable generators, and a cast of other items that didn't quite seem to fit into an environmentalist's agenda.

After waving at Hugh and stepping over the side of the boat, Jim hollered at Beanie LeFranc, "You guys doing some diving in the area?"

Beanie answered in his high pitched voice, "Only in the course of gathering data to aid in the protection of this planet and all her waters."

"Right. Tell your uncle to fix his oil leak, or I'll be back with a representative of the EPA." Jim descended the ladder and hopped into Hugh Eckley's boat.

As they sped away from Hooligan Arm in the direction of Craig, Hugh asked, "Did you find the answers that you were looking for?"

Jim flicked the nub of his cigar out the door of the cabin and into the white froth behind the boat. "Not even close. Those guys are complete clowns, and I don't trust them for a second. The boss-man up there wouldn't even dignify me with his presence. And that's after I kept him from getting harpooned by a gaff hook back at the town meeting. The nerve. Next time I'll let the townsfolk have at it with pitchforks and torches."

Jim sat across from Hugh and stared out the front window as the boat skirted across the water. They sat silent for several minutes, taking in the views that surrounded them, before Jim asked, "Hugh. How hard do you think it would be to put a bear onto the back deck of that boat back there?"

*The hardships inherent with traversing the trail were plenty. Whether by animal hoof or human foot, the path we followed had obviously been toiled previously, but the sheer magnitude of vegetation that encumbered my every step was only surpassed by the large volume of water that fell upon our heads. My rescuers of the land's first nation seemed unbothered by both plant and rain. I, however, found it a taxing endeavor.*

*Only when we entered open bogs filled with what I later learned to be a mossy, sponge-like substance called muskeg, was I able to enjoy brief respites from the constant prickling of twigs and thorns upon my sides. Instead, the muskeg fields gave way to a brutal wind that blinded me with its droplet filled sting. I trudged on, without knowledge of destination nor duration, step after step into the wilds of an untamed, untouched land.*

*The forests were full of trunks at every angle, some still full of life and some toppled by the environment long ago. The floor seemed covered entirely by moss, moisture evident in all aspects. Certain plants that grew up from the moss seemed innocuous, positioned only to please God's own aesthetic sensibilities. Others appeared out of spite; like the stinging, needle-infested shrub others would dub later simply as 'devil's club.' The only constant below the grey sky was the color green. It was everywhere, as far as I could see, deep into the forest, high into the tops of the trees. Varying shades of green had seeped its way into every crevice of this wet, virgin land.*

As another plane load of tourists made their way up the ramp from the seaplane float, the Cranbrook Culture Club was again in full regalia. Dressed to the nines in period attire, they attempted to recruit more women for their grand event titled *Traverse the Trail.* The experience advertised an afternoon hike through Alaskan rainforests, an overnight stay in canvas tents outfitted with the latest survival gear, and authentic Native Alaskan cuisine featuring smoked salmon and limpets, fern tops, and fresh picked berries.

The ladies' club hoped to have several such events throughout the season, but the inaugural trek was scheduled just a few days away. The three members of the CCC ramped up their advertising and had even hoped that a few of the local women might be able to attend.

They were billing *Traverse the Trail* as a unique experience for strong women. Dedicated to the late Ellen Cranbrook, the event propaganda advertised that the trail would follow a similar path through the woods from the village of Klawock to a campsite on the edge of Hooligan Arm where their namesake was rescued over a century ago; an experience reminiscent of the tale of feminine survival found within the pages of Ellen Cranbrook's personal account. In actuality, the three members of the CCC planned on bussing their customers up to a mountain in the rainforest and marching them six miles down an old logging road to a pre-stocked campsite clearing. It wasn't quite the adventure as billed, but it should prove to still be a truly Alaskan experience.

Shasta Wilford had funded the outfitting of the camp locale on the southern shoreline of Hooligan Arm. The ladies would march their patrons in, following closely on their four-wheelers, each armed with a can of bear mace. Upon arrival at the camp, they were depending on one of the locals that they had hired to have a fire burning and an authentic meal brewing. Reluctantly, they hired the only local they could find that was both willing and seemingly qualified for the job. The fact that he was a man was almost a deal breaker, but there was something about the ponytail, jean cut-offs, and his youthful enthusiasm that made them agree to make an exception.

Plans were rapidly moving forward as the date approached, but the members of the CCC were concerned. They only had a handful of committed participants, and time was running out. They needed to recruit at least four more customers to make the trip worthwhile. Although Shasta Wilford had a stash of money to cover initial expenses, she demanded that the club's first major activity had better bring in a significant chunk of cash. Between the four-wheelers, riding apparel, period attire, and camp outfitting, she had already dumped thousands into the project. It was time to stop the bleeding.

"Twavuuusssss the twaaaaaail." Angel Yu's broken English bellowed. The six tourists that were walking up from the floatplane cringed at the nasally timbred yodel. "You, too, can expewience the magical twip of Ellen Cwanbwook. Be a stwong woman and sign up now to enshuw a spot."

Phyllis Prescott gyrated to the disjointed syncopations of the ragtime music blasting on the boom box. Her panting was starting to cause a side ache, but the scene did draw attention from the intended marks.

Shasta Wilford announced, "Only three hundred and forty-five dollars ensures you an all-inclusive, true Alaskan experience. Follow in the footsteps of everyone's latest female hero from the Klondike, Ellen Cranbrook. Only four spots remain."

A pudgy, balding man in his late fifties approached the women. "I'm interested. When does the hike take place?"

Angel Yu chided, "Beat it, butta-ball. No boys. You too fat, anyway."

Dejected, the balding tourist shuffled away with a frown on his face. The last of the recent arrivals to the island reached the top of the ramp. They were identical twins from London, England, and both of the girls' faces featured matching massive noses. The two twin sisters from across the opposite pond bounded up to the Cranbrook Culture Club with overly eager expressions and each clutching their very own copies of *Muskeg Mama*.

Lucy Smelk bubbled with excitement. "Traverse the trail? Just like Ellen Cranbrook? Sign – us – up!" She spoke with a thick English accent.

Missy Smelk agreed in an accent that was as identical to her sister's as was her gigantic, crooked nose. "This is exactly what we are looking for. So exciting, sis." Turning toward the members of the CCC, Missy asked, opening her backpack, "Do you take Visa?"

"Cash only," snapped Angel Yu.

"Give us just a moment, if you please," said Lucy. The two sisters approached each other, throwing their arms around each other's neck, making a sort of two-person huddle. Low, mumbled whispers came from the two while they secretly discussed their financial situation. After a bit, they both nodded and broke their huddle with a clap of the hands. Reaching inside her backpack and retrieving some cash, Missy Smelk handed over seven crisp hundred-dollar bills. The bills were promptly snatched up by Angel Yu, disappearing quickly into a pocket of her late-eighteen-hundreds dress.

Again, in a quick, harsh manner, Angel commanded, "Exact change only. No cash back and no weefunds."

Shasta spoke up. "Here's a flyer explaining what to bring, and where to meet. We'll be embarking at exactly 2pm on the twenty-eighth. Please don't be late. As my colleague here explained, we do not offer refunds if you miss the bus."

The twin sisters giggled in excitement as they wandered toward their hotel in town. Lucy was overheard saying, "I hope they drop us in the water first, sis, so we can really feel what Ellen felt."

Missy bubbled back, "That would be just cracking. If not, we can always go for a swim on our own."

# Chapter 21

Had he been able to accept Visa cards for payment, Zeke Melon could have sold three times as many hooligan candles. As several thousand tourists strolled off the boats docked at the Ketchikan waterfront, Zeke had several of his candles perched atop his display, flames flickering in the breeze. His hand-painted sign read, "Zeke Melon's Amazing Hooligan Candles – Take Home an Authentic Alaskan Burning Fish - $15." Other than the bottom half of a beer can that served as a base for the candle, it was probably the only item sold on the waterfront that truly was authentically Alaskan.

The display alone seemed to capture the attention of about every twentieth person that walked by. Most of the camera-phone-toting sightseers were more concerned with the facades of the shops that surrounded them to notice the small, independent operation. Of the handful of people that did stop to inspect the flammable fish, only about ten percent inquired about purchasing one. Of those, over half either had foreign currency or were only armed with a credit card.

Still, with four large ships in port, and with over three thousand people disembarking per ship, Zeke was able to sell forty-two hooligan candles on his first day of sales. At fifteen bucks a piece, he was able to pocket over six-hundred dollars. Zeke's only concerning fiscal stat was that he burned through thirty-two demo candles throughout the day. That was almost as many candles as he sold. Something had to change.

After spending the entire Saturday peddling his wares, Zeke was exhausted. The previous night kept him up continuously for the eight-hour boat trip, and he had only managed about ninety minutes of interrupted slumber in the sleeping bag. Now, he was looking at either eating into a good chunk of his profits by renting a hotel room, or attempting to curl up and sleep on the docks next to his boat. Neither option sounded that appealing. He did spring for a nice meal at one of the waterfront restaurants, ordering cod tacos and garlic fries. The waitress was kind enough to overlook the fish stench emitting from his clothes and gave him a second order of fries on the house. With a full stomach and a half bottle of cold syrup in him, Zeke Melon curled up on the dock next to his skiff and slept like a rock. Even the rain shower that crossed over in the middle of the night didn't rouse him.

Waking up early, damp, and malodorous, Zeke decided that his sales tactics would need to improve if he was going to start raking in the big bucks. The mere sight of a sign and a couple of burning candles wasn't quite sufficient to attract the attention of enough patrons in order to make his weekend trip worthwhile. A little salesmanship was in order.

After again setting up his little tower of tubs on the cruise ship dock, Zeke walked to a nearby t-shirt vendor. He purchased an oversized sleeveless T-shirt that featured a comical looking salmon, smirking at a scantily clad woman, with the phrase, "Real men smell like fish!" scrawled in large red font. He also purchased a ball cap that had a fish head sticking out the front and a fish tail protruding from the back. He lit his first candle just as the morning's inaugural batch of potential customers ambled down the boat ramp, each wearing their standard matching rain parkas in anticipation of battling the famed Southeast Alaskan drizzle.

Before the horde approached, Zeke knew that his

showmanship would need to include a little more than a new shirt and hat. He downed half a bottle of Nyquil, took a deep breath in an attempt to calm his nerves, and chose his words carefully, hoping to avoid the most difficult verbiage for him to pronounce.

"Hoooooooligan c… c… c…" He paused, and breathed deep through his nostrils before again announcing, "Hoooooooligan c… c… candles! Light your life with hoooooooligan c… c… c… candles!"

The paying customers still seemed to come at about the same rate, despite his new look and vocalizations. Zeke needed something more, something to put his sales into another earning category. After a little more liquid syrup courage, he started marching back and forth in front of his booth, dried hooligan in each hand, improvising in song at the top of his lungs. He wasn't an experienced singer, nor did his voice seem to match pitch with any consistency, but the combination of his tall lanky features and red hair poking out under his hat, and with the nasally squelch discharging from his lips, a crowd of onlookers started to gather.

"Hoooo-li-gan. Hoooo-li-gan. Get your-self a fish caaaan-dle. Hoooo-li-gan. Hoooo-li-gan. Put them up on your maaaan-tle." Zeke sang and marched, sang and marched; only taking a break in the repetitive melody to accept cash from his patrons. He was surprised to find that singing put quite the damper on his stutter, and his catchy little jingle was so infectious, several of the tourists would even sing along periodically. He saw a couple of teenage girls singing the jingle as they giggled their way down the dock, arm in arm. The more he sang, the more he sold. The more he sold, the more he smiled. People of various countries of origin, from diverse cultural and ethnic backgrounds, and of varying ages all snatched up the hooligan candles, happily forking over fifteen bucks apiece.

By late in the afternoon, as the bulk of the tourists ambled back toward their ships, Zeke tallied that he had sold two-hundred and fourteen candles on the day. As the last of the cruise ship patrons strolled back up the dock ramp and onto their floating cities, the tall redhead was bursting at the seams with cash. He had raked in just over thirty-eight hundred dollars over the course of the weekend, and he could hardly wipe the grin from his cheeks.

Standing on the dock next to where he had moored his skiff, Zeke Melon stood proudly while he watched a huge cruise ship push away slowly from the city float. Zeke was elated, but also physically and emotionally spent. It was late afternoon and he was looking at another eight hour boat ride. He would be able to crash at his home at best for a mere handful of hours before he was due at the septic pumping job early the next morning. As he focused on the task of returning home, his epic smile faded.

After securing his tubs in the bow of the skiff, Zeke topped off the gas tank and fired up the outboard engine. Pushing off from the dock, Zeke checked his unofficial weather report by looking to the sky. Clouds were overcast, wind was light out of the southeast, and temperatures felt to be in the upper fifties. He was happy to think that there would be daylight left for the crossing of the wide open waters of Clarence Strait.

Off he buzzed, twenty-some miles-per-hour, pockets full of cash, and a grimace on his young face. Zeke Melon's first weekend excursion to market his wares was a success. He passed one of the large ships that was slowly exiting the Tongass Narrows. Zeke politely waved to the passengers standing on the upper deck. A couple of elderly tourists waved back from above as he passed. The skiff zoomed out of the Narrows and skirted the edge of Gravina Island. He stopped to top off the gas tank before taking his compass bearing and entering the open expanse of water. The boat was able to zoom a little faster across Clarence Strait on the return trip with the presence of daylight and much smaller swells tossing his boat than the previous crossing.

Zeke rounded Cape Chacon safely and had just begun the journey up the western side of Prince of Wales when he noticed a change in the weather. As the last remnants of daylight dwindled, the wind started to race, greatly impacting the rain that began to fall. Even the scent in the air seemed to change. Something was brewing in the atmosphere and Zeke still had about seventy-five nautical miles left on his trip. He hunkered down, fired up the handheld spotlight, and willed his small boat forward into the impending storm with sheer determination.

The Craig-Klawock highway bends to the north around a small bay as it leaves the Craig city limits. About a quarter mile north of town, just before the highway crossed Crab Creek, Jim turned right off the highway and drove his Crown Vic up a gravel drive that rose steeply for the first hundred feet. The driveway circled back and opened up to a small cabin-like structure elevated from sea-level enough to have a full view of the town below through a break in the trees.

Parking next to a rusted Chevy pickup, Jim donned his Stetson and made his way to the covered front porch of the cabin. Just before he knocked on the front door, Jim heard a voice holler, "I'm around here, Lieutenant."

Jim walked under the covered wraparound porch that led to a back deck with a fantastic overlook of the city's waterfront area and beyond. The cabin looked to be a little rundown and under market value, but the back deck featured a million-dollar view. A sandy haired man with grizzled beard stubble and an uncleansed appearance sat in a deck chair, sucking on the butt of a lit cigarette. An open beer can sat on a small deck table. Next to the sandy haired man, a hunting rifle with a scope was perched on a tripod, hanging down on the heavy butt-end, pointing its barrel into the air.

"Gretch, how're you doing this evening?" the Lieutenant asked.

After taking a long drag on the cigarette and letting the smoke float out through every facial orifice, Gretch Skully responded, "If you want to know the truth? I'm tired, Lieutenant."

"You're a hard working man, Gretch. Makes sense that you're a little tired."

"You wanna know what I'm tired of, Jim? I'm tired of paying more to work harder each year, for fewer fish." Gretch reached out and stole a swig from the beer can. "You hear me, Jim?"

"I hear you, Gretch." Jim was well aware of the recent struggles regarding the commercial fishing industry. He prided himself with staying in touch with the local economic trends. He was sympathetic as the fishing industry had been the lifeblood of so many residents, long before Jim ever stepped foot on this island.

After blowing smoke out his nostrils, the fisherman continued, "And after all that we endure, after working our fingers to the bone, seeing our lives pass each year on boats that suck up half our take… We get some little shit-ass punk and his band of merry Frenchmen spewing out their puke propaganda about environmental impacts, and damaging the waters of this Earth…" He let his small rant taper off at the end.

Jim walked up to the gun and inspected it, opening the chamber. It wasn't loaded. He looked through the scope and moved the barrel by swinging its aim on the tripod. It moved smoothly as he scanned the waterfront docks that sat on the city's edge below. "Quite the view through this thing."

"Better than a pair of binoculars."

Jim kept his vision fixed through the scope of the rifle while he asked, bluntly, "Gretch, did you blow up one of Planet Patrol's inflatable rafts?" Skully's only reply was to suck on the end of his cigarette and attempt to blow a smoke ring.

After a few seconds of silence, Jim said, "Because, you see. I've got this severed foot that the pretty new medical examiner informs me used to be attached to some guy that is most definitely dead now. And I've got a pretty good hunch that this guy may have been in one of the Planet Patrol's little white boats. And it seems to me, of all the people living on this island, you've got the most hatred built up for these guys."

Gretch Skully stood slowly, cringing from the muscles

of a man that worked hard for a living. He moved toward the rifle that sat on the tripod.

Instinctively, the Lieutenant put his hand on his side arm and said, "Easy, Gretch."

"Settle down, Jim. You know it's not loaded." The fisherman bent so that one eye met with the scope. He lowered the gun's aim in the direction of the waterfront and said, "I want to show you something." After focusing on his desired target, he moved his head away from the gun, but held it in place with one hand on the butt.

"Take a look," Skully ordered. Jim moved in and peered through the eye piece. It was centered on an old fishing boat in the harbor. The name *Lucky Lady* appeared on the boat's bow. A man wearing yellow rain pants was holding a bucket and a rag, wiping down the stern deck. Two children were taking turns climbing a ladder that led to the fly bridge.

"What I am looking at, Gretch?"

"Sig Hanson and his two boys."

Jim stood up from the gun's scope and asked, "What are you trying to say?"

The fisherman dropped his cigarette butt and squished it into the decking with the sole of his boot. "Sig is a longtime fisherman, and one of my oldest friends. He married a gal, had those boys. They used to have a nice little home just out the road. He's always fished hard, even harder than some of the rest of us. He's never been close to top grossing boat, or anything, but he's always managed to put food on the table and roof over his family's head." Gretch began fumbling with a pack of smokes, digging for a new cigarette.

Jim asked, "Okay, but where are you going with this?"

"People like Sig, there. And me. And quite a few other men on this friggin' rock. We don't know any other life than fishing, Jim. And when a tough season comes along, some of these guys can't survive."

"What happened?"

"Last season, we all had it tough. Fish volumes were low, and prices hadn't reacted to the market, yet. Low fish and low prices, well, you can imagine that it took its toll on everyone. Sig, there. He took it worse. For whatever reason, he had the season from hell. Just before the first opening, one of his engines conked out. So he started late and in debt after the repairs. And wherever he fished, it just seemed to be low grossing. One bad season and the man never recovered. His wife flew south shortly after they lost the house. He's raising his boys aboard that boat. Seems ironic that it's named *Lucky Lady*, doesn't it?"

Gretch inhaled another pull on his smoke and washed it down with the beer. "Those boys, there. He's prepared them to be his crew this season, which is cute and all, but that's dangerous work for a couple little munchkins, not to mention, they'll be almost a month late at starting up school this coming year. He's got no choice, though, Jim. What's he supposed to do? Leave the boys on shore for the summer while he's off fishing?"

Jim stepped away from the rifle and leaned on the railing of the deck, peering out at the view. A gill netter was passing by town, slowly churning a wake as it moved up the coastline. Fishing was a way of life for many of the island's longtime residents. These fishermen were good, hearty

Southeast Alaskans, and Jim understood the current threat to their livelihood. He also understood that any such threat didn't give someone license to commit murder.

Jim said, "I have to ask you a direct question, Gretch. I respect you and know that you are an honest man. So, I expect an honest answer." He stared directly into the fisherman's soft brown eyes. The man stood still, waiting for the question. The Trooper asked, "Did you have anything to do with blowing up the raft?"

Gretch laughed with a short snort out his nose. He shook his head and said, "I didn't do it, Jim. And I have no idea about who did. Don't get me wrong. Whoever did do it… I'd buy them a beer and shake their hand. But it wasn't me."

Jim kept his stare directed at the fisherman's eyes for several long seconds before turning away. "Thanks for your time, Gretch. Do me a favor, and keep that rifle unloaded, okay." Just before disappearing from the back deck of the house, Lieutenant Wekle stopped and asked, "Hey, you wouldn't know anything about a bear being released aboard the *Earth's Guardian*, would you?"

Gretch laughed. "A bear aboard that ship? That would be some feat."

"Yes, it would," Jim replied, noting that Gretch didn't deny knowledge of the event.

# Chapter 22

Jim felt bad about leaving his mother home alone on Mink Island for the bulk of the day. She claimed to have a few good books that she wanted to read, but Jim worried that she would get cabin fever, all alone on a small island. Before returning home, Jim stopped at the store and loaded up with groceries in preparation for a nice dinner. He tried calling his mother's cell phone while driving out Port St. Nicholas Road, but there was no answer. After parking his Crown Vic in the gravel lot and walking down to the boat dock, Jim fired up the outboard on the second crank. Halfway across, Jim noticed another skiff tied up on the Mink Island side. He rolled his eyes and exhaled.

"This ought to be fun," Jim said under his breath.

He secured his boat in the usual manner, grabbed the grocery bags, and made his way up the boardwalk to the yurt. Jim found his living quarters to be void of people. He stashed his groceries, changed from his uniform into jeans and a sweatshirt, and exited the yurt. After a short walk up to Lookout Rock, Jim found Maggie and his mother, each sitting in one of the wooden chairs. Kram sat upright on a cut stump positioned between the two ladies. He was smiling excitedly, vibrating with enthusiasm.

Bursting forth, Kram babbled frantically, "Jim-Kahn, so glad you're home. We've been chatting and I, no...*we* are so excited about this. I know you'll love this too. Only, you'll have to stay home. Only for the ladies, here, you know. I get to go, of course, 'cause I'm, well, special. But you can't go,

Jim. Don't worry, though, your two ladies here will be in good hands. Your best girl here, Maggie, and your wonderful parental unit, Vera, well, we've been talking. And they decided to participate in the big hike. I just called it in. They secured the last two spots on the trip. Isn't that exciting, Jim?"

Jim was a little stunned. "Uh… What big hike? What are you talking about, Kram?"

Still talking fast, buzzing with excitement, Kram said, "The big trek. You know, *Traverse the Trail.* Sponsored by the CCC. That's the Cranbrook Culture Club, not the Civilian Conservation Corps. Those are two completely separate CCC's. One's from the Nineteen-Thirties, put into place as part of Roosevelt's New Deal. Do you find it amusing, Jim, that the membership of the first CCC was only for single men, and this new CCC is only for single women? I find it completely fascinating."

Jim looked over at Maggie.

She shrugged and said, "Actually, it kind of sounds fun. A little hike in the woods, an overnight campout. Plus, it'll give Vera and me a chance to really get to know each other."

Jim turned to his mother. "But Mom. You're not single."

Vera Wekle replied, "Not according to the registration form that my man, Kram, here just filled out." She patted Kram on the shoulder. The ponytailed man stuck his chin out, grinning like a pleased puppy.

Oscar the mink ran up and wrapped around Jim's right foot, eager to see her provider. Jim wished he had brought

186

some crackers. He asked, "So let me get this straight. You two ladies are going to participate in an overnight hike?"

Maggie answered, "Yep."

"And Kram here... What... He's some sort of chaperone?"

Kram interjected, "Camp host, head cook and bottle washer. The pay's decent and I get to eat all the leftovers."

Jim shrugged. "What the heck is the Cranbrook Culture Club, anyway?"

Kram stood, put his hand over his heart and announced, "Dedicated to the legacy of the late Ellen Cranbrook, posthumously published author and survivor of the tragic sinking of the *SS Aberdeen*. Manuscript revised, edited and published by one, Greta Gleason, at the request and permission of the Cranbrook family."

Maggie chimed in with, "You know, Jim, it's that book that everyone's been reading?"

Vera held up a copy of *Muskeg Mama*. "I just finished it this afternoon. It's a stunning read, Jimmy, and all true. It all happened right here, you know."

Kram nodded. "It's a personal memoir."

"Haven't you noticed the influx of tourists, lately?" Maggie asked. "Everyone seems to want to come and experience a little of what Ellen Cranbrook had to endure. It's injected a little bit of life around this rock we call home."

"Stop!" Everyone stopped talking and stared at Kram. "Did you say... Tourists?" He made a grand, dramatic gesture, flinging both his hands high in the air.

Maggie shook her head. "Kram, who do you think's going on this hike? It's loaded with tourists. Haven't you noticed all the people wandering around town taking pictures? I heard that *Porty's* has rented out every room for more than a week."

Kram turned away and paced uneasily. Oscar the mink followed him, playfully mimicking each turn like a kitten. "Matching rain parkas, total disregard for traffic patterns, stupid questions about land elevations..." He raised his voice and announced each word with deliberation, *"You just stepped off a boat. The elevation is twelve, you twit."*

Jim attempted to interrupt, "Uh, Kram..."

Kram added flailing arms to his private diatribe. "What's next? Curios shops, shaved ice machines, roller skate rentals, horse drawn carriages, amphibious duck boats, overpriced hotdogs, bad music being played on crappy sound systems?" His voice picked up in both tempo and dynamic. "Scary clowns, deflated balloons, child movie stars, choco-tacos, Bulgarian belly dancers, men wearing Speedos, cats running amok in the streets, mass hysteria..."

*"Kram!"* Jim said sharply.

The man in jean cutoff shorts stared into the air between the trees, standing frozen in fear. Suddenly, he bolted straight out from Lookout Rock, diving into the water, swimming frantically for shore.

Vera Wekle asked, in a worried tone, "Where is he going? Will he be okay?"

"That's his standard exit." Jim put his hand on his mother's shoulder. "He'll be fine. I think the cold water helps."

"But, his little tirade. He's obviously quite upset."

"Mom, trust me. There's no reason to be alarmed every time Kram has a little overreaction."

Maggie said, "At least he left me the boat. Not a chance in heck *I'm* swimming off this island."

Pointing to the clouds that were thickening quickly with the increasing wind, Jim said, "Not that I want you to leave, but if you're planning on a boat ride across the bay into town, you might want to go soon. Looks like the weather is turning tonight."

Vera spoke up, "I'm a twenty-first century woman, kids. Maggie doesn't have to leave on my account. She is welcome to sleep over."

Jim blushed. "And with you on the bed, Mom? I'll give Maggie the couch and I'll take the floor. Not sure how 'twenty-first-century that sounds."

Maggie chimed in, "Don't worry. I'm heading back to the harbor tonight. And I think you're right about the weather. I should head out now." She leaned over and kissed Jim on the cheek. She said her goodbyes to his mother and disappeared down the boardwalk. Moments later, Jim and his mother watched as Maggie's boat buzzed quickly across the expanse of Port St. Nicholas. They followed the boat's journey all the way into town on the distant shoreline.

Vera Wekle stated, "She's really a great girl for you, Jimmy."

"Yeah, Mom. I agree."

The current Alaskan mission had had the scent of failure from the beginning for Beanie LeFranc. In all their previous eco-scams, Planet Patrol had pretended to attack issues that were actually quite real, seemingly deserving of their attention. In order to secretly search for old English antiquities off the coast of Nova Scotia, they had protested a factory that was dumping toxins into the bay. There wasn't a living mollusk on the coastline within a half-mile of the factory. Although their remonstration was a ruse, it had left Beanie feeling somewhat fulfilled by raising awareness of a grave injustice.

While supposedly fighting against Nicaragua's dumping of solid waste into the Caribbean Sea, the Planet Patrol crew had made midnight dives to a submerged Douglas DC-6 propeller plane rumored to have taken the plunge while returning to Cartagena, Colombia from Beaumont, Texas with two million in cash after a drug sale. Beanie and his uncle Pierre had incited a riot in the coastal town of Puerto Cabezas because of the unabashed poop pumping right into one of their own National Reserves. It wasn't until after Beanie led a dive mission down to the plane when he saw actual turds rising from the end of a large tube, that he became energized to continue the faux crusade.

This mission had been different, though. They needed an excuse to set anchor in close, just off shore of the Southeast Alaskan island, and his Uncle Pierre had chosen the local commercial fishing industry as their target. Beanie wasn't even sure what they were supposedly protesting, but his uncle ordered him to invent a bunch of statistics about water pollutants and declining fish populations. Beanie did as ordered, but it didn't sit well with the kid, especially after seeing the salt-of-the-earth faces their protest was impacting.

In addition to feeling guilty about the environmentalist assault, every other aspect of the Hooligan Arm recovery mission seemed doomed. Their midnight dive excursions proved both treacherous and stunningly unfruitful. It was normal to spend several days, if not weeks, mapping ocean floors, getting familiar with current and tidal trends, and conducting grid searches of large, dark, and deep bodies of water. What set this particular mission apart was the extreme conditions in which they worked. Depending on the tides, currents would tear through the cove, making diving excursions difficult, if not dangerous. Water temperatures were colder than on any previous mission, dive depths bordered on extreme, and visibility was low, despite the state-of-the-art underwater LED lamps they used.

Added to the severity of the conditions, was the fact that not a single remnant of a shipwreck had been located. In fact, the Planet Patrol missions that Beanie LeFranc had led didn't recover any human-related evidence of any kind on the bottom of Hooligan Arm. Given that the ship may have moved with the currents, the range of the salvage excursions was widened. Still, there was no sign of the *SS Aberdeen* and its sunken trove of Klondike gold.

Beanie and his Uncle Pierre read, and reread the recently published memoir, scanning for indicators in the manuscript that might better direct their search. They even considered the fact that maybe the late Ellen Cranbrook had identified the wrong cove altogether. But the indicators were all there. The author described in detail the lagoon at the head of the cove, the rock that protruded in the middle, even an indentation in the shoreline where she had clung to the last thread of her life as she was rescued by a Native clan. Every time that Beanie read the chapter that described the shipwreck, he became more and more convinced that they were in the right area. Hooligan Arm had to be the spot.

Another grave setback with regard to their current mission was losing a crewman and raft in an explosion during their third night of diving. The crewman was floating in the inflatable on the surface, having just released Beanie and another diver over the side. They were fairly close to the lagoon as the early search excursions started by shore and moved outward each night. The explosion was huge. Even Beanie, who was forty feet down and fifty feet out, felt the shock wave. The other inflatables in the area quickly came to offer aid, but there was nothing substantial left of the boat or its inhabitant. Small pieces of the raft floated in the bay, but with the darkness of night and the current increasing with the tide change, there was absolutely no body to recover from the blast.

His Uncle Pierre was convinced that the explosion was a strange accident, probably related to the gas tank that sat at the foot of the raft's driver. The dead crewman did smoke cigarettes. Beanie's uncle hypothesized that the guy must have opened that gas tank in order to check the fuel level when his lit cigarette fell from his lip, instantly incinerating him in a massive explosion. Uncle Pierre insisted that they all keep the unfortunate mishap a secret, as reporting the incident would certainly raise questions as to why they were diving in Hooligan Arm in the dead of night.

Beanie LeFranc never quite bought the cigarette-in-the-gas-tank theory of his uncle. Beanie, himself, was responsible for ensuring that all tanks were full and all equipment was in prime condition before every night mission. There was no reason for the dead crewman to check the tank. Also, Beanie had given strict instruction to his crew that lights of any kind were only allowed when submerged deeper than ten feet. Lighting up a cigarette on the surface would have been in direct violation of the young first-mate's orders, drawing unwanted visual attention to their secret salvage mission. The third reason that Beanie had doubts about the explosion was that he felt strange in Hooligan Arm; almost as if they weren't alone. It seemed that every time Beanie led a dive search, there was someone there, watching their every move. He didn't have proof, or even a visual sighting to back up his suspicions. It was only a feeling, a sense from deep within him, that they weren't the only people that occupied Hooligan Arm in the late, dark hours of the night.

Beanie LeFranc had these same feelings as he loaded into an inflatable raft for yet another middle of the night trip. A storm had moved in and rain pelted the cheeks of the dive crew as wind blasted them from the opening of the cove. Taking a break from diving, Beanie was manning the surface raft on this stormy night mission. After checking coordinates on a handheld GPS, he dropped off his crew over the side of the boat. Looking for shelter from the wind, Beanie ran his small craft over close to shore, tucking just inside a small indentation in the rocks. The spot provided him with some protection from the storm, and he sat on the bench seat, bobbing along on the waves, eyes fixed in the direction of where he'd dropped off the divers. Given the stormy conditions, Beanie authorized the divers to use their lights at the surface in order to facilitate a signal for safe retrieval.

With his vision focused on scanning for an indicator from his dive crew, and his mind concerned with keeping the raft out of the direct path of the storm, Beanie LeFranc failed to notice a string of bubbles rising from the depths of the cove, stringing from shore and headed in his direction. He failed to see the black gloved hand lift a football-sized waterproof package from the dark seawater. When the package landed in the floor of the raft next to his feet, Beanie was more curious than concerned. After illuminating his head lamp and curiously examining the plastic wrapped object on the floor of the boat, the young first-mate still didn't realize his impending doom. When the package detonated, instantly incinerating his feet and launching his body into the fast moving currents, Beanie LeFranc's last earthly thoughts were filled with a bewildered peacefulness as blood drained quickly from his body until only cold lifelessness remained.

# Chapter 23

The darker it became, the more the wind and rain seemed to increase. Zeke Melon's vision was seriously impaired by the stinging water pellets that blasted him in the face. The handheld spotlight illuminated more rain than it did shoreline. Waves tossed the fourteen foot Smokercraft like it was a bath toy. Zeke attempted to keep the bow into the coming breakers, but they seemed to come at him from all angles. Cloud cover was so thick, not even a flicker of moonlight could penetrate. The conditions were treacherous and Zeke sensed that he was in serious danger.

Without releasing his grip from the outboard tiller, Zeke clicked on his head lamp and laid out a nautical map on the bench seat, securing it from the wind by sliding it under his leg. He took turns with his view, studying the map and scanning the shoreline with his spotlight. With the conditions such as they were, he couldn't get a bearing on his location. He knew that he was on the west side of Prince of Wales, and he was considerably south of the town of Craig, but that was about all he was certain of. The bow of his skiff suddenly slammed down on a wave, and the spotlight's beam caught just a glimpse of a rock outcropping directly in front of the boat. Zeke blasted the tiller arm out, turning the boat sharply on the crest of the next wave, barely missing the rocks with his bow.

The near miss with the rocks scared him. Zeke was smart enough to know that his life was in danger. There were no other boats, no town, no other human life of any kind. If he capsized, he would die out here alone. He decided that he had better find a safe haven to wait out the storm before he and his skiff succumbed to the storm and went down in the chilled, churning currents.

Abandoning his efforts to use the nautical chart, Zeke attempted to find the shoreline of the main island and follow it until it turned inward. He would look for protection in some sort of cove, or even a narrow inlet. In the darkness, there was certainly a greater risk of running into shallower water and taking out his lower unit on a submerged rock, but he was willing to take that risk. It was better than taking water over the side from the massive storm-driven ground swells.

Using his spotlight and flinching from the onslaught of rain, Zeke muttered a prayer and guided the aluminum Smokercraft close to the shoreline. Given the conditions, he was forced to vary the throttle speed as the boat rose up and crashed down on the waves that confronted him. After several long minutes of hugging the rocks, the shoreline turned sharply inland to the right. Hopefulness overwhelmed him. Zeke adjusted course and turned the boat to the right, heading into the cove. The inlet wasn't big, but it was just what he was looking for. After about two hundred feet into the small arm, the shoreline again took a sharp right, creating a very tiny, but protected, hook of land. The tiny protection was about as big as a tennis court. It had tall trees that surrounded it, creating a much needed wind shield. It would be the perfect respite from the damaging gusts and crashing waves of the storm.

Letting the throttle die to an idle, Zeke scanned with the spotlight, looking for a place to beach his skiff. There appeared to be a stretch of gravel, only about ten feet wide, but perfect for allowing him to come ashore. As a precaution, Zeke raised the outboard engine so the propeller was barely submerged, and he slowly motored in toward the landing spot. The boat's metal hull made a grinding sound as it successfully made contact with the gravelly beach.

Killing the engine, Zeke Melon exhaled loudly, calming his frayed nerves. The wind and rain whistled above his head, but the protection of the tree-lined cove certainly weakened the storm's impact. Out of curiosity, Zeke lifted the gas tank that was attached via a hose to the outboard engine. It was pretty light. He shook it back and forth, hearing only a small amount of gasoline sloshing back and forth. He was probably minutes away from running the tank dry. Zeke had a full spare gas can in the bow of the boat, but he knew that powering down the engine to fill the fuel tank in the middle of high seas would probably have been his death. Without the ability to keep the skiff from turning broadside to the larger waves, he knew that he would have taken on water, if not capsized.

After securing the bowline of his skiff to a tree on shore, Zeke retrieved a tub that held his sleeping bag, clothes, and food. Drenched with rainwater, cold, and hungry, Zeke moved his personal items into a wooded area, changed into dry clothes, and gobbled down a couple of granola bars. He wrapped himself in his sleeping bag and curled up in a ball next to a moss-covered log. Sleep wasn't much of an option for him, but the warmth of the sleeping bag was comforting. He laid there in the dark, in an unknown cove, curled up below tall evergreens that dripped droplets of rainwater onto his face, waiting out the storm.

Zeke listened to the wind move the tree branches above him and thought of the wad of cash that sat protected from the elements inside his dry bag. He smiled at the success of his first weekend of sales. His thoughts drifted to his job as a septic pumper. His boss was not going to be happy with him. There was no way he was showing up on time in the morning, and there was no way to call in a report. It was all right, though. If he got fired, Zeke knew that he had enough cash on hand to cover his expenses for at least a month or two. He thought of the rest of his hooligan candles. He hadn't even sold a quarter of them yet.

Zeke considered quitting his job as a septic pumper and focusing on his enterprise full time. The only problem was that his inventory was limited. The hooligan spawn was tailing off and soon he wouldn't have any way of making more candles. He thought of the family and life he'd left behind in Pennsylvania. He thought of the prayer he had muttered earlier, and it seemed as though it had been answered. As he huddled alone below tall trees, seeking refuge from a storm, in some unknown inlet far from civilization, Zeke Melon reflected on his young life; deep thoughts in an unknown cove.

When his eyes opened, he was amazed to see daylight. It wasn't just daylight, but rather beautiful clear skies and bright sunshine. The fact that he had slept out the remainder of the storm amazed him, especially when Zeke realized that he hadn't even taken a sip of his medicinal crutch.

The young man with damp, red hair exited his sleeping bag and walked out from the trees onto the gravelly shore. The water in the small, protected cove was like glass. A bit of steam-like fog rose from the smooth surface. His aluminum skiff was high and dry as the tide had gone out, but Zeke wasn't too worried about his ability to slide it back into the water. He put on another layer of clothing, but still couldn't escape the chill of the dampness that all of his belongings seemed to possess. After loading up his skiff, refilling the gas tank, and exerting a little bit of effort to get the boat back into the water, Zeke sped away, the bow of the craft keenly cutting through the smooth surface of the sea.

What a difference a night made. Just hours earlier, the water that he'd navigated had churned violently. Now, he felt as though he was cutting through virgin sea that was completely at rest, only to be disturbed by his running bow. With visibility at a premium, the mariner was quick to get his bearings. He was several hours south of Craig. Zeke Melon felt like the king of the ocean, his small vessel slicing its way through clean water, with cool moist air in his face. He sang the song that had given him such success in sales the previous day. At the top of his lungs, with no other human ears to listen, Zeke bellowed, "Hoooo-li-gan. Hoooo-li-gan. Get your-self a fish caaaan-dle. Hoooo-li-gan. Hoooo-li-gan. Put them up on your maaaan-tle."

Mile after mile passed, and the song seemed to push his boat faster. He sped past the inlet that fed into the village of Hydaburg. He quickly weaved around a small fleet of chartered boats disembarking from a fishing resort. He saw two porpoises arching their backs above the surface about fifty yards off his starboard. A small fish jumped near his speeding bow. Zeke was less than ten miles from his home port when he saw something floating in the water.

It wasn't a log. The color was off. The closer that Zeke got, the more he sensed that something was amiss. Whatever it was that was floating didn't seem to belong in nature. He cut the power to his engine and his boat bogged down, rapidly reducing speed. With the engine in gear, Zeke idled up close to the strange looking object that floated in front of him.

Whatever it was, it had strange color markings. It was colored in blue, red, and white. The way the colors moved in the water suggested some sort of fabric. As Zeke moved in next to the object, dread filled him and a tingling sensation filtered down his spinal cord. Face down in the ocean, motionless, and adrift… It was a human body, peacefully floating with the tide, arms spread out with the hands sinking slightly below the surface. It appeared to be a young man wearing a shirt that resembled the French flag. The man wore a red scarf tied around his neck. The most disturbing part of the sight, and the sole fact that would haunt Zeke's nightmares for years to come, was what he saw below the dead man's waist. Just below the knees on both legs, jagged flesh and bone drifted in the sea.

The dead man was missing both feet.

Two ladies with identically large noses waited eagerly outside the front doors of J&Z Outfitters as a bald man in his mid-forties wearing a name tag that read "Steve" walked up with a key. Ignoring them, Steve unlocked the doors with one hand while rubbing the back of his neck with the other. Steve had barely retrieved his key from the lock when the two ladies bounded through the door with the tenacity of a couple of bulldogs.

"Good morn, my good man. I say, it's about time you opened up shop," said one of the ladies in a thick British accent.

Pushing through the doors past the store attendant, the other lady informed him, "You are two minutes and thirty-eight seconds past due. We've been counting the seconds."

The two women were identical in appearance, from their naturally curly hair and awkwardly built bodies, to their huge schnozes that protruded from their faces. The pair were as closely matched as any twins could be. They even dressed similarly, wearing white tennis shoes, blue jeans, and colorful sweaters.

Walking up to the store's lone attendant, taking note of his name tag, Lucy Smelk said, "Steve, is it? We happen to fancy apparel and supplies appropriate for a little adventure outing that we've enlisted in. From the looks of things, we've come to the right place."

Steve's response was more of a low groan than a courteous reply. "Oooaaahhh uhhhh…"

J&Z Outfitters was contained within a fairly small building, but the store was jammed to the gills with merchandise. Two aisles were dedicated to fishing gear, with poles elevated and angled over the aisles like rafters, creating the feeling of strolling through the grand promenade of angling. One side of the store held outdoor clothing on hangers. Brown Xtratuf rubber boots lined the floor while every shade of flannel draped from above. One aisle was devoted to hunting supplies, target practice gear, and animal meat processing. A small, tidy section of camping and survival gear was wedged between a row of gun ammo and an archery display.

Steve stepped behind a glass counter that displayed

various handguns. Numerous rifles of assorted makes and models hung on the wall behind the store clerk. Steve was nursing a massive hangover and the Smelk sisters were a little too bubbly for his mood.

"You ladies have a look around. Let me know if you need something. I'll be over here." They were the first actual words that Steve had spoken on the day. His voice came out low and coarse due to the copious amounts of Yukon Jack and unfiltered cigarettes that he had consumed the previous night. Steve began fumbling with a Mr. Coffee in the corner of the store while the Smelk sisters began trying on hats.

"This is simply delish, wouldn't you agree, sis?" Lucy percolated as she tried on a tan safari-style hat.

"Absolutely divine," Missy agreed, selecting an identical model.

The twins piled up supplies on the glass counter with fervor, amassing quite a haul. Tan fishing vests that matched the safari hats, two pairs of brown Xtratufs, two spray cans of bug dope, two folded packs of foil survival blankets, two orange whistles with orange neck straps, two pump-style water filtration systems, two backpacker's first-aid kits, two compasses and two topographical maps of the area were all laid out on the counter at the front of the store. After a few sips of coffee, Steve's mental cobwebs started to clear. He began to estimate the commission he was about to snag from the two British birds. Commission potential always helped a hangover.

After selecting matching Swiss-Army knives and adding them to the pile, Missy Smelk held up an aerosol-style can with a triggering system attached to the top. She asked,

"Does this stuff really work, Steve?" There was a picture of a menacing grizzly bear shielding his face from a stream of chemical spray on the front of the can.

While picking sleep out of his right eye socket, Steve answered, "They say it does. I really wouldn't know. I tend to rely on a little more fire power, myself."

Lucy perked up. "Oo, guns. What a wicked idea."

Missy asked, "But isn't there some kind of permit or waiting period for buying a firearm here in the States? We are a bit from out of town, one might say."

Lucy finished her sister's thought by saying, "I'm not even sure it's accepted for us to buy a weapon."

Steve mentally calculated the added commission of a possible firearms sale. "I'll sell you two anything. Besides, you're in Alaska. Not a ton of regs up here."

Lucy replied, "Oh, a bit like the wild west, I say."

"How delightfully fiendish," Missy added, with a snicker in her voice.

The two British twins looked at each other and announced at the same time, "Huddle!" They looped arms around each other's necks and placed their heads close, leaning in ear to ear. Slight mumbles followed by squeal-like giggles arose from the two person scrum. Every once in a while, the two would break from whispering and crane their necks up to scan the glass counter that held all the handguns.

Steve sipped his coffee and squinted his eyes to help deal with the headache that was pounding. He was slightly amused at the scene before him, as the twins squabbled back and forth about the merits of gun ownership. Suddenly, they released each other and announced simultaneously, "We'll do it!"

Scanning the pistol display in front of them, both women giddily went along, pointing as they came across handguns that caught their eye. Stopping at a little .38 snub nose, Missy chirped, "That is such a cute one. I think it would look good on my hip."

Lucy looked up from the glass case and peered over her colossal snout at Steve. "What do you think about that cute little revolver there, Steve?"

Steve replied, "We sell that one with a little salt and pepper."

Missy was confused. "Salt and pepper? What on Earth for?"

Steve continued, "So it will taste a little better when the bear crams it down your throat."

The sisters cackled joyously at the store clerk's joke. Playing along, Lucy asked, "Do you have any *bacon* flavored revolvers?" More cackling.

Eventually, after near hyperventilation, Missy stated, "Why don't you show us something that would stop a bear."

Lucy added, "Something with a bit more bang, I'd say."

Steve bent over and selected a Smith & Wesson Model 500 revolver. He gently placed the handgun on top of the counter. The silver revolver had black handle grips and a 6.5 inch barrel. Both ladies took turns holding the gun in the palm of their hands, feeling the sheer weight of the weapon with mystified expressions. Lucy practiced taking aim at a mannequin displaying rain gear. Missy pretended to shoot a deer head hanging on the wall, making little gunshot sounds in her throat.

Lucy said, devilishly, "It's a bit like Dirty Harry, don't you think, sis?"

Missy held the gun next to her right ear, pointing the barrel toward the ceiling, "Go ahead, make my day." Both girls laughed heartily. Steve rolled his eyes.

Steve slapped a box of .50 caliber S&W Magnum shells on the counter. He added a matching belt and holster, a gun cleaning kit, and a brochure sponsored by the State of Alaska Department of Safety titled, *Your New Gun and You – Ten Easy Steps to Happy and Safe Gun Ownership in the Last Frontier.*

After charging close to two thousand dollars each on their Bank of London Visa cards, both women dressed in their new garb before departing the store. They changed out of their white tennis shoes for the rubber boots, wrapped on their new fishing jackets, and donned their safari hats. After a brief argument over who got to wear the holster first, Lucy wrapped her new gunbelt around her waist and snugged the holster up tight to her right hip. Lucy took their new revolver out of its case and secured it in the black hanging sheath, while Missy fumbled with the box of shells.

"You can't load your new weapon in here. Store policy," Steve said, fighting through a new wave of whiskey induced head pain. "Take it outside if you want to put live ammo in that thing. And try not to shoot yourself. That thing'll blow a hole the size of an apple in your foot."

The twins giggled at the thought of an apple-sized hole in their foot. They stuffed the rest of their purchases into a couple of brown handled bags and the sisters departed J&Z Outfitters by saying, "Tah tah, Steve. It's been a hoot."

"Yeah, tah tah," Steve replied as he fumbled with the cap of an aspirin bottle.

They stepped outside and breathed in the fresh, Alaskan air, smiled at each other, and hastened toward their hotel rooms. They strutted proudly, hoping to be noticed in their new garb, brandishing their new toy that hung from one of their hips.

Half a block down the street, Missy turned to her sister and asked, "Is it my turn, yet?"

# Chapter 24

The bright sun on a gorgeous Monday morning in late May gave way to a bustle of activity on the waterfront town of Craig, Alaska. Trooper Brandi Sitzel parked her State issued Jeep Cherokee on Water Street and walked down the sidewalk toward a small dockside café. She and Stilly had both been assigned highway patrol for the morning, but Brandi decided that stopping for a cup of coffee would put just the right amount of distance between her and her partner. When on patrol together, Stilly tended to circle back around several times just so that he could wave to her like a school boy. He was nice enough and a decent Trooper for a young guy, but Brandi Sitzel needed a little space from the interoffice infatuation.

The *Water Street Café* was packed. There were only six tables in the small restaurant, and each one was full. Brandi walked up to the counter and ordered her usual. A waitress that knew her by name said, "One Sitzel, coming up." A packet of hot chocolate mix was emptied into a to-go cup. The cup was topped off with black coffee and a dollop of whipped cream. The waitress crammed on a lid and stuffed two skinny straws through the sip hole. Brandi dropped three crisp dollar bills onto the counter, thanked the waitress, and exited the café.

After walking half a block back towards her Cherokee, Brandi stopped to lean on the metal sidewalk railing and peer out over the harbor. She briefly contemplated her life's path while staring at the water, looking north toward several small, tree-studded islands.  She had grown up a true Alaskan, just a hundred miles south of the Arctic Circle.  After completing her academy training in Sitka and matriculating at the top of her class, Trooper Sitzel started her career in Detachment D, headquartered out of Fairbanks.  The assignment seemed like a dream come true as the station was in her hometown.

As she sipped her hot beverage, Brandi considered the transfer request that led to her assignment on Prince of Wales Island.  Being a young Trooper was hard enough, but a stunning blonde woman in a man's world proved to be more than she could take.  Her old captain in the Fairbanks Detachment grabbed her ass daily.  The other male Troopers teased her relentlessly about the fact that the sound of her full name matched up with a well-known porn star, Brandy Sizzle.  She even considered starting to pronounce the silent 't' in her last name, but knew that would only add fuel to their fire.  The assignments she caught from dispatch were always the bottom of the heap.  Any major case that she stumbled upon was immediately reassigned.  Soon, it became more than she wanted to endure.  Trooper Brandi Sitzel put in an immediate transfer to the only station that had an opening at the time.

Lieutenant Wekle had proved to be a good man and a good boss.  He was someone she could trust.  He wouldn't tolerate any harassment of her for being a woman, for her stunning appearance, or for her namesake.  For that, Brandi Sitzel was eternally grateful and extremely dedicated to her current assignment.  But she wanted more.  Brandi was due for a promotion to corporal.  She wanted to be handed more of a role in the investigations that took place, but Jim appeared unaware.  She desperately needed a title above Trooper, as being considered equal to the young Trooper Brett Stilhaven was hard to accept. The kid panted like a dog when they were in the same room together.

As the Trooper continued to sip on her drink at the sidewalk railing, Frightening Frankie's floatplane rumbled overhead. He was making an approach after his morning run into Ketchikan. The seaplane banked and landed just offshore from the town. As the plane taxied through the calm morning waters, something strange on shore caught Trooper Sitzel's eye. A large, strange looking plant of some sort seemed to be moving on the wooden pier. It crept closer and closer to the ramp that led down to the seaplane dock.

"What the hell is that?" Brandi mumbled to herself as she watched the odd configuration of random vegetation move across the wooden planks for several feet before pausing and standing perfectly still. After several seconds of inactivity, the plant-like object scurried again, getting ever closer to the edge of the seaplane ramp. Brandi strode swiftly up the sidewalk. The de Havilland Beaver was tethered to the dock and Frankie was helping his patrons out of the floatplane below as Brandi Sitzel approached the anomalous entity.

As she neared the entrance to the pier, Trooper Sitzel was able to discern what the object was. Two short segments of chainlink fencing had been attached in the middle, creating a V-like structure. Stuck into the various square holes in the chainlink fence were random boughs of cedar, hemlock, fir, and spruce, with a few fern branches added in as well. The branches stuck out in numerous directions from the fence, creating a visual barrier, hiding a solitary person that sat tucked away inside the V of the fence. Once more, the makeshift camouflage rose slightly off the surface of the pier and inched closer to the top of the seaplane ramp.

Brandi stopped about twenty feet from the scene and leaned against a street light pole, more curious than concerned. Six tourists, each wearing heavy jackets despite the clear skies and warm temperature, slowly ambled up the ramp from the sea-level dock. They were scanning the horizon, analyzing points of interest, and searching for bald eagles flying overhead. After reaching the top of the ramp and huddling close by while awaiting their luggage, all six tourists seemed completely unmindful of the man that crouched behind a conifer-lined portion of fencing, just several feet away.

A ponytailed man wearing jean cutoff shorts sprang out from behind the cedar blind. He was holding an electric guitar that was attached to a small, battery powered amplifier that hung from his belt. The man shouted "Hot damn," as he struck a pose behind an unsuspecting middle-aged woman from Peoria, Illinois. The woman jumped in fright as the ponytailed man slammed his right arm across the guitar strings, creating the squealing crunch of a heavy metal power-chord. As the guitarist lit into a shredding tirade of distorted scales, he gyrated around the group of tourists, causing fear and confusion. The tourists shuffled away from the crazed musician, but the guitarist moved swiftly after them, pelvic-thrusting with each burst of rhythmic eruption. As the six tourists shifted their direction in a desperate attempt to dissuade their tormenter, the guitarist jogged quickly, positioning himself directly in front of the group, resembling a cat cornering its prey.

The man with the guitar howled out a melodic growl, his voice equaling the volume of the dynamic thrashing from the amplifier: *"Keep on rockin' in the free world…"* Although the vocalization mimicked an old Neil Young song, the arpeggiated fragments coming from the guitar more closely matched something similar to Yngwie Malmsteen. Just as a teenage dockhand reached the top of the ramp with the luggage cart, the wild musician jumped back and sprawled across the suitcases. With his back resting on a pair of matching Samsonites and his hairy bare legs pointing straight into the air, the ponytailed man worked up to the climatic conclusion of his musical tirade.

He vamped on four chords with a pulsing rhythmic groove while belting, "Sha-na-naaaa-na. Sha-na-naaaa-na. Hey-hey-hey. Good-bye," repeatedly. The ponytailed guitarist hopped off the luggage cart, slipped in behind the evergreen boughs of his makeshift fence, and ducked out of sight. The camouflaged fencing lifted off the ground and quickly backed away. The tourists stood stunned, mouths agape. One lifted a cell phone and snapped a picture. Trooper Sitzel followed the disappearing fence-man.

She caught up to the fence and stood directly behind the crouched, ponytailed man. "That was an interesting performance, Kram."

Turning, with his standard sheepish grin, he said, "You saw it, huh? I may need to fine tune it a bit. Was the pelvic thrusting a bit much?"

"Not at all. The luggage cart was a bit over-the-top, but I really liked the Bananarama quote."

"I think I need to work on the middle part a bit. It's missing an edgy punch."

"Kram, can I ask you a question?"

"Shoot." He looked up from behind some cedar

branches with genuine interest.

"What in the hell are you doing?"

Hopping up straight, still holding the guitar, Kram said, "It's called the tourist deterrent and tormentation project. I call it the TDTP for short. I'm thinking of having T-shirts made.

"Again… What the hell are you doing?"

Kram developed a look of sincerity. "Aren't you concerned with the recent influx of extraneous beings infiltrating our city streets? Aren't you concerned that soon we will be overrun with camera-toting, gin-swilling, convulsion-inducing, rodent-breath, tourists all over this beautiful island? Well I am, and I am taking matters into my own hands. The art of deterrent is really a finely honed craft. It takes dedication, precision timing, and commitment to the moment."

"Just… keep it under control." The Trooper started to walk away. She stopped, turned, and said, "I'll talk to Jim about this. In the meantime, don't give anyone any heart attacks, okay?"

"Roger, over and out." Kram dropped straight down on his knees and slinked away under cover down the pier to the edge of a nearby building, hiding in the shadows.

Trooper Sitzel walked away from the wooden pier toward where she had parked her Jeep Cherokee. She unlocked the Jeep and was about to open the door when she heard shouting.

"What is it now?" the Trooper said quietly to herself.

In the distance a voice sounded frantic, "Help! Come quick!"

The Trooper released her grip on the Jeep Cherokee's door, hit the lock button, and jogged up the sidewalk. The voice came from up Water Street, past the floatplane dock, close to where the marina was located. There was a woman waving her arms and running toward the Trooper. Brandi quickly approached, meeting the woman on the sidewalk.

"What's the problem, ma'am?"

The lady breathed hard from running. She caught her balance by holding onto the sidewalk railing. "A man just pulled up in his boat. There's..." She paused to catch her breath. "There's a dead body layin' across the bow."

# Chapter 25

Peter Gorski was born in Chicago, Illinois in 1967. His father made a mint in the dry cleaning business with fourteen different shops sprawled across the Windy City. Pete's mother had left the family early in his childhood when she hooked up with a sausage maker and member of a rogue biker gang. Claiming to be attracted to the scent of fennel seed and motorcycle exhaust, she loaded up on the back of the sausage maker's Harley and bolted out of town, breaking the hearts of her husband and two boys.

Pete's father was a respectable man, and raised his two boys in Chicago, grooming them to someday take over the dry cleaning franchise. Gorski men never did seem to know how to pick their women, as both Pete and his brother chose wives that split shortly after the requisite three years ran out on the standard Gorski pre-nup.

Several years into adulthood, Pete's father and brother passed away together in a tragic car accident. Pete suddenly found himself inheriting the family business, the family fortune, and the only other remaining family member, his young nephew named Bradley. Pete attempted to make a go of it as a dry cleaning tycoon, but bitterness swelled in his heart. He was angry that his mother had left him at such a young age. He was outraged that his wife had divorced him. He was livid that his father and brother had died, leaving him holding the bag, and he was especially incensed that he was now responsible for raising a little snot named Bradley.

As the bitterness grew over the years, so did his

disdain for law and order. The honest money being generated by the family business was ample enough to live a luxurious life, but the job itself was about as enthralling as a turnip. Peter Gorski soon found more action and excitement in the field of loan sharking than he ever did running a bunch of laundromats.

Over the course of several years, Pete managed to hire several trusted henchmen that made sure his loan recipients paid in full. His special trademark incentive became known throughout the Chicago underworld as the "Gorski Manicure." Whenever someone wouldn't pay up, their right hand would be forced into a bucket full of toxic dry cleaning chemicals. The secret concoction of acidic cleaning agents would burn the skin right off the hand, if it was held under long enough. The beauty of the "Gorski Manicure" was that it allowed the poor sap on the receiving end the ability to relent at any time depending on how much skin damage they could endure before agreeing to double the interest payments.

The organized crime division of the local Chicago Police Department soon became all too aware of the famed "Gorski Manicure," and made a move on the loan sharking businessman. With the help of the Feds, law enforcement officials started closing in on all aspects of the Gorski empire, both legitimate and illicit. The writing was on the wall for Pete Gorski. He liquidated as many assets as quickly as possible, gathered up several million in cash, and headed for the international terminal of the airport with his nephew in tow.

Landing in Paris, France, and making it through customs before the government had time to red flag his passport, Peter Gorski and his nephew holed up in a small apartment while he waited for the dust to settle. Amazed that several million dollars in cash had made it through in his checked baggage, Pete considered the good fortune a sign and he decided to make a complete overhaul of his life. Pierre Lemieux and Beanie LeFranc were born after the two split a bottle of Chianti and played rock-paper-scissors over who got to pick their new name first. At the time, young Beanie was just fifteen years old, but Pierre figured that was old enough to learn to guzzle red wine in Paris.

Carrying a hefty wad of cash proved useful in obtaining legal-looking documents that would solidify their new identities, but the suitcases full of bills also seemed like quite a liability to Pierre. After making their way to the southern coastal city of Marseille, Pierre invested a huge chunk of the cash in a large, sea-going vessel. Pierre and Beanie spent the next year hiring a crew, learning to operate the ship, and hatching a master plan of how they would live their newfound lives. During that time, Beanie became quite a skilled scuba diver, and managed to get tight with the diving community in the area.

After creating an organization called Planet Patrol, developing quite an online presence to give the façade of legitimacy, and fully outfitting the vessel to be self-sufficient over the course of long voyages, the new captain, young first mate, and small crew of irreverent divers, set out from their home port of Marseille. They embarked on a mission under the guise of eco-friendly warfare, but set out with a handful of destinations earmarked for making them a second fortune.

Peter Gorski, aka Pierre Lemieux, was raised not only by a shrewd Chicago businessman, but also under the tutelage of a treasure hunter. Although Pierre's father never embarked on any actual treasure seeking missions, the man was obsessed with rare, old books that described locations of shipwrecks. Several of these shipwrecks had been marked as "locations of serious interest." His old man used to love sitting down with young Peter, turning pages, examining maps, discussing long lost sunken treasures that were ripe for the taking. These sessions from his youth stuck with the man, and once he decided to recreate his life, spending his father's fortune on treasure seeking missions just seemed appropriate.

Out of fear that meeting various international salvaging laws would lead to the discovery of his real identity, Pierre Lemieux developed the hoax of making port in nearby communities and spewing forth a silver streak about some pertinent environment-related crusade. His nephew, the newly dubbed Beanie LeFranc, proved quite gifted at coming up with region-appropriate campaigns. In truth, Beanie actually believed in many of the causes that he pretended to fight for, so the charade came quite naturally to the kid. The *Earth's Guardian* would drift in to some unsuspecting port town, put forth a large enough stink to get asked to remove itself from the area, and then set anchor close by the shipwreck. The crew, led by Beanie, would conduct nighttime dive missions in an attempt to recover any items of value.

Missions had varied success. An old warship off the coast of Valencia, Spain provided a small chest of gold coins and remnants of several antique weapons. A supposed pirate ship near Costa Rica was never located. An exploration vessel from the seventeen hundreds had already been stripped clean off the tip of Cabo San Lucas. A yacht that recently sank near the Catalina Islands produced a pouch full of German bearer bonds and a brick of cocaine. As Planet Patrol worked their way up the west coast of the United States, their reputation for eco-warfare grew. By the time they took port just outside the Seattle waterfront, Pierre was lamenting the fact that most of the promising "locations of serious interest" from his father's old notes had already been checked off the list. Fearing that he might have to resort back to his loan sharking days in order to pay the bills, Pierre just happened to stumble across a new bestselling work of non-fiction.

The book, *Muskeg Mama: Memoir of a Klondike Girl*, was prominently displayed in the window of a Seattle tourist trap. The cover art quickly captured his attention as it was a black and white photo montage that included images of gold nuggets and old steamships. He stayed up all night in the wheelhouse of his ship, entranced by the storyline. The next morning, Pierre Lemieux informed his crew that they were pulling anchor and heading north for Prince of Wales Island.

*The gold. Oh the gold. I saw it drive men to their death. I saw it turn a clean heart black. Its allure was more than most could resist. It grew grand cities out of rock and ice. It created paths over mountains that were never meant to host such travails. It turned church elders into mean drunks. And it sank ships without regard nor prejudice.*

*I watched the men load crate after crate, struggling with all their might, into the cargo hold of the SS Aberdeen. The sheer weight of their haul was evident, as it took all these strong, burly servants of the north could muster in order to complete their task. My new love interest, Wally, my rescuer from the treacherous dance halls and loathsome men of the gold rush, watched keenly over the loading procedure. He was quick to notice an odd eye or sly hand when it came to his gold. His obsession was obvious, but I believe, mildly controlled. He was a generous man, ready to share his good fortune with those close to him. He was one man that didn't deserve the fate that befell him. But in the end, it was the gold that did him in. It was the gold that guided that ship off course, that corrupted the captain's judgment, that conjured the storm, and it was the gold that sank that boat and all its men; forever were they laid to rest at the bottom of the sea.*

# Chapter 26

A small crowd had assembled on the dock close to where Zeke Melon had moored his skiff. Walking up to the scene, Jim scanned the faces in the crowd, recognizing most as locals. Jim wondered momentarily why Kram was standing on the dock behind a small fence covered in cedar branches, but dismissed the man's quirkiness as standard operating procedure. Brandi Sitzel was there, doing a good job of keeping the crowd back and keeping Zeke isolated off to the side. Jim was glad that she had waited for him before starting the inquiry process.

"What'chya got, Trooper Sitzel?" Jim asked after pushing his way through the crowd of onlookers.

"Zeke here, pulled up in his boat with that laying across the bow."

Jim looked to where Brandi pointed. There was a blue tarp covering the front section of the Smokercraft. Jim stepped into the boat and pulled away the tarp. A lifeless, legless young man was sprawled across several plastic tubs. The man wore a shirt reminiscent of the French flag and had a red scarf wrapped around his neck.

"This body belong to that foot in the morgue?" Brandi murmured.

"I don't think so. I know this kid," Jim said quietly to his Trooper. "This is Beanie LeFranc. I just spoke with him the other day."

"Zeke, here claimed to have found him floating like this, early this morning, just south of Hooligan Arm. He claims to have pulled the body out of the water and headed straight here."

Jim stepped out of the boat, turned to Zeke, and said, "We need to stop meeting like this, young man."

Zeke struggled to speak. "I p... p... p... promise. I have n... n... n... no idea..."

Kram perked up from the back of the crowd. "Fascinating."

Jim turned and said, "Kram, this isn't the time."

Zeke said, "I f... f... f... found him with n... n... no f... f... f..."

Kram shouted, "Face. Fish. Film. Father-in-law."

"Kram!" Jim ordered.

"Feet," Zeke finished.

Jim asked the redhead, "Where have you been, Zeke? I almost had the Coast Guard out looking for you."

"K... k... k... k..."

Kram attempted to help, again. "Kite flying. Kilt wearing. Kettle corn eating. Kiln working."

"Ketchikan," Zeke finally got out.

Concerned, Jim asked, "You went all the way to Ketchikan in that little boat? Didn't you get hit by the storm last night?"

Zeke nodded. "Spent the night on the b... b... b...

b…"

Kram yelled, frantically, "Barbeque.  Barnacles.  Belly dancers."

"Beach," said Zeke.

Jim turned to Brandi and said, "I'm going to take Zeke back to the station and get his statement in private.  You stay here.  Call Stilly to give you a hand.  I'll contact the M.E. and get her down here quick to remove the body.  Take as many pictures as you can, and keep this crowd back, okay?"

"You got it boss."  Turning to the small crowd of onlookers, Brandi ordered, "I need everyone to head ten feet up the dock.  We are going to need a little space here."

Jim grabbed Zeke by the arm and said, "Come with me."

"W… w… w…"

"Water.  Wedgy.  Woodstock.  Woodrow Wilson."

"Wait."  Zeke pulled away and stepped into his boat.  He grabbed a dry bag that sat close to the gas tank in the stern.  The clear, plastic material of the dry bag gave a clear view of its contents.

"That's a lot of money, Zeke," Jim stated.  "Looks like we have a lot to talk about."

Jim led the young man up the ramp and put him in the back of his Crown Vic.  Before getting into the driver's seat, Jim pulled out his cell phone and dialed a number.

"Hi, Hugh.  Looks like I need another ride out to Hooligan Arm this afternoon.  Yeah, I know.  Just send me the bill."

Cliff Barr became a professional writer right out of college. After graduating with a journalism degree from the University of Alaska Fairbanks, he got a job working for a newspaper in Juneau. He proved to be an average journalist at best, but during his off-duty hours, Cliff managed to piece together a fairly decent mystery novel. The book was set on a college campus near the Arctic Circle and drew from his first-hand experiences as a student in Fairbanks. The book, titled *Frozen Murder*, followed a college professor who teamed up with a detective in order to track down a serial killer that was targeting innocent sorority girls. The two-man investigative team never caught the perpetrator, and in a sharp twist of the plot, the novel's last chapter revealed that the serial killer was actually the college professor all along.

The book was actually picked up by a middle-level publishing house and sold fairly well over the first few years. The book's unsettling ending set up perfectly for a sequel, and fans of *Frozen Murder* have been demanding the story's resolution for over a decade. Cliff had embarked upon a second book countless times, but couldn't ever get past the first chapter. Convinced that he wasn't just a one-hit-wonder, but rather a victim of severe writer's block, Cliff sought refuge from all distractions by moving to a much more remote locale. He had visions of buying a small cabin in the woods with a view of the ocean and digging into *Frozen Murder II – The Search for Professor Wiggins* whole heartedly. With royalties from his first novel waning, Cliff eventually had to settle for renting the left half of a duplex on Williwaw Drive, and taking on odd writing jobs for various monthly publications just to help pay the bills. He had just hit 'send' on a 2500-word piece about skunk cabbage and was looking forward to working on his second mystery novel when the sounds of the four wheelers interrupted his chain of thought.

"Damn terrorists. They're back." The furry eyebrowed man jumped up from his writing desk, grabbed a bag full of cardboard tubes, and ran for the door. "I'm ready for you bastards, this time. Bring it on."

Standing in front of the duplex, Cliff set what he was holding on the ground next to his feet. He selected one of the cardboard tubes from the bag and held the Roman candle in his right hand, waiting for the perfect moment before lighting the fuse. He could hear the four-wheeled machines tearing up gravel as they sped toward his driveway. Cliff positioned himself halfway down his driveway in perfect view of his brand new mailbox. This time, he opted for a simple, grey box perched atop a basic four-by-four post. It wasn't the fanciest or sturdiest of designs, but one that he hoped would lure the four-wheeled menaces perfectly in range of his trap. Cliff readied his wind-proof lighter, holding it next to the fuse, while angling the Roman candle straight down the gravel driveway to where the mailbox stood as bait. Seconds before he estimated the four-wheelers to be within view, Cliff flicked the lighter and ignited the fuse.

As sparks sizzled from the fuse of the Roman candle, three ATV's came tearing around the corner, spewing gravel from their tires as they turned at Cliff Barr's mailbox. The three motorists again wore riding gear from head to toe, completely disguising their identities. As the fuse disappeared into the tub of the pyrotechnic, Cliff grimaced in preparation for ignition, aiming the tube parallel with the ground from his outstretched arm. This first colored fireball detonated, shooting backwards, blazing just past his torso and in through the open door of his apartment. In shock and disbelief, Cliff remained frozen, still not fully comprehending that he was holding the firework backwards. The second shot blasted from the tube, and again made it through the open door of the duplex, this time igniting a stack of handwritten notes that sat on his writing desk.

"Aaaaack," Cliff screamed. "My notes!" He dropped the Roman candle on the ground and galloped frantically toward his apartment. The rocket continued to launch different colored fireballs back toward the duplex, sizzling by Cliff's feet as he ran.

Inside his living space, flames rose from the stack of notebook papers. A smoke alarm squealed loudly. Cliff located a fire extinguisher and blasted the blaze with white powdery spray, nailing his open laptop computer in the process. Outside, the last of the fireballs shot from the Roman candle and pelted the side of the duplex with a solid thud.

With a decade's worth of notes dedicated to his second novel in ashes, his laptop ruined, and a smoke alarm piercing his cranium, Cliff Barr slowly exited his home, dragging the empty extinguisher on the ground behind. His mouth was agape, and bottom lip quivering. His left eyebrow was singed. One of the four-wheelers sped up the driveway toward his house. It immediately made a sharp u-turn, spraying gravel on the side of Cliff's blue Toyota Rav4. Cliff watched his new mailbox bounce spastically down his driveway pulled by a chain behind the ATV.

Cliff heard a female voice with a thick Chinese accent

yell, "See you next time, asshole." The three ATV's turned out of his driveway and roared away. Eventually, the sound of their engines eroded into the quietness of the day. Still standing, motionless and stunned, Cliff Barr heard a crackling noise behind him. He turned, and again screamed, "Aaaack," as flames rose from the outer wooden shingles of the duplex.

# Chapter 27

"You listen to me, young man. No more trips to Ketchikan in that little skiff of yours. You'll use the ferry crossing from now on, right?" Lieutenant Wekle lead Zeke out of the interrogation room into the heart of the Trooper station.

"I'll take the f… f… ferry from now on." Zeke's face was still white as a sheet. Finding the dead floater alone was enough to rattle the guy's already unstable nerves, but after a spending a stormy night on the beach and being interrogated by a State Trooper, the kid was nearing a breakdown.

"And no more bodies or body parts, okay?"

"I'll t… t… t…"

From across the station, Kram suggested, "Table dance. Taco stand. Torment puppies."

"Try," Zeke finished.

Jim snorted, "Kram. Stuff it." Motioning toward Stilly, he said, "Alright, Zeke. Trooper Stilhaven will give you a ride back to the dock. Collect your things from your boat and go home and get some rest. Don't worry about your job today. We've already contacted your boss. He's not expecting you until tomorrow morning."

Trooper Brett Stilhaven got up and led the redheaded man out of the station. Jim turned to Kram. "What are you doing here?"

Kram smiled. "I'm just stopping by to extend a courtesy to you and yours. Dinner, tonight… Your place."

Jim looked at Maggie, who shrugged and smiled in return. "Better make it a late meal, buddy," he said. "I'm up to my ears right now."

Growing into his best puppy dog expression, Kram reproached, "And your mother is sitting out there on that island, all alone. Hungry, cold, wet, sad…"

Maggie piped up. "We'll be there. Seven o'clock sound good?"

"Seven it is." Kram began dashing around in little circles. "I've got shopping to do. Hope the store still hasn't run out of lard." Kram bolted for the side door of the station and exited in a flash.

Sitting down in a chair next to Trooper Sitzel's desk, Jim said, "That boy's innocent."

Brandi Sitzel raised her eyebrows. "Kram? He's a lot of things, but innocent…?"

"I'm talking about Zeke Melon." Jim told Trooper Sitzel about the midnight run to Ketchikan, the success of his hooligan candle sales, and the eventful return trip.

Brandi said, "A story like that, it's a little too odd to be made up. So you think it's totally by chance that the same guy found both a severed foot and a footless torso, at two different times, from two different bodies floating in the water?"

Maggie chimed in from her dispatcher's desk, "Not totally by chance. Both recoveries have proximity to Hooligan Arm in common. And Zeke seems to have been spending a lot of time in and around there lately."

"Precisely." Jim leaned back in his chair, lifting the

front legs off the ground. "Both the foot and the body connect to the Planet Patrol boat, which just happens to be anchored in Hooligan Arm. That's two dead bodies, both unreported, from the same boat. That's easily enough for a court order to search that vessel."

Brandi asked, "Are you sure that the recovered severed foot is from a separate body than the one found today? Maybe that French kid was wearing a prosthetic or something."

"I know it's two different deaths. The floater that was brought in today was definitely Beanie LeFranc. I just spoke to him the other day, and he was walking around just fine, using both legs without issue. All the while, the severed foot sat in a cooler here in town."

"What is causing these guys to get their feet detached from their bodies, anyway? That seems extremely odd to me," Maggie added.

Jim said, "That's the million dollar question. To be honest, I don't have much of an idea there, yet. Now that we have new evidence, I'm hoping the M.E.'s office can help with that one. I'll stop there before we head out to search the ship." Jim stood up, grabbed his Stetson and walked toward the side door of the station. "Maggie, I want you to call Cheryl Lawson and make sure she's got that court order ready. Tell her to meet us at the marina by Hugh Eckley's boat in an hour."

Jim was halfway to the door when Brandi stood and said, "Hey, boss. Can I have just a minute of your time first?"

Nodding toward his office door, Jim answered, "Sure. Come on in." Both of the State Troopers entered the office.

Jim sat behind his desk while Brandi shut his door. She turned and stood at attention in front of the desk.

Brandi took a deep breath, and then went into her prepared speech, talking fast without pause, "Boss, I would like to officially request a promotion to corporal. I've been a Trooper now, long past the standard time limit for promotion. My former captain, well, you know the story there. When I filed the request for this transfer, I knew that I'd have to put in a bit of time first before promotion, but I feel that I have been a pretty good Trooper for you, and it's been a year now. I appreciate being a mentor to Stilly, but honestly, it doesn't feel as though I am truly his superior while we share the same rank. Now that he is past his probationary period, we are actually considered equals, and I think he knows that, which seems to undermine any authority that I once had. You know as well as I, that I have a lot to learn still, but I feel that I…"

Cutting her off mid-sentence, Jim said, "Trooper Sitzel."

Brandi paused. "Yes?"

"I disagree with you on one point." Jim waited, allowing the tension to build.

"What's that, boss?"

"You have not been a 'pretty good Trooper' for me." Jim again allowed time for an awkward silence. Brandi's expression turned grim. Jim finally said, "You have been an *exceptional* Trooper for me."

Brandi Sitzel couldn't hold back a smile, "Thank you, sir."

"Don't call me 'sir.'"

"Sorry, boss."

"Here, have a look at this." Jim lifted a paper off his desktop and handed it to her. "I sent this in last week. I haven't received official confirmation yet, but I have no reason to doubt."

Brandi scanned the document. It was an official request for her promotion to corporal. She beamed.

"I just hope they don't take your raise out of my budget," Jim said, smiling back.

With earnest eyes, she replied sincerely, "Thank you, Jim."

"You earned it."

Brandi turned towards the door while saying, "I'll make sure we have that court order and I'll meet you at the boat."

"Wait a sec. I have a question for you." Jim turned his head, looking out the office window toward the dispatcher's desk. "I expect an honest response, Brandi."

The Trooper nodded.

"What are your thoughts on Maggie working here?"

Without hesitation, Brandi said, "She does a good job."

"I know that she's a good employee. That's not exactly what I was getting at. I mean with regard to…" Jim paused again.

"You mean… the two of you."

"Exactly."

"I find it easier to ignore that part of the interoffice workings here."

Jim rubbed his temples. "I can't ignore it. I know it's weird sometimes. Heck, it's weird for me. I'm supposed to be her boss on one hand, but in our personal relationship, we should be equals."

Brandi suggested, "Well, maybe you need to give her the upper hand in something."

"Not following you."

"Most men don't get it. In most relationships, the man has the upper hand in more than a few ways. You guys do the heavy lifting, pay the bills, kill the spiders. What do the women get? They get the final say around the house. You know…which couch to buy, which shirt the kids are going to wear, what food you should be eating. In many relationships, it balances out. Both have an equal hand in things."

Jim nodded, thinking about it. He said, "But we're not married, we don't live together, we don't have kids. We don't have a house…"

"Exactly. You have the upper hand at work, and that's totally cool. She can accept that. But when does it ever equal out?" Brandi raised her eyebrows.

Jim said, sincerely, "Thanks, Brandi. I appreciate this."

"Let's not make a habit of it. I don't do relationship stuff very well." Trooper Sitzel walked away from her boss and out the office door.

Jim followed close behind. He tried to catch Maggie's

eye on his way out, but she was on the line with someone. Jim almost reached the side door of the station when Maggie called out, "Jim, just a minute."

The Lieutenant stopped and turned. Maggie held her finger on the mute button of the phone and said, "This is Cheryl Lawson. She's got the court order, but she can't meet you at the harbor."

"Why not? Isn't she the Harbormaster?"

"Apparently, she's tied up at home. Wants to know if you can stop by and pick it up."

Jim donned his Stetson. "Text me the address. I'm meeting with the M.E. first. Then I'll pick up the paperwork from Cheryl. Tell Hugh that I might be a little late for our boat ride."

"Sure thing, boss." Maggie turned her attention back to the switchboard.

Jim hated it when Maggie called him, "boss." Before leaving, Jim said, "And, Maggie. Don't worry. I won't be late for dinner."

She smiled. "You'd better not. Kram's pretty excited to cook for your mom. He's buying lard."

"So I heard."

# Chapter 28

After ten years' worth of handwritten notes went up in a colorful blaze on his kitchen table, Cliff Barr was a little more than distraught. He was fairly certain that the damage deposit he'd plopped down before renting the duplex was a total loss now that a third of the wood siding on the front of his house appeared to be quite charred. His plans for launching Roman candle fireballs at the hoodlum four-wheelers had literally backfired. His new mailbox was gone, and he was nearing a conniption fit.

The cops had proved to be completely worthless. Cliff had called them multiple times to no avail. The rogue ATV's still tormented him regularly. He had decided to take matters into his own hands, and had driven up to Klawock in order to visit an expert in fireworks. After lying to the clerk behind the counter by saying that he desired to scare some unwanted wildlife intruders without actually killing anything, the clerk had been all too eager give Cliff some hands-on training in the fine art of Roman candle shooting. Cliff had done everything exactly like he'd been trained, and the result was tragic. Someone was about to get an earful, at the very least. Cliff loaded up in his Toyota and set out for the highway with a large chip on his shoulder.

The ponytailed clerk working behind the counter of *Big Al's Fireworks Emporium* wore jean cutoff shorts and grinned widely as Cliff approached. The ponytailed man grabbed a firecracker off the shelf, lit it, and yelled, "Fire in the hole!" as he threw the tiny sizzling bomb at Cliff's feet. The author danced wildly in place, attempting to lift both feet simultaneously off the ground. The firecracker exploded inches from his right shoe. The loud popping sound caused a temporary ringing in Cliff's right ear drum. The ponytailed clerk yelled, "Hot damn!"

"What are you, some kind of idiot? You're not supposed to do that here." Cliff Barr pointed to a sign that read, "*Do not light fireworks within 100 feet of this establishment.*"

"Not to worry, my long-faced friend. Big Al, himself, has authorized me to provide onsite training and first hand demonstration of the product. This is high-grade, premium stuff, straight off the boat from China. None of that cut black powder stuff that fizzles out halfway through the bang. This is the real thing, baby. I've got Kablooyee Bazookas, Fire Sticks, Bengal Mortars, Death Blasters, Sticky Flickies, the Red Flower of Hell, and even these." Kram held up a black sphere, about the size of a croquet ball. A thick fuse came up from the center of the sphere and bent over in a sagging loop. "This thing is the Ball of Thunder 3000. This sucker's illegal in forty-nine states. Want to get rid of that nosey neighbor that always borrows your tools, but never returns them? Launch one of these puppies into his next backyard barbeque and watch people dive for cover. Problem solved. It…will…rock…your…world."

Finally with a break in the sales pitch, Cliff interjected, "Well, actually. That's right along the lines of what I wanted to speak to you about. I was here a day ago, and mentioned that I needed something to get rid of some unwanted pests. You gave me that onsite training that you're so proud of. Well, I followed your ass-wipe training to a tee, and it nearly burned my house to the ground. Just look at my eyebrow…"

"Apparently, you need more training, different tactics, a whole new approach. You came to the right place, sir. Kram's the name, flame's the game. Now, tell me. Just what kind of pest are you trying to get rid of? Bears? Mosquitoes? Politicians?"

Cliff waited for a moment, considering whether or not to punch the firework clerk square in the lip. Instead, Cliff said, "A rogue gang of four-wheeled menaces. They've been terrorizing me for days, now."

"Ah, a revenge game, eh? You should have mentioned that the first time. You'll need more than the old 'backwards Roman candle gag.' You've got yourself a nasty little infestation there, sir. And when you've got an infestation, there's only one solution." Kram paused, waiting for a reply.

"What's the solution?" Cliff Barr finally asked.

"You need an exterminator. You've come to the right place, Cliffy. We have much to discuss." Kram gathered up a few select rockets, mortars, and croquet sized balls. He placed them into a plastic bag and announced, "That'll be sixty-three dollars, please." Reluctantly, Cliff Barr dug some bills out of his wallet.

After closing up the fireworks stand, Kram stated, "We'll hammer out the plans over dinner tonight. I'm hosting a little dinner party at my yurt, and you're going to be there." Kram walked toward his Vespa scooter, popped on his helmet and asked, "You like mussels fried in lard, don't you? Never mind. You're going to love 'em. Cliffy... That just doesn't have the right ring to it. You ever consider a name change?"

The trip out to Cheryl Lawson's home took a little longer than Jim had expected. He had to travel way out the road before turning on to what appeared to be a fairly new driveway. His Crown Vic drove up a paved, tree-lined drive that opened up to a spacious parking lot in front of an immaculate home. The main house featured a tall, V-shaped roof and stone siding. Large vinyl-framed windows stood beautifully encased by the stone siding. The lot for the home had been cut into a sheer rock wall that encased the back side of the property. A construction crew had parked several trucks next to the house and the logo on each of the trucks' doors read *K Diamond Construction*. Several men busily worked on what appeared to be a fancy guest house connected to the main home via a tall breezeway. As Jim stepped out of his State Trooper's vehicle, the front door opened and Cheryl Lawson appeared in the covered entryway.

"Jim, thank you for driving out here. I had to stay home in order to go over some slight changes in the blueprints with the foreman." The Harbormaster wore form fitting jeans and a tight, blue sweater. Her wavy, black hair flitted over her shoulders.

"Not a problem, Cheryl. This is quite the home you have here."

"Come on inside. I have the signed court order on the kitchen counter."

Jim followed Cheryl Lawson in through the main entry and down a well decorated corridor. The hallway led to an open expanse that included a living room and kitchen area. All furniture and appliances appeared to be brand new. The hardwood flooring sparkled and the counters were made from freshly polished granite. Tall windows on the opposite side of the house gave a spectacular view over the tree tops of sparse islands and the open sea beyond. It was a dream home, and it certainly caught Jim by surprise.

While pulling a manila envelope off the kitchen counter, Cheryl said, "I know what you must be thinking. How could someone afford all of this on a harbormaster's salary?"

"I guess the thought crossed my mind, even though it's none of my business."

Handing the envelope over to the Lieutenant, Cheryl said, "Let's just say, I've come into a little bit of money lately. Actually, I inherited a nice little nest egg from a long lost relative. Rather than retire early and be bored to tears, I decided to invest in a little real estate project."

"Makes sense to me." Jim took the papers out of the envelope and examined them. "This should get me full access to their boat. Thanks, Cheryl. I really appreciate it."

"No problem at all. The judge was happy to sign it." Cheryl Lawson flashed a pretty smile and said, "Now. Go nail those bastards."

"Not sure there will be anything to nail them on. They seem to be the victims here."

She shook her head. "I don't buy that for a second. You and I both know that something's going on out there."

Turning back toward the main entry, Jim said, "I

would agree with you on that point. I'll let you know what we turn up, Cheryl. Thanks again."

Before Jim got too far down the hallway, Cheryl offered, "Come back again when you can stay longer. I'd love to have you over for dinner sometime."

"That'd be great. Can I bring a date? Maggie would love the view from up here."

Frowning, Cheryl said, "Not exactly what I had in mind, Jim."

"I know." Jim nodded and saw himself out the door.

# Chapter 29

Preparations for *Traverse the Trail* were in full swing.
The three members of the Cranbrook Culture Club sat in
*Porty's* at a corner booth to discuss the final plans. The bar was
abuzz with the usual afternoon clientele, but also supported an
influx from the newfound tourist boom. Most of the locals
either sat at the counter drinking cans of beer or stood close to
the dartboard sharing pitchers. Many of the tourists gathered
around tables or in booths. One could tell the difference
between the locals and the tourists simply by the way they
dressed. Two bottles of champagne sat open at the corner
booth, one empty and one recently popped.

"I say we make 'em suffer." Phyllis Prescott's words
slurred. The first bottle of booze had gone straight to her
head. "It wasn't no picnic for Ellen Cranbrook. So why
should this be any different?"

"Because, we're actually hoping for a couple of good
Yelp reviews." Shasta Wilford was trying to be the level head
in the group. "It's all Yelp reviews these days, ladies. If we
show this first group of *Traversers* a good time, encourage them
to give us five-stars with comments, we won't have to do
nearly as much recruiting down at the floatplane docks for our
next adventure outings. I bet ladies would be flying in here
exclusively for our event. Soon, we could triple our fee."

Angel Yu topped off their three glasses. "I want to
talk about our next time to Cliff Baah's house. We need more
explosives. Make his mail box go boom again."

Shasta said, "Focus, ladies. This meeting of the CCC is to discuss our final preparations for the TTT. Now, did either of you buy batteries for our handhelds…"

Phyllis blurted, "Remind me, what do you got against that guy, Cliff, anyway." She belched loudly from the champagne. "I mean, besides being a man, of course. Why are we sticking it to him so bad?"

Loudly, Angel Yu said, "He bad writer. He bad man. Cliff Baah need to pay." Angel Yu guzzled the contents of her champagne flute and reached again for the bottle.

Determined to keep the club's meeting on track with the agenda, Shasta said, "Okay, I guess it's agreed all the way around. Cliff Barr is a man-pig and will continue to be the focus of our CCC community cleansing outreach program, however, we need to finalize our shopping list for…"

"He man-pig shit-weasel." Angel started to giggle.

"Shit-weasel." Phyllis burped again, and joined in the laughter.

It was obvious that the champagne had gotten to two-thirds of the club's membership. Shasta Wilford needed to take a break. "Excuse me for a moment, ladies." She got up from the table and made her way toward the restroom. Halfway across the bar, Shasta was accosted by two identical looking women with big noses and matching safari hats.

"We are so looking forward to the little adventure outing," one of the women said in a British accent.

The other twin chimed in eagerly, "And we are quite prepared for anything that might befall us during the excursion." Both women patted a holster that hung from just one of their belts.

Shasta's eyes widened as she took in the major heat they were packing. "Not sure you'll be needing that thing, ladies. We should have everything under control." After realizing the sheer magnitude of the side arm, she added, "That gun's huge. You know, we are going to be doing a lot of hiking. Doesn't it weigh you down with it hanging on your hip like that?"

"We take turns," the first twin replied.

The second twin added, "And you can never be too sure about what might be lurking in the shadows. Tah tah." The Smelk twins giggled as they shuffled towards the bar to schmooze with the locals.

One twin leaned into the other and asked, "Is it my turn yet?"

Entering the cold back room of the medical clinic, Jim walked up close to the metal exam table, taking his stance next to the tall, blonde coroner with black rimmed glasses. The fluorescent lights on the low ceiling buzzed overhead. A moveable, circular exam light was positioned above the table, shining a bright beam straight down upon a deathly white corpse with no feet. A towel had been place over the naked body's midriff.

"Dr. Dooley, what have you got for me?" Jim peered over the shoulder of the tall lady doctor.

In a calm, calculated tone, Kim Dooley replied, "You

already know this, but I have confirmed that the foot recovered earlier does not belong to this young man. I haven't had time to perform the autopsy yet, but I have a pretty good sense of cause of death."

"Explosives?"

"Yes. Look here." The coroner pointed with a gloved finger to several lacerations on the torso. "These were made at the time of death. There are several just like it all over the body. These weren't caused by shrapnel of any kind, either, but rather by the sheer force of a blast."

Jim asked, "So, we're ruling out pipe bombs?"

Moving her finger down toward the upper thigh, Kim Dooley said, "And look here. Floating in the water for a time certainly had a cleansing effect on the body, but there are still several burn marks evident. They appear to be consistent with nitroglycerine burns."

"Nitro? Then I guess these burns aren't likely a result of a gasoline explosion? I kept thinking someone was torching the gas can of the inflatable rafts."

"Not likely. That may have been a residual effect of the initial blast. Also, I think it is likely that the body was launched pretty far in the air as a result of the explosion. Look at this bruising." The doctor pointed out large dark patches across the rib cage. "Again, this was caused at the time of death, and there are no matching indications on the victim's backside."

Jim stepped away from the table. "Best guess, doc."

"Dynamite. I'm not an expert here, but I'd say one or two sticks, detonated at close proximity to the shins. All indications support that theory." The pretty, blonde doctor pushed her glasses up with the knuckle of her gloved right hand.

"Dynamite? Isn't that a little too…Yosemite Sam?"

"Hey, I just call 'em like I see 'em."

"Two sticks of dynamite and…*that's all folks.*" Jim made the phrase sound corny.

"That's Porky Pig."

"Close enough." Taking another step back, Jim asked, "I know you said that the foot we brought in previously doesn't belong to this body, but are the wounds consistent?"

Kim nodded. "Absolutely. The break patterns of the leg bones, tear patterns in the flesh and muscle… It's a match. I would conjecture that both of these men died in the exact same manner. A dynamite charge was detonated at close range to both of their legs below the knee." The doctor's voice changed from official to caring, "What's going on out there, Jim? Is someone making dynamite landmines or something?"

"I don't think so." Pacing next to the cadaver, Jim thought aloud. "So these Planet Patrol guys are buzzing around in their little inflatable rafts, and someone, somehow gets close enough to drop in a couple sticks of dynamite at their feet. Does the bomber just ride up in another boat? How does the dynamite get detonated without impacting the bomber?"

"You're the investigator. I'm just the pretty doctor."

Jim smiled at the coroner. "Didn't you mean to say that I'm the handsome investigator."

"Down boy. I'm happily married."

"And I'm happily in a relationship."

"Then it's agreed. Just friendly flirting." The smirking doctor pulled her gloves off, tossing them into a trash can.

Jim popped open his cell phone and punched a couple of buttons. After a few seconds, Jim said into the phone, "Stilly. I want you to check something out. Locate every source of dynamite on the island. Every blasting company, or supply outlet. Check with the barge lines for incoming shipments. There's got to be some pretty intense Federal regs on this stuff, so it should be easy to track. Also, find out if any dynamite has been reported stolen or missing recently."

After hanging up his cell phone, Jim made his way for the door. "Thanks, Doc. You do good work."

"Say hi to Maggie for me. And I heard that your mom's in town. How's that going?"

"I feel like I'm neglecting her. If only people would stop getting blown up by dynamite."

"If only…" Kim Dooley flashed her smile as she again pushed up her black rim glasses with her knuckle.

# Chapter 30

The hum of a portable generator filtered in through the walls of the log cabin. A single light bulb dangled from the ceiling, gently drifting above a table littered with wires and small tools. Two maroon tubes were being gently held by gloved hands while black electrical tape was wrapped tightly at both ends. Two wires bent away from the tops of the blasting caps that had been secured onto the two maroon tubes. The wires were tied and taped together, and then attached to a small, radio-controlled ignition device. The small electronic device was taped securely in place, centrally positioned between the two sticks of dynamite. A battery was inserted into the electronic igniter, and a small, red LED light illuminated just below a tiny, but thick antenna.

The explosive device was gently laid on top of a wooden table and swaddled tightly in plastic wrap. The killer's gloved hands carefully placed the bomb inside a clear, plastic bag. The open end of the bag was fed into a slot of a vacuum sealer, and soon, the bomb was perfectly watertight. An epoxy mix was applied to one side of the explosive package and a circular magnet, about the size of a hockey puck, was firmly adhered to the plastic encasement. The sealed dynamite bomb was gently placed on a high shelf in order for the epoxy to set, securing the magnet in place. Lying next to the explosive device on the shelf was a waterproof radio trigger. Hung close to the high shelf was a black wet suit, black diving gloves, scuba mask, and regulator. Below the wet suit sat a scuba tank and fins. On a low shelf to the side of the scuba tank sat a fresh copy of a lone book. The book's cover displayed the title, *Muskeg Mama: Memoir of a Klondike Girl.*

Lieutenant Wekle and Trooper Sitzel stood on the back deck of the *Earth's Guardian* while Hugh Eckley's Boston Whaler drifted just off the starboard side of the larger ship. Jim served Pierre Lemieux with the papers that legally authorized a complete search of the vessel. Lemieux's eyes were bloodshot and his cheeks ruddy. His wispy hair appeared disheveled. He had the look of a forlorn man.

"Looks like you are down to only two inflatables, Mr. Lemieux," Jim said after scanning the back deck and seeing four empty stalls.

Staring off the side of the ship, not making eye contact with either of the Troopers, Pierre Lemieux said, "Casualties of war."

Jim asked, "And just what war is that, Pierre? The war to protect the environment? Or is there something else going on? It seems to me you've lost momentum with the local anti-fishing movement, yet, here you are. Still floating around Hooligan Arm." After getting nothing in response, Jim instructed, "Pierre, I want all of your crewmen on deck immediately. I will question you and your men while Trooper Sitzel conducts a full search inside your ship. As you can see by the court order, this is a legal search process. This search is in response to evidence that suggests two of your crew have been killed recently, and we have reason to believe these deaths were not an accident. Do you understand, Mr. Lemieux?"

Eyes still fixed on the horizon, Pierre calmly

responded, "Do what you must. I will do the same."

Jim nodded at Brandi, signaling her to get to work. He turned back to the short, white haired man. "Now, just what does that mean?"

"Do you believe in the Yin and Yang of the universe, Lieutenant Wekle? The concept that true balance is inevitable?" Pausing for effect, Pierre continued, "Well I do. And I also believe that we often must find that balance on our own. The universe doesn't always hand you that balance on a silver platter, but, rather, sometimes you must go out in search of balance independently."

"I'm not sure what you're getting at, Pierre."

Pierre finally moved his eyes and fixed his gaze on Jim. "They took my own flesh and blood, Lieutenant."

"Who? Who did this to your nephew? That's what I'm here trying to determine, and anything you can say on the subject would certainly help."

Continuing as if Jim's questions were never asked, Pierre said, "And now they will pay. The universe will balance itself, Lieutenant. I'll see to that."

After parking his Toyota Rav4 in front of his recently charred duplex, Cliff Barr squeezed on a pink and purple helmet and straddled the rear half of a Vespa scooter seat. Kram pulled out of the Williwaw Drive with the scooter bogging down some, riding a bit top-heavy. They buzzed along Port St. Nicholas Road with Ciff Barr clutching on dramatically from behind, pressing the side of his helmet into the driver's back. After parking in Jim's empty gravel lot, the two men jogged down the boat ramp to the Lund skiff that bobbed alongside the dock.

"Come here and help me. We might need one of these." Kram busied himself with the removal of one of the potato canons from the starboard gunwale of the boat.

Fascinated by his newfound friend, Cliff asked, "What the hell is that thing?"

While turning the handle of a socket wrench, Kram answered, "This, my friend, is liberty. Life. The American way. Good old fashioned ingenuity."

"It looks like a septic drain pipe."

"It's a cannon, my eyebrow enhanced Bohemian, and it might be just the thing we need to exact revenge on those Hell's Angels of Williwaw Drive." Kram finished removing the potato gun from the boat and carried it up the ramp, allowing it to rest against the side of his scooter. "When this is all done, I might have to see about mounting this sucker on the Vespa."

After returning to the boat with a couple of grocery bags that were stored in the scooter's rear compartment, Kram hopped in the skiff and fired up the outboard. "Wait here," he instructed as he pushed off, leaving Cliff Barr to watch him cross over to Mink Island.

Kram reached the dock on the small island, lifted the grocery bags safely from the skiff, and quickly crossed back over to the Prince of Wales side of the bay. After securing the skiff to two boat cleats, Kram stepped out of the boat and walked to the edge of the dock. He dove into the water headfirst, popping up seconds later to holler, "Come on Cliff. Let's go."

"What the hell are you talking about? That water's freezing."

"The skiff needs to stay here for Jimbo. He gets a little testy when I don't leave him the boat. Come on, let's go. We need to start cooking if we are going to have dinner ready in time." Kram spoke in an earnest tone, treading water.

"Why did you run the boat across a minute ago?"

"Well, I couldn't just let the groceries get all soggy, now, could I. Have you seen what saltwater does to lard?"

"Couldn't you have dropped me off with the grocery bags?"

In an ordering tone, Kram said, "You, my friend, are in training. Proper revenge tactics takes proper education. I am prepared to offer you the full Kram experience. Remember my previous comment regarding liberty, life, and the American way? I am about to impart my secrets for obtaining all three of those topics. This is a once in a lifetime offer, Cliffy. All you have to do is trust my tutelage and get in this water."

After taking a moment to muster the courage, Cliff Barr ran straight off the end of the dock, feet and arms still flailing when he hit the water. Once surfacing, he let out a high-pitched wheeze, "Aaaaack."

"Hot damn," Kram shouted at the top of his lungs. His voice echoed off the mountains surrounding the cove. "Let it out, Cliffy, my boy. Hot damn!"

After fighting off a shiver and gathering his strength, Cliff Barr squeaked, "Hot damn!"

"That's it, my protégé. You've just taken your first step towards a better life. Now swim, dammit, swim. Swim like the dolphin that's in your soul."

The two men made a beeline through the saltwater, plunging their arms into the chilled sea as they made the short crossing to the small, tree-covered island. Halfway across, Kram stated, "Again, we've got to do something about that name. Cliff Barr... Sounds like something out of an old episode of *L.A. Law*."

# Chapter 31

Jim, Maggie, and Vera all sat at Lookout Rock beneath tall cedar boughs, surrounded by moss, ferns, and blueberry plants. They gazed out at a receding tide that exposed a long stretch of orange-brown seaweed on the rocks across the bay. Oscar the mink hung close to Jim's leg, hoping for a snack to be dropped. Maggie sat on a wooden chair close to Jim. Vera Wekle sat opposite, bundled up head to toe in winter garb.

"Are you still cold, Mom?"

"The blanket helps. Thank you, Maggie, for bringing one out to me. You're such a sweet girl."

Maggie squeezed Jim's arm in a pleasing way. She said, "Doesn't feel too cold to us locals, but I guess it's usually a little warmer in San Diego."

Vera Wekle replied, "So nice of your two friends in there to prepare us a special dinner. I feel honored."

"You are an honored guest, Mrs. Wekle," Maggie said.

Directing the reply toward her son, Vera said, "She's so nice and polite, Jim. Hang on to this pretty young lady."

Suddenly, Kram sprinted down the boardwalk holding a bucket. He frantically bypassed Lookout Rock and went straight to the rocky shoreline. He grabbed hold of a thick rope that was tied to a tree branch. The rope extended away from the shore and into the water. Kram pulled the rope in, hand over hand. Soon after retrieving several feet of line, small, black crustaceans appeared on the thick rope. Kram removed individual mussels from the rope, dropping them into the bucket at his feet. After harvesting several dozen shellfish, Kram pulled the remainder of the rope in, exposing a fairly small cement weight that was attached to the end. He lifted the weight and heaved it like a shot-put back out into the seawater, allowing the rope to fully extend from the shore.

"Doesn't get any fresher than this. Won't be long now," Kram exclaimed, jogging past Lookout Rock back to the yurt.

After Kram disappeared, Maggie asked quietly, "Who is this guy that's helping Kram cook tonight?"

Vera replied, "Claims to be a…and I quote…'protégé in training.' Kram made him swim out here."

Jim said, "His name's Cliff Barr. I met him a few days back on a call."

"Oh, the four-wheeler guy. He seemed pretty fragile back when he called in," Maggie said.

"I'm sure Kram will whip him into shape." Turning his attention to his mother, Jim asked, "You sure you still want to go on this overnight hike tomorrow, Mom? If you're cold now, it won't get any warmer in the middle of the night. Plus, what if the weather turned crummy? I'd feel bad if you got drenched and spent the night shivering."

"I'll be fine. Besides, I checked the weather report. The forecast looks good."

Jim smiled at Maggie and said, "And we all know how accurate weather forecasts are in Alaska."

Maggie said, "I'm looking forward to a little girl-time

with Vera, tomorrow. I think it'll be fun. By the way, thanks for the day off tomorrow, boss."

Vera chimed in, "He'd *better* give you the day off tomorrow. Should be a *paid* vacation day, too."

"Let's not get carried away, now, Mom."

Soon, Cliff Barr appeared on the boardwalk, holding a wine bottle in one hand and a coffee thermos in the other. He gave both ladies a refill on their wine glasses before filling Jim's empty coffee mug. Standing tall like a waiter, clothes still damp from the swim, salt beginning to crust on the tips of his matted hair, Cliff spoke in a rehearsed monotone, "Dinner will be served in three courses this evening. First, I will be delivering smoked sockeye on brie, followed by the main course of breaded mussels deep fried in lard with Chef Kram's special spicy mayonnaise, and lastly, I will be serving a salmonberry tart, prepared with sugar-crusted lemon zest. After-dinner entertainment will feature the Rainforest Drum and Dance Troupe. Will you be needing anything to make your meal more enjoyable at the Mink Island Bistro?"

Maggie gave him a wide smile. "That sounds lovely, Cliff. Thank you very much."

Again, in an almost hypnotic monotone, "I've been instructed to inform you that, from now on, I shall be called C-Barr the Seadog. Thank you." The writer-turned-waiter spun around and returned to his duties in the kitchen.

"C-Barr the Seadog?" Maggie muttered.

Jim nodded. "Sounds like Kram has found himself a little project. It's probably good for both of them."

Dinner was fantastic. Each course's visual

presentation was only outdone by the savory flavors. C-Barr proved to be a reliable aid to Kram's culinary craft. Jim, Maggie, and Vera enjoyed the pleasant evening of food and conversation. They laughed as Vera told stories of the trials and tribulations of a young Jimmie Wekle. The ladies found common ground when it came to teasing their man. Maggie asked Vera all about Jim's upbringing, elementary school bullies, junior high awkwardness, high school prom dates, his extended family, father, and siblings. Jim let his mother do most of the talking, with small interjections from time to time. They smiled, laughed, and enjoyed the moment.

Soon after dessert dishes were cleared, C-Barr the Seadog appeared before the diners. He had black and red warpaint streaks on his cheeks. Cliff took an uncomfortable pose, freezing in place, and said, "I have been instructed to tell you that the entertainment portion of the evening is about to begin. Please forgive me. He's making me do this."

Kram leaped from behind a bush and dramatically stuck a landing on the boardwalk. He had matching warpaint on his cheeks and carried a wooden African-style drum. Kram burst into an enraged solo on the instrument with his hands blasting into the goat-hide drumhead in a furious blur. After reaching the climax of his introduction, Kram slammed one last hit with his palm and deeply yelled, "Hah!" The sound of Kram's guttural projection startled Mrs. Wekle. Maggie caught Jim's eye and they both offered a flirtatious smile. Kram froze in place, building tension, then slowly started an infectious groove.

As soon as the slow groove began, C-Barr the Seadog slithered his shoulders and gyrated his hips. The man's impromptu dance moves eerily mimicked that of a boa constrictor sneaking up on an unsuspecting prey. Kram bellowed out an innocuous melody in a mix of Spanish, Swahili, and English. Kram's melancholy song floated above the drum beat as his newfound friend slinked awkwardly before the small crowd.

"See-ya-hamba ku-ka-ne-kwen-kos, nos vemos mas tarde, C-Barr the Seeeea-dog." Kram crooned his mixed dialect verbiage as the drum beat slowly increased in intensity. As the rumble of the African drum rose in tempo and timbre, C-Barr's gyrations steadily became more spastic. The hand drum pattern soon became quick and skilled, rising to a high intensity peak. The dancer's improvisations reacted to the change in rhythm by jerkily turning from side to side, arms out in front as some sort of mix between the robot dance and Frankenstein on speed.

"Movimiento, Senor C-Barr." Kram repeated the melodic fragment multiple times as the drum bursts flashed, faster and faster, increasing to a fury previously unmatched. C-Barr the Seadog's bodily reactions resembled a mix between a weeble-wobble and a windsock. Suddenly, without warning, Kram slammed both hands into the drum twice, screaming each word in rhythm, "Hot - Damn!"

On cue, the dancer froze in place, his left arm extended and his right hand covering his crotch. Cliff's facial expression was one of placid disbelief. Kram stood and announced, "The Rainforest Drum and Dance Troupe. Thank you, thank you. Enjoy the rest of your evening here at the Mink Island Bistro. Let's hear it for C-Barr the Seadog and his inaugural improvised torso convulsions. Thank you, thank you. C-Barr…C-Barr…C-Barr…"

All three patrons of the Mink Island Bistro offered steady applause. Maggie put her thumb and finger in her mouth and whistled loudly. After taking a grand bow, Kram pushed the still-frozen dancer off the boardwalk toward the shoreline. Both men ran frantically, splashing into the cold water, swimming away toward the opposite shore.

"That was…unique," Vera Wekle commented, searching for the right adjective.

"Kram is…unique," replied Jim.

Maggie added, "He seems legitimately excited to have a new friend."

"A Kram-in-training? I don't know about that. This island might only be big enough for one." Jim chuckled. "It's good for him to have a project, I guess. I think he's been bored lately. Kram's started taking on part-time jobs all over the island."

"Hasn't the man had steady income in the past?" Vera asked. "How does he pay the bills? How could he afford to own this island, not to mention other property, without income?"

Maggie replied, "You know that song from the early eighties, *Hair of the Frog*? By the band, Axe Attack?"

Vera nodded. "I'm not much for rock 'n roll, but I think I recognize the title."

"I'm sure you've heard it on the radio a hundred times or more. It's even been used in several movies," Jim interjected.

"Anyway, he wrote that song," Maggie said. "And

many more like it. He was the founding member of Axe Attack."

"He was the heart and soul of that band and they made quite a bit of money," Jim said.

"They've toured the world."

Vera asked, "How did he get to be so…odd?"

Jim took over. "A combination of things. Hard to pinpoint. Some of it, it's just how he is, I'm sure. But he experienced some pretty tough stuff back in Vietnam. Things that would make most men run and hide. Kram won't open up about his service to me very often, but when he does, it's pretty shocking. He was in a unit that, well, I guess they got called in only for special assignments. And believe me, they got things done. He made it out, though. Both physically and mentally. Honestly, I think he survived it through music. And now, he's surviving by being one of the most unique characters on an island full of eccentricity."

"I can tell that he loves you very much, Jim. You're lucky to have such a friend." After a slight lull in the conversation, Vera stood and said, "It's getting late and we have a big day tomorrow. I'm going to turn in. You two enjoy some peace and quiet out here, okay?" She kissed both Jim and Maggie on the cheek before shuffling off toward the yurt.

Maggie scooted her chair close to Jim and leaned on his shoulder. "Alone, at last."

Putting his arm around her, Jim said, "I have something I want to tell you."

"Okay. What is it?"

"I'm glad that the two of you are going on the overnight hike together."

Maggie seemed to lean into Jim a little more. "Oh, yeah?"

"In fact, I'm glad that the two of you are getting to know each other. I know that Mom wouldn't be up here now if it hadn't been for you. You've taken the initiative to encourage her being here, and her getting to know you. Honestly, I think that's great."

"I wasn't so sure you felt that way."

"I do. And I think you should keep making those kind of independent decisions regarding our relationship. Thanks, Maggie."

Maggie beamed. She lifted her head from Jim's shoulder and stared into his eyes. She leaned in and they kissed passionately, alone on Lookout Rock.

# Chapter 32

Clouds steadily rolled in through the night, covering the moon in a blanket of darkness. Pierre Lemieux had given his orders to the skeleton crew that remained. They lowered the two surviving inflatable rafts from the stern of the *Earth's Guardian* to the surface of the water below. He had lost two of his crewmen, including his own flesh and blood. He had lost four of his small boats; two to explosives and two due to an enraged and confused bear. His organization had been attacked repeatedly, his vessel the subject of a search warrant, and his files and logs confiscated as evidence. In addition, his current enterprise had been a complete bust. Nightly dive missions had provided absolutely no evidence of a sunken steamship. No gold was recovered, nor anything of value. Expenses were mounting and cash flow deteriorating. Pierre Lemieux was exasperated, humiliated, angry, and at the end of his rope.

Stepping off the ladder and into the lead raft, Pierre instructed his crewman, "Hit it." The outboard engines of the two inflatables throttled up and the men sped away from their ship in the direction of the City of Craig. It didn't take long before the lights of the town glistened across the water. As they neared the breakwater that protected the marina, Pierre gave the cue, and both outboard engines were killed. Aluminum oars with plastic paddles quickly appeared and the two boats made a near silent approach in past the breakwater.

Knowing full well that there were several boats in the harbor that housed live-aboards, Pierre knew that their current mission would require complete stealth. Armed with power tools pertinent to their usual underwater missions, three crewmen wearing scuba gear, quietly slipped off the side of the rafts into the water. Pierre Lemieux selected the targets by relaying hand signals. Underwater lights were illuminated and the divers submerged.

Three divers, each carrying an underwater drill, selected locations near the keel of the three separate commercial fishing vessels that their boss had chosen. One was a smaller craft with markings of a hand-troller. The other two boats were large purse-seiners, each with a small metal boat pulled up on the stern below the large wheel of the net pulley. With the bulk of the sound insulated by the depth of the water, three large drill bits simultaneously spun into action. Dull grinding sounds rose to the surface from the three boats, but within seconds, the sounds stopped and the divers emerged. Handing up lights and tools first, the divers were pulled back aboard the inflatables by the dry crew that remained. The two boats made a silent exit from the marina under oar power before outboards were fired up outside the breakwater. The two inflatable rafts sped away from town towards their anchorage in Hooligan Arm, leaving behind three fishing boats, moored in the harbor, severely taking on water into their bilges.

A diver wearing a full wetsuit, mask, tank, and fins carefully slipped into the water from the rocky shore, hidden by the darkness of the moonless night. The diver submerged several feet below the surface and kicked hard with fins, propelling through the current toward the middle of the bay. As darkness consumed the diver's path, a small waterproof light was illuminated, allowing the diver to monitor directionality. It took several minutes of hard swimming, but soon a wide, white object curved down from the surface, plunging several feet into the water. The diver followed the white ship's hull from the bow to the stern, inspecting both sides of the vessel.

Selecting a place close to the dormant ship's propellers, protected from the ever-changing currents, the diver reached out a gloved hand and secured a waterproof package to the hull of the *Earth's Guardian*. The magnet grabbed onto the metal hull of the ship, quickly slapping into place with a muffled clang. The diver then extended a narrow, insulated wire antenna from the waterproof bomb packaging. The antenna was brought up the stern of the boat, quietly secured just above the surface of the water with a marine adhesive. Knowing full well that radio frequencies do not penetrate saltwater well, the diver positioned the triggering system so it could connect through open air.

The diver turned, submerged, and kicked hard, swimming back toward the shore across the cove. After removing fins and climbing carefully up the rocks, the diver made a short trek into the trees, returning to the rustic cabin that was fully hidden in the woods. With a desire to fully view the carnage, the diver would wait until daylight before hitting the radio-frequency detonator, sending the Planet Patrol vessel on a fatal plunge into the icy depths of Hooligan Arm.

At five-twenty-eight in the morning, Jim's cell phone rang next to his head as he slept on the couch. He grabbed the phone, hoping to not wake his sleeping mother, Jim punched a button and softly said, "Wekle." Trooper Sitzel informed her boss that she had received a call from Emergency Call Center regarding a situation down at the marina in town. Being the on-call Trooper for the night, she had already geared up and investigated the scene.

"You should probably get down here, Jim. It's pretty ugly. People are starting to gather, too."

"I'll be there in twenty minutes. Better wake up Stilly and get him down there. Try to keep a lid on the situation in the meantime."

Foregoing the shower, Jim dressed in a matter of seconds and was securing his pistol when his mother sat up in bed and asked, "Duty calls?"

"Yes, Mom. I have to run. Maggie will be out to pick you up in a couple of hours. You be safe, dress warm, and have fun on your hike." Jim bent down and gave his mother a hug.

After a very quick crossing in the skiff, Jim fired up his Ford Crown Victoria State Trooper's car, and tore onto the highway, lights flashing and siren blaring. Given the early morning hour, the road into town was empty and Jim pulled up to the marina in record time. A small horde of people had amassed on the docks, several taking pictures with their phones. Hanging from dock lines tethered to wooden slips that were visibly sunken due to the added weight, three of the commercial fishing boats docked in the marina bent at unnatural angles as they were partially submerged with the inside of their hulls full of water.

Jim jogged down the ramp, coming up next to his Trooper with a blonde ponytail hanging below her Stetson. "This is really bad, Jim."

"Any fatalities or injuries?"

"No, we're lucky there. All three boats sat empty last night. But it's pretty obvious this was malicious. Two purse seiners and a hand-troller just happen to take on water and sink, on the same night, in the same harbor, all by chance? No way."

Jim was concerned. "Agreed. Any idea on the cause, yet?"

"They didn't wait around to find out," Trooper Sitzel answered.

"What do you mean?"

"Gretch and his boys loaded up in Sig Hanson's boat and pulled out a couple of minutes ago. They were carrying guns, Jim. I think they mean business."

Reaching in his pocket for his cell phone, Jim replied to his Trooper, "I don't doubt it. There's a war about to take place and you and I are about to put ourselves in the middle of it."

As Jim punched a couple buttons on his phone, Trooper Stilhaven pulled in and ran down the ramp. Brandi filled in the younger Trooper while Jim spoke on the phone.

Pocketing the phone, Jim said, "Stilly, you get on your cell and wake up the Harbormaster. We need her down here to assess the damage and make a plan for recovering these boats. Also, get her to download last night's video footage from the breakwater cam. I want to see exactly who it was that sank these."

"I could give you a pretty good guess," Stilly said.

Sternly, Jim said, "Well, I want proof. I'm not going off half-cocked like Gretch and the boys. Stilly, I want you down here on the waterfront all morning. If any other pissed-off fishermen load up in a boat carrying guns, don't let them out of the harbor. Any info you get, call me immediately. You may have to use the marine radio if we get out of cell range."

"Sure thing, boss. Where are you guys heading?"

Jim pulled a cigar from his shirt pocket, bit off the end, and said, "Hugh Eckely's on the way to take us out on his boat. Brandi, go pull the shotguns from our cars. We need to put a stop to this before there's any more damage. We're heading out to Hooligan Arm."

# Chapter 33

As much as it made his brain hurt, Zeke Melon did the math. He sat in his odor-laced one-bedroom hovel and crunched numbers on the back of a gas pump receipt. He calculated that, if he could sell two hundred and fifty hooligan candles per week he'd make more money by the end of the summer tourist season than he would after an entire year of pumping septic tanks. Both jobs tended to be extremely smelly, but Zeke would take the seasonal stench of oily fish drying over the smell of year-round festering poop any day. The problem was with supply. He didn't quite have enough of the little fish in order to meet his projected sales, and the window for the Hooligan spawn was quickly coming to a close. Zeke needed to go fishing, and soon.

So he called up his boss and requested an extended leave of absence due to the recent traumas of recovering various dead body parts. After Zeke laid it on thick, conjuring up quite the flair of stuttered words, his boss didn't have any trouble buying the story and fully granted his leave request. Zeke gathered up his dip-net, cooler, snacks, and a generous supply of Nyquil and loaded it all into the back of his Datsun pickup. He pulled away from his home just as a ponytailed man parked a baby-blue Vespa scooter in front of his neighbor's side of the duplex.

Zeke parked close to the pier and carried his gear down the ramp at the marina. He noticed that a rather large crowd had gathered on the docks next to some damaged fishing boats. As he passed the crowd on his way to the

Smokercraft, a young State Trooper eyeballed him suspiciously.
Ignoring the stink-eye from the law enforcement officer, Zeke
loaded up his boat, topped off the gas tank with one of his
jerry-jugs, and fired up the outboard engine. Tossing dock
lines into the bow and stern, Zeke Melon slowly putted out of
the marina and past the breakwater before gunning the engine
and steering his boat toward Hooligan Arm.

After watching a Datsun pickup leave the other side of
the duplex, Kram hopped off the Vespa scooter and trotted up
to Cliff Barr's front door. He quietly tried the door handle and
found it to be unlocked. Cracking open the door several
inches, Kram stuck a handheld boat horn inside the small
apartment and pulled the trigger, filling the duplex with a high-
decibel squeal that would wake a hibernating grizzly bear.

Kram pocketed the boat horn and yelled, "Come on,
C-Barr. Early eagle gets the humpy carcass."

A blurry-eyed man wearing flannel pajamas opened
the door wide and said, "I don't know about today, Kram. I've
got a deadline to meet. Two thousand words on humpback
whale bubble feeding for the *Alaskan Gazette*."

"Nonsense. Today's a big day in your training. We've
got a camp-host gig out the road, and not a moment to spare.
I'll start packing your car. You go get dressed."

Rubbing sleep from his left eye socket, Cliff asked,
"What kind of training is this, exactly? I thought you were
going to help me with defending against the four-wheeler gang.
Don't get me wrong. Last night was kind of fun, except for

the swimming and interpretive dance..."

"You want full-buck C-Barr the Seadog status don't you? Well, that kind of title isn't just handed out, gift wrapped with a purdy little bow on top. And it certainly can't be achieved by sitting around mashing down keys on a typewriter."

"I use a laptop, actually..."

"Suck it up, C-Barr. That's an order. We've got a few stops to make before heading out to the campsite." Turning his attention to the Toyota Rav4, Kram said, "Good to see you've got a tow-package on this thing. How does it handle off-road? I guess we'll find out. All-wheel-drive might come in handy today. You ever push your suspension to its limits? Now go inside and fetch me your best pair of blue jeans while I strap the potato canon to the roof of your car."

Cliff disappeared back into the duplex while Kram busied himself with the potato canon. Moments later, the writer opened his door and handed out a brand new pair of Levi's. Kram whipped out an old pocket knife laced in fish scales and bounded up to the door. Snatching the jeans from Cliff's outstretched arm, Kram made quick work out of turning the pants into a fresh set of jean cut-offs.

Tossing the ragged shorts back inside, Kram hollered, "Put these on immediately and get out here. Our day is just beginning."

Maggie used Jim's skiff to pick up Vera Wekle from Mink Island. After going through a mental checklist of items in their backpacks, Maggie drove to the pier near the floatplane dock where the two women loaded into a short, chartered bus with several other female passengers. The bus left the docks and made its way south, down the island, turning onto an old logging road that meandered deep into the rainforest. After traveling several miles down the bumpy path, the bus stopped at an open clearing where three elderly ladies stood, each holding a helmet under their armpits, with one foot propped up on a four-wheeled ATV. The three ladies were decked out head to toe in full riding gear. The passengers disembarked from the bus, mounted up their backpacks, and awaited instructions from the event organizers.

One of the group leaders straddled her four-wheeler and announced, "Welcome, ladies, to an adventure of a lifetime. We will now traverse the trail that was once followed by Ellen Cranbrook, herself. You will see firsthand the rugged beauty of this land and will begin to understand the trials and tribulations that Ms. Cranbrook must have experienced back in that fateful summer of 1896."

Another lady shouted with a thick Asian accent, "We will begin our hike now. Follow me as we delve deep into the woods on the jooney to Hooligan Ahm, the sight of the faaaamous sinking of the *SS Abe'deen*." The Chinese woman started up her ATV and punched it into gear, slowly rolling up the logging road, heading further south into the trees. The backpackers all followed on foot, beginning their adventurous hike with the other two four-wheelers following close behind.

Vera said, "This is so exciting. Thanks for doing this with me, Maggie."

"I'm glad to be here, too, Vera. It is great to get to

spend time with you, especially on a hike like this."

"You know, my Jimmy really cares for you. I can tell."

Maggie let a small grin show. "I hope so. Vera, I really like him."

In a confident tone, Vera Wekle replied, "I know."

A woman hiking just behind, wearing a safari hat and a holstered sidearm, said in a British accent, "I hope we see some bears."

An identical looking woman dressed in matching attire, but without a holstered weapon replied, "Of course you do, you're wearing Clint. Isn't it about my turn yet?"

Maggie turned. "Did I hear you right? You named your gun, *Clint?*"

One of the British birds replied, "Of course."

The other added, "For obvious reasons."

Into the Alaskan wilderness, the caravan of women traveled. They took breaks every half-mile or so, sharing their thoughts about the experience and recounting their favorite parts of the book they had all previously read. They traded snacks along the trail, took pictures of the scenery, gabbed mildly about their personal lives, and truly enjoyed the hike, growing ever closer to their campsite along the shores of Hooligan Arm.

# Chapter 34

*The young Native children would sneak up and touch my arm before scurrying for cover behind the thickets that surrounded the trail. I deduced that their purpose was not to mock or provoke me in any manner, but rather to see if my flesh felt any different than their own darker skin. The women would periodically offer food or dry clothing, nothing more than a piece of dried fish or a hand-woven shawl, but the gesture was much appreciated. The men set the pace, carried weapons of various sorts, and seemed to make the decisions in the group.*

*We traveled only moderately, but I soon came to realize that it was I who slowed their pace. What kindness displayed by my rescuers to alter their traditional travel rate for this alien, white-skinned woman. I pushed forth, making every effort to increase my pursuits of the trail. I stubbornly couldn't accept that I would hold them back in any way. No matter how I tried, though, the elements of our island seemed to best my efforts. When the terrain turned to rocks, I would stub my toe. When it opened to fields, my feet would sink through the moss. When the trail was overtaken by branches, I would snag and tear my clothing. When the rain would fall, it seemed to only soak my clothing. When the wind would blow, it only seemed to chap my lips and cheeks. Were my rescuers impervious to such elements, or were they simply accustomed? On we stepped, unknown to me the purpose or destination. Simply from blind faith and respect did I press on, sensing in my heart and soul that my life would soon achieve purpose. My thoughts propelled each step. "I am a strong woman! I have a purpose in this forsaken land!"*

The twenty-eight foot Boston Whaler with twin Mercury engines barreled through the chop with ease. The white fiberglass hull planed perfectly, creating an amazingly smooth ride at such a high rate of speed, especially considering the small whitecaps that were present on the water's surface. Hugh Eckley's silver hair glistened from the sunlight that glinted through the starboard side window. The boat's operator pushed the throttles hard while sitting behind the wheel of his new boat.

"They've got a bit of a head start on us," Brandi said, sitting in a tall chair across from the skipper.

"We'll catch up to 'em. This thing flies at triple the speed of a purse seiner," Hugh said in a strong voice that carried over the sound of the engines.

Standing on the open back deck, smoking his stogie while holding on to a high handle, Jim spoke loudly, "Hugh, we need to put ourselves directly between the *Lucky Lady* and the Planet Patrol boat."

"This is my brand new boat, Jim. I'm really not fond of the idea of taking bullet holes through the fresh fiberglass."

"Don't worry, Hugh. This is an official trip, so you're protected under the State's insurance plan. The deductible's a little high, but bullet holes surely must be covered."

"Great," replied Hugh, sarcastically.

Trooper Sitzel said, "You really think we are about to head into a war zone, Jim? Would these guys really start shooting?"

After puffing on his cigar, Jim replied, "Do I really think that our local fisherman would shoot someone for deliberately putting a hole in three of their boats? Yes, I do. Our job is to prevent that from happening."

"Are we going to arrest Pierre Lemieux for sinking those boats?"

Jim nodded. "Eventually. I hope so. And we may indeed have to take him into custody right now, just to keep the peace. But first, let's play it cool as we're a little shy on evidence."

"Isn't there a breakwater camera?" Hugh asked. "Shouldn't we be able to at least place Pierre's crew at the marina last night?"

"Absolutely. That's why I ordered Stilly to get in touch with Cheryl Lawson immediately. As soon as Stilly has something, he's supposed to call. He may be calling on VFH if we're out of cell range." Jim turned his head and puffed his imported cigar so that the smoke didn't drift into the covered seating area of the boat.

"I can't figure out what the deal is with this Planet Patrol, boss," Brandi said. "When we searched their ship, we found a ton of diving equipment, underwater electronics, winches and heavy lifting gear. They had the standard array of modern digital navigation, of course, but what I didn't see that you'd expect from an environmental protest boat, was a lab of some kind. Don't you think they'd be taking water samples, soil samples, even marine life specimens, and testing them for data collection? Plus, where were all the scientists? You saw the handful of crewmen on board. Those guys couldn't pass a ninth-grade algebra class, let alone interpret data sets. I really didn't find much of anything that I expected to see."

"I actually found pretty much everything that I expected."

"You don't think their main agenda is related to the

environment, do you boss?"

"No. And I haven't thought that for a while, now." After a puff, Jim continued, "Don't you find it a little odd that, for years, Hooligan Arm has been a fairly uneventful body of water? Then, several months after a new book gets published naming Hooligan Arm as the location of a sunken ship full of Klondike gold, we've got body parts floating up next to a foreign ship full of crooked men and scuba gear."

"You read *Muskeg Mamas*, boss?" Brandi was surprised. "I didn't think it was your kind of read, what, with all the 'woman-power' overtones."

"I skimmed it. Kinda skipped over those woman parts."

"I don't think you should use the term, *woman parts*, in open dialogue, boss."

Hugh Eckley spoke up. "I refuse to read it."

Trooper Sitzel turned her head towards the skipper and asked, defensively, "Why, Hugh? Don't you think it's good to celebrate a woman who persevered through that many hardships? Especially when it occurred right here in our back yard?"

"Of course it's good. But not when it didn't really happen."

"Why do you say that, Hugh?" Jim asked. "I read most of the book. The facts and descriptions of the area all seem authentic to me. With the details presented, the author obviously had spent some time on this island. She did the Hooligan Arm description to a tee."

"Descriptions, true. Storyline, complete fiction," Hugh said gruffly.

"I have a hard time buying that, Hugh. The book's been at the top of the nation-wide non-fiction charts for a few weeks now. What makes you so sure?"

"I have lunch with David Martin every week."

"Who's David Martin?" asked Brandi.

Jim answered, "He is a longtime island resident, and a Tlingit elder."

"The Tlingit clans from this island are tremendously proud of their history," Hugh continued. They've passed detailed stories down through generations, some of which are hundreds of years old. They pride themselves on this tradition. Look, David Martin is eighty-two years old. His father was only a young child in 1896, but his grandfather was an active member, and leader in Klawock. This family lived through the era that was set in this book. There was no Klondike gold rush steamship that sank in Hooligan Arm. There was no Ellen Cranbrook that made it ashore and nursed back to health by the local Tlingit clan. There was no famous trek from the shores of Hooligan Arm to Klawock. In fact, according to David, the clan didn't even fish that cove. The tidal currents were too strong for the techniques they used. There would have been no reason for them to even be there. Look, the book might have a good story in it, and I might have read it if it was billed as fiction. But claiming to be a true happening? I don't buy it, and neither should you."

"There they are." Jim pointed straight through the front windows of the Boston Whaler. The *Lucky Lady* chugged forward, black diesel fumes billowing from the stacks, just about to round the point and turn into Hooligan Arm. Hugh's Boston Whaler was closing on them in a hurry.

Brandi said, "They haven't quite reached the *Earth's Guardian* yet. Looks like we'll get there in time."

"In time for what?" Hugh interjected. "That's the question."

Jim ordered, "Sitzel, you grab both shotguns from under the bow. Hugh, see if you can cut them off quick. Knowing these guys, they might just ram the ship at full speed."

"Great." Again, Hugh with the sarcastic tone.

Lieutenant Wekle shoved the cigar butt into his mouth, chomping down on it with his front teeth. He accepted the shotgun that his Trooper handed to him and held on tight to the handle with his other hand on the back deck. They were about to make a fast turn.


The Boston Whaler blew past Zeke Melon's skiff like it was a jet plane. Zeke had to turn into the wake in order to keep the boat from taking waves over the side.

"S...s...s...some people. Jeez, where's the f...f...f...fire," Zeke muttered to himself, slowing to rock over the wake.

He felt guilty about not showing up to work. The extra, self-induced stuttering that he'd conjured up while speaking on the phone to his boss seemed to have stuck. The combination of guilt and the extra stutter wreaked havoc on not only his nervous system, but also his gastro-intestinal tract.

After his fourth attack of severe flatulence, Zeke decided to medicate. He finished off his first bottle of cold medicine before he even made it halfway across the opening of Port St. Nicholas.

Weaving between small islands, taking the most protected route, Zeke feared that his tolerance for Nyquil had become an issue. Motoring past a small inlet that featured a creek trickling over rocks and emptying into a kelp bed, the redheaded fisherman popped the top on his second bottle of the morning. He snugged up close to shore and slowed his engine while fighting with the childproof cap.

"S...s...s...stupid piece of sh...sh...sh..."

Eventually, after guzzling half the liquid in the bottle, Zeke jammed the throttle open, and quickly planed the aluminum craft, pointing back on course toward his destination. He passed by another cove's opening, bow bouncing in the white-capped chop. Wind whistled through his red hair and across his pale cheeks with an almost mesmerizing effect. Soon, a medicinally charged warm calm crept through his body as he neared the point of land that hid the sight of his destination. He felt relaxed for the first time that day, and felt at one with the rugged nature that surrounded him.

As the point of land that he would soon veer around grew closer into his view, Zeke again opened the bottle of Nyquil, this time chugging every last drop. He tossed the empty bottle at his feet, where it sloshed around in the dirty bilge water with the other bottle he had polished off a few moments before. The intoxication due to the sheer magnitude of drugs in his system mounted as Zeke rounded the corner and pointed the bow of his skiff into the heart of Hooligan Arm. His eyelids grew heavy and his brain fogged. He moved the tiller on the boat's engine as if his arm was forced to push through thick pudding. The wind in his face felt like feathers tickling at his lips and cheeks. He was wholeheartedly stoned.

He had read stories online of youths boasting about the hallucinogenic effect of a Nyquil overdose, but Zeke Melon had always dismissed that as an urban myth. The sight that laid out before him in the middle of the cove suddenly made him consider the validity of such claims. In multiple visits to his favorite fishing grounds, Zeke had seldom seen a lot of boating activity. He was more than surprised to be heading straight for three vessels, all within close proximity to each other, floating in the center of Hooligan Arm.

The large white ship, anchored with the double-p flag flying, he had seen before. It seemed to move in and take residence during several prior fishing trips. The fishing boat that boasted the name, *Lucky Lady*, he had never seen before. The Boston Whaler that sat between the two other crafts was the same boat that had blasted past him just minutes before.

"What the hell is going on out here?" his voice smoothly pronounced. Zeke didn't know what surprised him more, the ease with which he muttered the words, or the sight of people standing, holding rifles, on two of the boats.

The fishing boat held four men on its stern deck below the giant wheel of the seiner's pulley system: one with an auburn beard, one wearing yellow rain pants, one with a large beer belly, and another holding a tall, spiked gaff hook. Auburn beard and yellow rain pants each held a hunting rifle, barrels pointing off to the side. Beer belly and gaff hook each sported pistols that were positioned at the ready in holsters on their belts.

The Boston Whaler had only two people on its back deck, with a third sitting at the wheel inside the covered cabin area. The two people on the back each wore the uniform of an Alaskan State Trooper, one male and one female. Zeke recognized them. They both held shotguns at bay. The male Trooper had a cigar in his mouth and held a bullhorn in his free hand.

A solitary figure was visible high up by the white ship's wheelhouse. On the upper walkway, protected by a thin railing, a short, older man with red cheeks and messy white hair stood somberly while looking down on the commotion. The short man wore white from head to toe, and his hair fluttered in the breeze like sinewy strands of corn silk blowing on a mid-western farm.

Zeke let go of the throttle, allowing the skiff to bog down into a slow drift. He killed the engine and angled his head, attempting to hear anything that made sense out of the confrontation. He thought he heard the white haired man on the large ship yell, "Ass-wipes," but he wasn't sure. Zeke floated silently, allowing the narcotic effect of the cold medicine to fog his brain. He felt removed from reality, almost as if he were attending the drive-in theater back in the hometown of his youth. Several other words were shouted from the boats before him, but nothing that he could comprehend. Suddenly, it became all too real. The cobwebs of his lubricated mind shattered when the adrenaline stormed in. One of the men from the fishing boat and one of the State Troopers in the Boston Whaler had pulled their weapons, taking direct aim at each other.

# Chapter 35

A gloved hand lifted the radio detonator off the shelf inside the remote cabin. The detonator was carried through a wooden door, down a couple of steps, and across a narrow path leading to the rocky shoreline. Crouching near the trunk of an evergreen tree, hidden from sight by its low hanging boughs, the person holding the detonator made sure that the view to the middle of the cove was unobstructed.

A steady breeze created foam-peaked crests on the surface throughout Hooligan Arm. The *Earth's Guardian* stood stoically perched on the water, moving only slightly in the breeze as it hung on the anchor chain. Surprisingly, there were other boats there, too, but that didn't matter. The mission at hand would proceed.

A gloved thumb pressed a switch on the detonator that caused a couple of LED lights to flash to life. It was primed and ready for the final code to be input into the keypad. The person holding the small radio device drew in a steady breath through the nose, exhaling slowly past pursed lips.

In a quiet voice, the person said, "You should have taken the hint, you bastards."

On the quiet, secluded shores of Hooligan Arm, a person sat crouched, hidden in the trees, holding a gloved thumb above a radio device's keypad, ready to press in the ignition code, initiating a destructive blow to the hull of the *Earth's Guardian*.

Kram drove the dark blue Toyota Rav4 with reckless abandon down a Forest Service road barely fit for an off-road vehicle, let alone a modern car. The enclosed trailer that they hauled bounced violently with each pothole they slammed across. He flashed by a row of alder branches that repeatedly slapped the windshield and streaked down one side of the car. Cliff Barr sat stiff as a board in the passenger seat, pretending to jam his foot into an imaginary brake pedal with each looming obstacle.

"Gotta hand it to you, C-Barr. You know how to pick your automobiles. This thing corners like it's on rails." Kram sat upright behind the wheel, hair pulled back into his standard ponytail, grinning like a school boy. The road suddenly curved sharply to the right. Kram rapidly turned the wheel while goosing the accelerator. Gravel spewed from a couple of the blue car's tires as they careened around the curve. "Dynamic torque-controlled all-wheel-drive. Electronically cooled, six-speed transmission. Bet this puppy's fun in the snow."

Cliff said, "Slower is good. We can decelerate, now. Less bumpy. Less of a chance of death."

"Nonsense, C-Barr the Seadog. The topic of today's lesson is, 'lighten up and go with the universal current.' You know, we're all connected by a universal string, quite similar to a guitar string." Kram slammed the accelerator to the floorboard as the Forest Service road began to climb a steep hill. Cliff Barr's face turned white.

Kram babbled on, "This string is floating in space and

time, and, when plucked, creates all kinds of wonderful harmonic overtones that filter through quantum gravity. All living creatures have finely developed microscopic tuning forks that are in sync with these harmonic gravitational overtones." Nearing the apex of the hill at a high rate of speed, Kram refused to let off the gas pedal. As the car and trailer continued to gather momentum, Cliff Barr approached a catatonic state.

"There is a concept in string theory called, super-symmetry. This concept is one that I wholeheartedly agree with. It basically relates force to matter in all things. My take on it, is basically this. If we force it to happen, it won't matter. If we simply lighten up our force on things and go with the universal flow of current, our lives will begin to matter." The car reached the curved top of the hill doing close to sixty miles-per-hour. It shot off the surface of the road, jumping several feet into the air, trailer in tow. Holding onto the steering wheel, Kram yelled, "Hot damn!" The car slammed back to the road, jolting both passengers, barely in time to make the next sharp corner.

Kram continued, "C-Barr, basically, my theory of life is this: Lighten up and go with the universal current. Are you comprehending this over there?"

Cliff replied, "I might barf."

Kram said, "Good. That's all part of the experience. It's actually a pretty common reaction when one first realizes the deep secrets of the universe. I'm sure even the physicists have a similar response." The car hit a deep pothole and pounded violently. Cliff Barr groaned.

"Speaking of barf, did you know that digestive tract

health is deeply bonded to an emotional musical response? That's why I always recommend experiencing music in some capacity during or immediately after consumption."

The road that Kram chose to travel circumvented the path that the *Traverse the Trail* expedition was on. This allowed Kram and his protégé to reach the campsite and prep the area long before the ladies arrived. The rustic Forest Service road tied in to the end of the main highway and ran up, over, and around various small mountains as it snaked its way south. After arriving at the edge of Hooligan Arm, the gravel road curved to the right, heading west while following close to the shoreline. Kram slowed a bit as he guided the Toyota Rav4 past a rustic cabin perched on the shore not far from where they would camp. A yellow Jeep Wrangler sat empty, parked next to the cabin.

"Someone must be staying at the Beaker Homestead," Kram said, as his car and trailer pushed by the property.

Close to a quarter-mile up the rocky beach past the cabin, Kram hit the brakes hard and threw the Rav4 out of gear. He hopped out of the car eagerly, bouncing around like a playful kitten. "This is it, C-Barr. Get out here."

Cliff oozed out of the passenger side of the car. The two men stood in a clearing surrounded by tall trees. Water glistened between round trunks as Hooligan Arm was visible to the south of the clearing. A path that had been cut through shrubs and ferns entered the clearing to the north. Pointing at the path, Kram exclaimed in a boyish tone, "That's where the hikers will come in."

Standing in the center of the clearing next to a makeshift fire pit, Kram turned in a complete circle, scanning the area. He pointed to where the tents were to be erected, where the cooking station was to be set, where camp chairs should be placed, and to where the firewood should be stacked. Orders were given such as an Army General would command his troops. Kram stood as the visionary, while Cliff maintained status as the errand boy.

While carrying an armload of split firewood from the back of the Rav4, Cliff said, "This wood's making a mess out of my car."

"Good."

While carrying a heavy bottle of propane, Cliff asked, "How much are we getting paid for this?"

"*'We'* is an interesting word choice, C-Barr. Remember, you are in training. Now go get the tents, cots and sleeping bags from the trailer and set them over there."

# Chapter 36

"Gretch, you don't want to do this," Lieutenant Wekle yelled into the bullhorn.

"Like hell I don't," Gretch Skully yelled back, aiming his hunting rifle above Jim's head toward the top of the Planet Patrol ship. The Boston Whaler floated directly between the *Earth's Guardian* and the *Lucky Lady*.

With his partner aiming her pistol squarely at the man holding the hunting rifle, Jim shouted back, "Put down your weapon, Gretch. I am here to take Pierre Lemieux and his men into custody. If they sank those boats, they will pay for it. Trust me on this one."

From the railing of the *Earth's Guardian* wheelhouse, Pierre Lemieux yelled, "And who's going to pay for the killing of my men? That psychopath down there murdered my nephew, and now he's here to kill me. Why aren't you taking him into custody, Lieutenant Wekle?" The short man stood alone outside his elevated wheelhouse. His three remaining crewmen stood atop the stern deck, looking down on the scene while wearing their ridiculously matching blue, red, and white shirts.

Turning toward Pierre, Jim said, "One thing at a time, Lemieux. Now shut your mouth and go inside your vessel before you get shot."

Jim turned his attention back to Gretch Skully, who still held his hunting rifle, taking high aim through the scope. Brandi Sitzel aimed her pistol, marking a direct target through the sites at Gretch Skully's midsection.

Jim yelled, "Gretch, you know how hard it is to hit something with a rifle from a moving boat? You pull that trigger, chances are, you miss your shot. But, did you know, we actually practice firing from a boat? You pull that trigger, Trooper Sitzel, here. She won't miss you, Gretch. And I would hate to see that happen."

From above, Pierre yelled, "What are you waiting for? Shoot that asshole."

With three other fishermen standing tall beside him, Gretch said, "You don't sink someone's boat, Jim. You just don't do that. We just want a chance to defend ourselves. We want justice."

Jim said, "You're right to want justice. So do I. Put your rifle down, Gretch. Let us take care of this."

"How are you going to prove it was him?" Gretch hollered.

"That's our job, Gretch. Trust us."

"He's gonna walk Jim. Snakes like this guy... They know how to work the system."

"Put it down, Gretch. Don't do this."

They all stood on their respective boats, frozen in place for several extremely tense moments. Trooper Sitzel maintained her aim, ready to put down the fisherman at the first sound of his gun firing. Gretch remained focused on his scope, finger on the trigger, contemplating his shot. Tension built as everyone held their pose, unmoving and unrelenting. Suddenly, without warning, Gretch Skully dropped the barrel of his rifle, holding it at rest.

"Good choice, Gretch. Now you and your buddies go put your guns away inside the cabin of your boat."

A blast unexpectedly rocked the entire cove. Water exploded from under the stern of the *Earth's Guardian*. The force of the blast sent spray high into the air and rumbled shock waves through each of the other boats nearby. Being fairly close to the discharge, Jim and Brandi instantly fell to their knees from the force of the explosion. Gretch and the other fishermen cringed and shielded their heads as water and hull fragments sailed through the air in their direction. A large wave pushed out from the stern of the tall ship, dramatically rocking the other vessels.

The force of the explosion caused two of the crewmen standing on the stern of the *Earth's Guardian* to lunge violently forward into the deck rail. They caught the rail squarely in their stomachs, knocking the wind from their lungs. The third crewman, who stood closest to the back of the boat, missed the rail and sailed off the edge of the ship, crashing into the water with a sharp slapping sound. The crewman landed only a few feet away from where the vessel was taking on water through a gaping hole in its stern.

Without allowing time for his clouded brain to comprehend what he had just witnessed, Zeke Melon sprang into action. The sight of a man plunging overboard due to the force of the explosion caused a humanitarian reaction from deep within Zeke's brain. He fired up his outboard and buzzed past two other boats en route to the man that needed rescuing, his body bobbing in the surf.

Motoring up close to the floating body, Zeke said in a smooth, stutterless voice, "Don't worry, I gotchya." Zeke reached over the side of his skiff and slipped both hands under the arms of the floater. With his feet positioned against the sidewall of his skiff, he pulled back while pushing out hard with his legs. The boat bent to the side with the added weight, but soon the body slipped over the gunwale, falling lifelessly into the bottom of the skiff.

Considering whether or not he could conjure up his CPR training from a distant past, Zeke pulled the man's body into a position in which he could examine him fully. The man's eyes were open, staring past Zeke's face, focused on nothing. The man's lips were slightly apart and a wet, gurgling sound came from his mouth. Leaning down to inspect whether or not the man was breathing, Zeke finally saw it. Stuck deep in the side of the man's neck, a metal piece of shrapnel from the ship's exploded hull was covered in blood. It had savagely pierced a main artery in the neck and death had already consumed the man.

# Chapter 37

Jim was having a hard time keeping his cigar lit with all the commotion. Now that the situation appeared to be under control, the State Trooper stood on the Boston Whaler, attempting to get his Bic lighter to work in the breeze. While Jim fiddled with his cigar butt, Brandi Sitzel and Hugh Eckley were leaning over the starboard wall of the Boston Whaler, attempting to pull the dead body up from Zeke Melon's skiff.

"Thanks for all the help, there, boss. It's not like this guy's heavy or anything," Brandi chirped sarcastically.

"You guys do good work," Jim replied, finally getting some smoke to puff out the end of the stogie. He was amazed at how fast the ship had gone down. The *Earth's Guardian* sank in less than three minutes, but it seemed even faster to those watching. It had completely disappeared from sight, leaving behind a rainbow ring of fuel as its only visible remnant. The ship's remaining inhabitants had had no time whatsoever to grab anything of value from the boat.

A wet, shivering Pierre Lemieux sat handcuffed next to two of his crewmen in the enclosed bow of the Boston Whaler. His thin, white hair plastered to his forehead, Pierre let out repeated groans. The *Lucky Lady* slowly chugged around the point, leaving Hooligan Arm with all of its original passengers. Pierre watched out the back of the Boston Whaler as the fishing boat rounded the corner.

Pierre yelled, "You hold me and my men in handcuffs,

while you let those shit-eating barbarians leave. They blew up my ship." The more he screamed, the more his voice turned thin and raspy.

"Shut up," yelled Jim and Brandi simultaneously.

The dead crewman's body had successfully been pulled on board. Brandi shouted toward the bow section of the boat, "They didn't blow up your ship, dumbass. I had eyes on them the entire time."

"Then, tell me, geniuses. Who's been killing off my crew? Who just sank my ship? If it wasn't those ass-wipes, then who?" Pierre's question was a good one. No one had an answer for him.

Breaking the silence, Jim asked, "Time to come clean, Pierre. You're not here to protest the environmental impact of commercial fishing, are you?"

"Whatever," the white-haired man replied.

"You've been diving Hooligan Arm for days, now, haven't you?" Brandi said.

Jim accused, "Your intentions were to create a diversion so that no one here knew what you were really doing, right?" Pierre shrugged. Jim asked, "What I don't get, though, is why go through the hassle of the environmentalist guise? It's not illegal to dive in Hooligan Arm, and salvaging rights do exist in Alaskan waters. Why not just anchor here and conduct your search missions in the light of day?"

Pierre finally responded. "Let me ask you this, Lieutenant: Have you ever witnessed the frenzy that a hunt for sunken treasure can create? Let's just say... It's not very conducive to a quality recovery mission."

"Let me get this straight," Brandi said. "You read the book about a steamship sinking here on the way back from the Klondike Gold Rush, you putt all the way up here in that hunk of junk white ship of yours, rile up the locals, get kicked out of town, and have the entire cove to yourself in order to search for your sunken gold. Is that about it?" Pierre shrugged again.

Hugh Eckley stepped in from the stern and said, "And let me guess. You didn't find a sunken steamship. You didn't find any gold. You didn't find a damn thing down there, did you?"

Pierre didn't respond, but the look on his face confirmed Hugh Eckley's suspicions. Hugh looked at the Lieutenant and said, "I told you Jim, that book is pure fiction."

As Hugh and Brandi wrapped the dead body in a tarp on the stern of their boat, the Boston Whaler's VHF radio sparked to life. Trooper Brett Stilhaven's voice cracked loudly through the radio's speaker.

After responding in the appropriate manner and changing stations from the marine hailing channel, Jim said into the mic, "Stilly. What've you got for me?"

Stilly's voice came through with standard VHF static. "I couldn't ever get in touch with the Harbormaster, but I did get her assistant to help me. She's here with me now in the Harbormaster's office. We were able to fire up the breakwater cam footage from last night, and sure enough, it shows us something interesting. The Planet Patrol boats entered the harbor just before three o'clock in the morning. I am currently staring at a zoomed-in still shot that shows Pierre Lemieux running one of the inflatables with a guy in the bow wearing diving gear and holding some sort of cordless power tool with a large drill bit attached."

Jim Wekle looked into the bow, shaking his head at Pierre and the boys.

Pierre groaned, "That doesn't prove anything."

Jim leaned his head down and said towards the forward berth, "That's felony malicious destruction of property, and attempted manslaughter."

"Manslaughter?" Pierre barked.

"An old man happened to be sleeping on board his fishing boat when you decided to start drilling holes in his hull. You're going to jail, dumbass." Turning his attention to the two young men sitting next to Pierre, Jim said, "And whichever one of you spills his guts first gets the shortest sentence."

Stilly continued, "I've called Ross Land and Sea. They're putting together a plan to salvage the three fishing boats. They think they can plug the holes, pump out the water, then float 'em over to dry dock. Thinks they'll be able to save them."

Jim punched the mic and said, "That's good news. Got anything else for me?"

"Actually, yeah, I do. You remember the other day when you asked me to look into sources of dynamite on the island and any reports of missing or stolen explosives?"

"What'd you find?"

"Well, I just got a call from the Feds. I guess licensed blasting companies are required by Federal law to report any lost or stolen pieces of explosives. Well, a construction company here on the island filed paperwork a few weeks ago. They had purchased the explosives for blasting out rock for a new home foundation when an entire box of dynamite turned up missing from their work site. The company's name is *K Diamond Construction*."

Jim stood frozen, his complexion losing color. He muttered to himself, "Oh, no."

"What is it, Jim?" Brandi asked in concern.

Jim spoke into the mic, "Is the Harbormaster's assistant still there, Stilly?"

"Yeah, she's here."

"Ask her if she has any clue where we can find Cheryl Lawson."

After a few seconds of silence, Stilly's voice came back through, "Not sure, Jim. We both tried Cheryl up at her home, but she's not there. The assistant says that Cheryl owns a remote cabin and heads there sometimes. I think it's actually out close to you guys. It's the old Beaker Homestead."

Suddenly, an explosion echoed from shore, surprising the boat's inhabitants, causing them all to turn their heads in the direction of the sound.

Jim said, "Maggie." Then, as his face displayed even more concern, he muttered, "Mom."

He ran to the back of the Boston Whaler and looked over the side into the water. Zeke Melon's head bobbed along as he sat in his Smokercraft, floating next to the other boat. Jim quickly asked, "Zeke, can you get us over to that shore in a hurry?"

"Sh... sh... sh... sure." Zeke was disappointed that his stutter had returned. He was out of Nyquil.

Standing back upright, Jim ordered, "Hugh, you take these idiots back into town. Radio Stilly and have him meet you on the docks to take them into custody. Brandi, you and I are heading for shore. Grab the shotguns."

# Chapter 38

After completing their duties of setting up the campsite, Kram and Cliff got bored and decided to start blowing things up. At Cliff's expense, Kram had brought a grab-bag with him from the fireworks stand that contained an array of items, including several small, round, black spheres called the Ball of Thunder 3000. The boom from one of these little bombs was so powerful, the two men could feel the ground shake at fifty feet. The first thing that they blew up was Cliff Barr's charred laptop computer.

"Now, don't you feel liberated," Kram asked, rummaging through the front of the Rav4, looking for something else to bomb.

Approaching a stump that sat behind the camp's dishwashing station, Cliff Barr looked forlorn as small shards of Apple product crunched under his feet. Reaching down and picking up a letter "w" key from the ground, Cliff replied, "Not really. Maybe we shouldn't have done that."

"Nonsense. The first thing you need is to break the bonds that tie you to your former pain. We'll call it the *emancipation of C-Barr the Seadog*," Kram said, heading back to the stump.

"Say, isn't that my cell phone?"

Soon, Kram got tired of exploding stationary objects, and started to examine the possibilities of launching the little bombs. He opened the loading chamber of the potato canon and determined that the diameter of a Ball of Thunder 3000 was just barely under the diameter of the cannon tube. "A perfect fit. In theory, the hairspray detonation would launch the mortar, igniting its fuse at the same time. Another theory is that the whole thing will explode, taking me with it. C-Barr, you just might receive the honor of being nominated to launch the inaugural exploding cannon projectile."

A low hum came from the forest in the near distance. Soon, the sound of twigs breaking accompanied the small engine noise. A four-wheeler slowly pushed through the brush surrounding the trail and parked on the edge of the clearing. Several female hikers, each wearing backpacks, entered the clearing looking weary and a bit relieved to have arrived at their destination. Two other ATVs followed the group, parking next to the other four-wheeler. The group organizers dismounted and removed their helmets.

Shasta Wilford looked over at Kram and exclaimed, "What the hell is with all the explosions? Sounds like World War Three around here."

Angel Yu locked eyes with Cliff Barr, shocked at his presence. She grumbled, "You... What you doing here?"

Cliff Barr appeared equally shocked at the sight of his motorized terrorists. "You're a bunch of old ladies? You've got to be kidding me?"

Two State Troopers holding shotguns accompanied by a redheaded lanky kid holding a long-handled net appeared in the clearing from the beach side of the campsite.

Surprised, Maggie said, "Jim. What are you doing here?"

Vera Wekle waved, holding her pack. "Hi Jimmy. We made it."

The sound of a car engine drifted through the trees from down the beach. Jim looked at Kram. Kram instantly sensed what Jim's questioning look meant. Kram said, "There was a yellow Jeep parked back at the Beaker cabin."

Jim handed his shotgun to Brandi, saying, "Keep this secure. I'm going after her." Turning his attention to the three ladies of the Cranbrook Culture Club, Lieutenant Wekle ordered, "Ladies, I'm going to commandeer one of those four-wheelers."

Brandi handed both shotguns to Kram and said, "Lock these inside the Toyota." Turning to jog toward the four wheelers, Brandi said, "I'm coming with you, Jim."

The two Troopers set their Stetsons on one of the camp tables and mounted two of the Yamaha Grizzlies. After a quick inspection of the machines, ensuring they understood the nuance of operation, the Troopers nodded an affirmative towards each other. The ATVs were started up, slammed into high gear, and driven quickly out of the camp's clearing, disappearing into the Forest Service road that led past the nearby cabin.

Cheryl Lawson drove the Jeep away from the homestead cabin at a moderate speed. The vehicle handled the rough nature of the road well, bouncing over potholes with ease. The driver's side window was down, causing the woman's flowing, black hair to twist in the breeze behind the

Jeep's headrest. With a stoic, self-assured expression, Cheryl Lawson guided her vehicle up the road, completely unaware that two State Troopers on ATVs were only fifty yards behind and closing fast.

After doing a double-take in her rearview mirror, the Harbormaster had to quickly come to a much unexpected decision. How Jim and his underling came to be following her tail on four-wheelers, she hadn't a clue. It was obvious that the Troopers wanted her to stop, as they both periodically waved an arm high above their heads. Cheryl Lawson momentarily considered outrunning them. She was confident that her car could top their speed, but she doubted her ability to outmaneuver given the precarious road conditions. She considered pulling over and playing dumb, but figured that if the Troopers were already tracking her down, the jig was up. She could just keep driving, as really, what could they do on four-wheelers? But Cheryl knew that the island's road system would get very limited for her, very quickly.

After a fast consideration of her options, Cheryl Lawson decided to make a run for it on foot. She slammed down the gas pedal of her Jeep and sped up a straight stretch in the road. She figured that, given their reaction time, the quick burst of speed would give her a very small, but crucial head start. Without pause, Cheryl released the gas pedal and slammed down hard on the brakes, causing the Jeep to skid on the gravel and turn slightly to the right. Snatching the duffle bag from the passenger seat, she flew out the driver's side door, leaving the Jeep's engine running and door swinging on its hinge. She darted off the road, disappearing into the thick foliage of the Alaskan rainforest.

Behind her, as she ran hard through the dense brush,

Cheryl heard the two ATVs slide to a stop. She heard her Jeep's engine being shut down. She ran harder, deeper into the woods, scraped by branches and thorns across her cheeks and arms. Behind her she heard a man's voice shout, "Cheryl. Come back. We need to talk." The sound of the voice made her run harder, ignoring the tattering of her pants and shirt by the sharp twigs that she bolted through. Again, Jim's voice echoed through the trees, this time a little fainter, "Cheryl. I'd like to hear your side of the story. Come back and let's talk."

Clutching the duffle bag in her hand, Cheryl Lawson didn't turn back. She didn't stop running through the rainforest until she was well away from the road. Pausing to assess the scrapes and cuts along her body, Cheryl leaned against the trunk of a fir tree. Her mind raced. She was in deep, and she knew it. Her options were waning. She unzipped the duffle bag and peered down. Staring at the only item that sat at the bottom of the bag, Cheryl reached in and removed the pair of red tubes that had been taped together and prepared with caps and a fuse. Turning it in her hand, allowing her eyes to scan and inspect, she placed it back in the bottom of the duffle bag. Armed with one more bomb made from stolen dynamite, Cheryl Lawson zipped the bag closed and calmly started making her way through the woods, heading in the direction of the waters of Hooligan Arm that peeked at her through the trees.

# Chapter 39

"I don't get it, boss. Why would Cheryl Lawson be our killer?" Brandi asked while the two Troopers conducted a search of the Beaker Cabin. She carefully sorted through wires, tape, small radio devices, and other bomb making paraphernalia. "I mean, obviously it's her. I just can't imagine the motive here, though."

Jim inspected the scuba diving equipment that lined one the walls of the tiny cabin. "I'm pretty sure I've got most of the pieces. There's just one thing I can't quite figure out."

"Why don't you enlighten me, boss? 'Cause I'm missing more than a couple of puzzle pieces here."

A sudden noise by the side of the cabin startled the Troopers. They drew their pistols, taking aim at a window. Cliff Barr's head popped up into view of the window. His voice cracked as he said, "I've been instructed to inform you that supper is ready. Please don't shoot me."

Both pistols were holstered as Cliff disappeared, running away from the cabin, emitting a small whimpering sound.

Jim asked, "You hungry? It's been a long day. We should probably eat something."

"Famished. Okay to leave the cabin unattended?"

"Why not? There's no more explosives here. Let's hope she used the last of the dynamite with the *Earth's Guardian* bomb."

"Well, then, let's eat. You know, you still owe me an explanation for the motive here."

The two Troopers walked the short distance on the Forest Service road from the cabin to the group's campsite. They entered the clearing to find the group of women sitting on camp chairs in a circle around a campfire, each holding a plate and fork. The food smelled fantastic.

Vera Wekle said, excitedly, "Jimmy, this is so much fun. You should grab a plate of food and join us."

Jim crossed to the cooking station and took a plate. "You know how I feel here, ladies. There is a suspected murderer at large in the area. You all should've packed up and left an hour ago."

A woman with a large nose and a British accent, said, "Just adds to the sense of adventure, don't you agree, sissy?"

An identical woman wearing matching clothes replied, "Indubitably." Patting the large revolver on her hip, she said, "Wouldn't mind getting a crack at this lunatic on the loose, myself."

Brandi said, while getting a plate, "You ladies just keep that gun in its holster before I take it away from you, okay?"

"A bit of a sassy cracker, that one is," Lucy Smelk said, invoking giggles from both twins.

Missy Smelk turned to her sister and said, "Times up. My turn to wear Clint."

Cliff Barr scooped various entrees onto two plates for the Troopers while Kram busily put the finishing touches on the presentation. Jim accepted the food, kindly saying, "Thank you, gentlemen. What are we eating this evening?"

Kram nodded at his protégé. "C-Barr, would you like to do the honors?"

Cliff stood upright and announced in an official tone, "This evening's menu features several ingredients harvested from the nature that surrounds you. Limpets steamed in herbed garlic broth. Fennel crusted baby fern tops sautéed with leeks and capers. Kelp salad drizzled with a salmonberry vinaigrette. And the star of this evening's culinary experience, thanks to our special friend, Zeke Melon, cedar smoked Hooligan, served on a bed of jasmine rice."

Sitting in a camp chair, Zeke waved and said, "Th... th... th..."

Kram interrupted abruptly, "Thistle. Theremin. Thelonious Monk."

"Thanks," finished Zeke.

Everyone at the camp happily ate their meal around the campfire. At one point, Shasta Wilford expressed her mild disapproval over how many men were present, but reluctantly deemed it acceptable given the situation. Phyllis Prescott complained about the lack of champagne. The Smelk twins told stories around the campfire of old English folklore, laughing more at their own jokes than anyone else. Kram ordered C-Barr the Seadog around camp, cleaning dishes, and filling everyone's coffee mug. Zeke Melon avoided speaking. Angel Yu kept giving Cliff Barr the stink-eye.

As Cliff walked by the group with a metal coffee percolator in his hand, Angel Yu flipped him the bird.

Cliff stopped right in front of the Chinese woman and

exclaimed loudly, "What? What did I ever do to you? What could I possibly have done in some former life that caused you to allow such hatred of me to fester so much that you have made it your personal mission to make my life a living hell?" After finishing his tirade, all eyes were on the man who stood, panting, coffee pot trembling, in the middle of the camp circle.

"You Cliff Baah?" Angel Yu asked.

"Yes."

"You the writah, Cliff Baah, yes?"

"Yes, that's me."

"You killed my husband." Angel Yu's accusation shocked not only Cliff, but the entire camp.

Shaking his head, Cliff replied, "I don't have a clue of what you are talking about. I didn't even know your husband, and I assure you, I've never killed anyone."

Angel stood, taking a step closer to the man, "Did you wite a weview of the Cedah Cove Wesort? A weview that was published in the *Alaskan Tou'ist* magazine?"

Averting his eyes while searching the far reaches of his brain, Cliff finally responded, "I guess. Yes. That was years ago."

"Do you remembah what you wote about the food?"

Pausing to think for a moment, Cliff finally said, "If I remember right, I don't think I liked it very much."

"You called it 'swill not fit for a Boy Scout Camp.' My husband cook that food. He head chef. He vewy pwoud. Until you, with you one little phwase… It sent my husband into deep depwession. He stawt gambling. He stawt dweenking.  He died the next ye'ah fwom a hawt attack.  And it all stawted with you, Cliff Baah."

"It was just a simple review.  Just words on a page."

"Wohds are powahful.  People believe what they wead."

A tear streamed from one of Angel Yu's eyes.  Phyllis Prescott walked over and comforted her friend.  Cliff stood silent in front of the woman for quite some time before simply saying, "I'm sorry."  He wandered off and continued his duties around the campground.  The mood finally elevated and people once again began telling stories, laughing, and cajoling each other to believe the exaggerations common to campfire tales.

Jim sat comfortably between his mother and his girlfriend.  Maggie grabbed his arm and leaned in close as Kram strummed a guitar.  The evening sky was still bright as day, but the temperature had cooled a bit, creating a cozy scene around the fire.  Kram's expertise on the six-string even surpassed his culinary excellence.  As he crooned a love song to everyone's delight, nobody bothered to notice a rustling in the forest just behind the row of tents.

She was tired, sore, hungry, and disillusioned.  It was a dangerous combination, taking its physical and mental toll, and it drove Cheryl Lawson to the point of desperation.  She had approached the camp unnoticed, hiding in the brush just outside the row of tents that had been erected on the edge of the clearing.  Laughter and song had broken out in camp.  The cheerful sounds only further enraged the woman. She sat on her haunches, ready to move fast.

Choosing the right moment to make her move was easy. The ponytailed man had just finished his song and the rest instantly broke out in applause. She knew that the moment to act was imminent. Cheryl sprinted from her hidden vantage, holding an object in her left hand while lunging for the gun with her right. Before Missy Smelk could even recognize the situation as it unfolded, the English lady's Smith & Wesson .50 caliber revolver had been removed from her holster and pointed at the center of the crowd.

"Clint," Missy shouted, evoking terror from both her and her sister.

Cheryl stood tall, swinging the handgun around the circle of campers, while holding a pair of dynamite sticks above her head. She slowly moved to the center of the circle and set the dynamite on the ground, dangerously close to the fire. The crazed woman reached into her pocket and retrieved a small, black radio device, moving a switch with her thumb that illuminated the red LED ready light.

Cheryl said, her voice shaking, "No one move. No one run. Do you know what this is?" She held up the little black device. "This is a remote triggering device. Right now, you are all wondering about the blast radius of two sticks of dynamite. Well, I assure you, you don't want to find out."

The woman stood in the center of the campsite, waving the gun around the circle, displaying the black radio trigger for all to see. She held a crazed look as she jerked from one direction to the next. Most of the campers cowered in fear. The two State Troopers had drawn their weapons.

Cheryl Lawson was maniacally pleased that she had commanded the full attention of the entire camp. She was completely unaware that the ponytailed guitarist had silently slipped away, disappearing into the trees.

# Chapter 40

"Cheryl, don't do this. You don't want to harm any more people." Jim aimed his pistol at the woman's torso, but knew it was too risky to fire.

Standing next to the dynamite, still turning her aim around the circle of people, Cheryl Lawson asked, "Why'd they have to go looking, Jim? Why couldn't they just leave it alone?"

Jim kept his voice calm. "That's what people do, Cheryl. They like to see things, experience things, and look for things they find interesting. Look at all of these women here. You inspired them, Cheryl. They wouldn't be here if it wasn't for you."

Brandi asked, "What are you saying, Jim?"

Jim said, "Tell her, Cheryl. Tell them all. This is your fan club. Sitting right here, around this fire. You see, you can't lie to the world and expect the world to just blindly sit, passively accepting everything you write as the gospel truth." As Jim spoke, expressions around the fire turned from fear to confusion. "That's right, everyone. This is your so-called hero, standing right before you, threatening to end your life with a flick of the switch. This is Cheryl Lawson, Harbormaster by day, and novelist under the pen-name of Greta Gleason."

"Shut up, Jim. I swear I'll kill you all." Cheryl was obviously shaken.

Jim continued, "None of it's real, ladies. It's a good story, by a decent writer, but none of it's true."

Cheryl shouted, "Shut up. It's all true. Every printed word. Sure, I write under the name Greta Gleason, but the Cranbrook family hired me to publish their lost memoir."

"Then why didn't the divers find the sunken steamship, Cheryl? And why haven't the Tlingit tribal elders ever heard of this remarkable tale? Tell me, Cheryl. If your book is truly a work of non-fiction, where's the evidence?"

Cheryl's expression changed. The gun she held seemed to slump a bit from the weight. With her voice lowered, she asked, "How'd you figure it out, Jim?"

"Some of it was easy. You made the mistake of inviting me to your house. Obviously, you'd come into a lot of money lately. That much you couldn't deny. But you made the mistake of stealing your dynamite from the construction company that you still employed. They filed a report, Cheryl, and their trucks are still parked up at your property." Jim paused for a moment, then continued, "You may have overlooked that I was on the interview committee that hired you, Cheryl. Did you really think your service as a Coast Guard Salvage Specialist First Class would go unnoticed? I served in the Coast Guard myself, and I know firsthand the kind of training and experience that salvage specialists receive. That's where you learned to dive. That's also where you received training in underwater ballistics. You killed those men to keep your secret safe, Cheryl. And you had the training necessary to pull it off, too."

The large gun, heavy in her hand, shook as she spoke, "I watched them from shore as they dove from their rafts in the middle of the night. I knew what they were looking for. And I knew they wouldn't find it. I had to keep my secret, Jim. I had to scare them off. But they wouldn't leave. They kept diving, night after night, searching for something that wasn't there."

Jim said, "There's only one thing I don't understand, Cheryl. I know that you've killed three men. I know that you blew a hole in that ship and sank it today. I know about your training and experience that gives you the means to do all of this. I know about your recent purchase of the Beaker Homestead Cabin. That gives you opportunity. I know that your motive is to cover the fact that you were getting rich off selling a non-fiction work that wasn't true in any sense. That's motive, means, and opportunity, Cheryl. But there's only one thing I don't understand. Why didn't you just publish the book as a fictitious novel in the first place? Why did it have to be non-fiction?"

"That's easy to answer." The words didn't come from Cheryl, but rather from a man that crouched behind the camp's cleaning station. Cliff Barr stood up and said, "I'm a writer, too. And if there's one thing I know, it's this. People want to believe." Cliff slowly started to walk towards the woman with the gun. "Years ago, the public bought my book because it rang true to them. My novel was loosely based on real events. It put the reader into a place of believability, a place of trust in what was written on each page. That's why I haven't been able to continue my work. Who would believe it? I certainly wouldn't. People want to believe."

Cheryl let the gun fall to her side. She repeated what Cliff said, "People want to believe. This isn't simply about truth or fiction. It's about power. Women are capable creatures. We can survive. We can endure. We can succeed in a man's world. Just look at these ladies here." Cheryl motioned toward the members of the Cranbrook Culture Club. "They believe every word in my manuscript, and the results are obvious. They are confident women, with bolstered ambitions and goals. It changed them, Jim. It *is* real."

"Put the gun and transmitter on the ground, Cheryl. It's over." Even though the killer had lowered her gun, Jim was still very fearful of the triggering device clutched tightly in her hand.

Cheryl stepped backwards away from the fire. Trooper Sitzel instructed the campers to move quickly away, directing them to run down the Forest Service road safely away from the dynamite. Jim remained with his gun focused on the killer's chest.

Cheryl said, "You can shoot me, Jim, but I just might have enough time to push the button. Are you willing to take that risk, Jim?" She slowly kept taking steps backwards. Reaching the edge of the clearing, she stopped and raised the revolver, aiming it at the Lieutenant's chest. "Are you willing to risk it, Jim? Go ahead and take the shot. You'll live, unless you don't kill me instantly."

Both of Cheryl's hands started to tremble; one holding the Smith & Wesson, one gripping the radio trigger. Jim could see that she was losing it. She could fire the revolver or press the detonator at any second. If he were to act, it had to be soon. She was right. He could shoot her, but she would very likely have time to signal the bomb. Jim took aim, this time at her forehead. His best chance of survival was a kill shot. The more the woman's hands trembled, the more expressionless her face became. Jim could read the signs, she was at the end of the line and it was time to act. Jim steadily readied his aim and prepared to pull the trigger.

A whooshing sound came from behind him, followed by an excruciatingly loud explosion directly in front of him. Jim dove to the ground away from the where the dynamite still sat. As the sound waves from the explosion reverberated through the trees, Jim made a quick self-assessment, surprised and relieved to find that he was unharmed. Brandi Sitzel came running back from the road, pistol in hand, shouting, "Jim, are you okay?"

Rising to his feet, Jim replied, "I think so." With their guns drawn, the two Troopers walked over to where Cheryl Lawson used to stand. Lying in a bloodied heap on top of charred foliage, the Harbormaster lay sprawled, her left arm having been completely blown off by the explosion, palm open with the detonator lying on top. Jim reached down and removed the gun and trigger while Brandi checked her pulse.

"She's dead, Jim," said Brandi.

Jim turned toward the back of the campsite. Standing next to the Toyota Rav4, holding a potato cannon like a bazooka, Kram shrugged and said, "It was a Ball of Thunder 3000. Guess it did the trick."

# Chapter 41

Jim and Maggie held hands as they walked Vera Wekle to the floatplane dock. They exchanged hugs while saying their goodbyes.

"You know how to show an old lady a good time, Jimmy," Vera said, handing her suitcase to the dockhand.

"Say hi to Dad for me, okay, Mom. Love you, and thanks for visiting."

Maggie said, "Thanks for going hiking with me, Vera. Sorry that we almost got killed."

Giving the young lady a big hug, Vera replied, "It'll give me a story to tell around the bridge table, that's for sure." Releasing the hug, she looked straight into Maggie's dark eyes and said, "You are a wonderful girl and you make my son a better person. Now, if only he'll get off his ass and ask you to marry him."

Jim blushed and Maggie laughed as the woman stepped from the float up into the fuselage of the seaplane. Frightening Frankie waved to Jim and Maggie as he closed the plane's doors and hopped into the pilot's seat. After the de Havilland Beaver fired it's tremendously loud, rumbling engine and taxied away, Jim and Maggie climbed the ramp to the wooden pier. They waved as the seaplane rumbled over their heads on its way to Ketchikan.

Jim turned and grabbed Maggie by the shoulders. He leaned in, kissing her hard, holding her in a long embrace.

"What was that for?" Maggie asked.

"What are your thoughts on my Mom's last words?"

"What, about me being wonderful?" she said, playfully.

"Well, yeah. That, and the other."

"You mean, dare I say, *marriage*?" Maggie was obviously teasing him, and enjoying it.

"Yes, Maggie. What are your thoughts regarding that… uh… subject."

"Well, first, I think you should be able to say the word marriage. Second, I think you should man up and ask me."

They held hands and strolled slowly down the pier. Jim said, "I'm a man. I saved your life, didn't I?"

"Well, technically, Kram saved your life."

"I don't want to marry Kram," Jim said.

"I would think not. He is a good cook, though. Maybe I should marry him," Maggie bantered.

"I think that washing all those jean cut-offs would get old after a while," Jim said.

"Who says that I'm going to be doing the laundry?"

"You're not going to do the laundry?"

"Not a chance."

They walked for a few yards before Jim asked, "Do you think that me being your boss would get any easier if we were married?"

Maggie smiled, kissed him on the cheek, and replied, "Not a chance in hell, boss."


*With each experience that I endured, I left a piece of my soul behind. My cynicism and the ability to lock away all human emotion remained on the stage of the dancehall, left behind to spite the men who frothed over with sin brimming from their hearts. Fear was laid to rest on the bottom of the sea when the mighty SS Aberdeen went down, sinking its coveted gold into a terminal shrine. My desire for adventure was left on the trails that crossed this mighty island, through thicket and lush greenery. And my loathing for humanity drifted into the tree tops to be carried away by the wind and rain as I was welcomed with open arms into the fold of the Native inhabitants of this incredible land. I now, after trials and near death tribulations, have finally discovered what all mankind seeks. Peace.*

# Epilogue

After the only two surviving crewman of the *Earth's Guardian* turned State's evidence against their former boss, Pierre Lemieux was found guilty on charges of fraud, three counts of malicious destruction of property, and one count of attempted manslaughter. At sentencing, the judge, being from a family of lifelong Alaskan fishermen, gave a seven minute diatribe on the benefits of the commercial fishing industry. Halfway through the judge's speech, Pierre let an involuntary reflex slip as the word, "ass-wipe" was muttered just loud enough to be caught by the judge's ear. After adding on a contempt of court ruling, the judge threw the book at the man and sentenced Peter Gorski aka Pierre Lemieux to nine years in the State pen. In a complete twist of ironic fate, the former dry cleaning mogul of Chicago, Illinois was assigned to work the prison's laundry facility.

The membership of the Cranbrook Culture Club decided that, in light of recent events, they should abolish the existence of their club. Due to evidence of the fraudulent nature of the book that they had dedicated their club to, the three club members conducted a ceremony on the shores of Hooligan Arm where each of their copies of *Muskeg Mama* was wrapped in Klondike period attire and exploded into pieces by a Ball of Thunder 3000.

The three ladies, however, did keep the four-wheeled ATV's and riding gear. They formed a new club called *Four Wheels of Female Fury*, and ordered matching leather jackets with FwFF embroidered on the back. The ladies hired a local writer to draft a written charter, detailing their allegiance to enacted vengeance on any and all social injustice connected to the island's extensive Forest Service road system. As payment for drafting the official charter, the *Four Wheels of Female Fury* agreed in writing to refrain from any and all contact with the writer's mailbox.

Zeke Melon officially quit his job as a septic tank pumper and sold his blossoming hooligan candle enterprise to a local prospective businessman. After his experience with pulling multiple dead bodies and a severed foot from the waters surrounding the island, Zeke was hired by the local Medical Examiner's office. His duties were to assist Dr. Dooley in the acquiring, transporting, and processing of dead bodies, a job that the tall, lanky redhead seemed to excel at.

After catching wind from the local pharmacy concerning the amount of cough syrup being purchased by the job candidate, the Medical Examiner gave Zeke an ultimatum; give up Nyquil for good, or find another line of work. Considering the soothing effect that dead bodies were starting to have on his stutter, Zeke Melon gladly agreed to the terms and started working immediately. His clothing still reeked of dried hooligan, but that didn't seem to matter when working in the morgue.

News quickly spread concerning the fraudulent premise of the book *Muskeg Mama*, and copies were pulled from shelves. The estate of the late Cheryl Lawson, aka Greta Gleason, was hung up in probate. Without a last will and testament officially filed, no one was too eager to step forward and lay claim to the impending lawsuit that was building like a tornado over a Midwestern trailer park.

Although visitors no longer made the trek to Prince of Wales Island in order to pay homage to Ellen Cranbrook, an influx of world class divers soon began to hit the island. Due to the fact that the *Earth's Guardian* had sunk in roughly the exact location of the fictitious *SS Aberdeen*, divers from across the globe used rogue copies of the discontinued book in preparation for their adventurous Southeast Alaskan submersion. Between the remote location and the extreme currents, the Hooligan Arm dive soon hit the radar of almost every experienced deep-sea diver in the world.

The mystique of *Muskeg Mama* and the *Earth's Guardian* started to develop a cult following among the world's diving community, and any recovered piece of the submerged ship was said to be a badge of honor among the scuba elite. Hanging a shirt with colors of the French flag on your wall became an unofficial proclamation of submerging in Hooligan Arm. Sewing the "double-P" Planet Patrol insignia onto your wetsuit claimed that you had actually recovered an item from the shipwreck. Internet blogs boasted of treasures and knickknacks salvaged from various dives, and stories varied with exaggerations. The one detail that all divers seemed to agree on was how to locate the exact spot of the submerged ship. Just look for the oil slick.

A ponytailed man drove a Toyota Rav4 off the inter-island ferry boat, loaded with freshly made hooligan candles. He turned onto a road that led straight into the heart of the downtown Ketchikan waterfront, dodging tourists that randomly crossed the road without any regard to traffic. Choking down several cusswords and the urge to drive squarely over the top of several parka-clad sightseers, the ponytailed man made it to his destination, parking close to the cruise ship dock. He unloaded gear from the back of the car and carried several plastic tubs into the belly of the beast.

After setting up his display and lighting a couple of demonstration candles, the ponytailed man took out an electric guitar and plugged it into a small battery-powered amplifier that hung from the belt of his jean cut-offs. After launching into a series of scales and arpeggios, flying up and down the neck of his Gibson Les Paul, the ponytailed man followed close behind tourists, playing energetic power-chords relentlessly, until they reluctantly agreed to buy one of his hooligan candles.

In a recent business transaction, the ponytailed man in jean cut-offs not only obtained the hooligan candle enterprise, but he also purchased the rights to a song. Dancing around the Ketchikan waterfront, wailing on his electric guitar, Kram belted at the top of his lungs, "Hoooo-li-gan. Hoooo-li-gan. Get your-self a fish caaaan-dle. Hoooo-li-gan. Hoooo-li-gan. Put them up on your maaaan-tle."

# HOOLIGAN ARM

# Acknowledgements

To the friends of Jim and Kram, your encouragement and support are a constant source of inspiration. I never dreamed that I would have three of these things out there, but all of my readers have helped keep the fun going. Thank you.

I owe everything I know about potato guns to my brother-in-law, James Traynor. That cannon was one of the best gifts I've ever received.

I consider myself lucky to live in a town with so many talented and helpful people. Joanie Christian, you did it again. I love how your book covers continue to capture the spirit of Southeast Alaska, while meeting my simple vision. The cigar is pretty cool, too. Sarah Newman, you helped give polish to this manuscript, always with a smile and a positive word.

I have had the great fortune of finding an editor that is both skilled with the written word, as well as a true Southeast Alaskan. Tara Neilson is fantastic, and perfect for the Jim and Kram series. I swear that I know how to spell waving (wait… or is it waiving?).

My family is amazing. My wife, children, parents, siblings, in-laws, aunts and uncles have all been an incredible source of encouragement during the completion of this manuscript. They have all been anxiously awaiting Jim and Kram's third adventure and cheering for it all along the process. And I promise... none of you are the sole inspiration behind Kram.

Brent Purvis

# ABOUT THE AUTHOR

Brent Purvis resides in Colville, WA with his wife and two kids. In addition to writing humorous mystery novels, Brent is a music teacher and regular performer of jazz and blues as a trombonist and keyboardist. He has also written, composed, and arranged a full-length Broadway-style musical-comedy, which was recently produced with high acclaim.

Teaching music for over two decades has allowed Brent to live in some of the most beautiful places in the Northwest, as well as meet some of the most amazing characters along the way.

Growing up in Ketchikan, Alaska gave Brent a unique experience with life in the Last Frontier. After high school, his musical pursuits sent him south as he majored in music education at the University of Idaho. Upon receiving his degree, Brent landed a teaching stint on Whidbey Island, where he met his wife and started his family. They moved to Sitka, Alaska before settling in beautiful Northeast Washington.

You can find Brent's blog, Kram's Perspective, at: http://jimandkramrule.blogspot.com/

Made in the USA
Monee, IL
16 June 2020